JIMMY'S RULES

A SUSPENSE NOVEL

MICHAEL MAYO

coffeetownpress

Kenmore, WA

coffeetownpress

A Coffeetown Press book published by Epicenter Press

Epicenter Press
6524 NE 181st St. Suite 2
Kenmore, WA 98028.
www.Epicenterpress.com
www.Coffeetownpress.com
www.Camelpress.com

For more information go to: www.epicenterpress.com
www.mike-mayo.com

Jimmy's Rules
Copyright © 2020 by Micael Mayo

ISBN: 9781603816861 (trade paper)
ISBN: 9781603816878 (ebook)

Printed in the United States of America

*For
SDH and WBS
and, as always,
Marcia*

Author's Note

Like the other Jimmy Quinn novels, this is fiction based on fact. Virtually everything that Willie Seabrook says and does is a variation on something found in his own work and his confounding, contradictory, excessive life.

Readers who know Dashiell Hammett's stories and novels will find many familiar elements that have been borrowed, stolen, or repurposed.

Chapter One

1933
NEW YORK CITY

Willie Seabrook was the greatest liar I ever met.

He should be telling this story, not me. He'd make it fit together and he'd smooth over all the rough stuff and you'd be so taken in by his excitement and the screwy things he knew that you'd believe it, too. You'd know he was lying but you wouldn't mind because you were having such a good time. Me, I'm stuck with what happened. I'll make the best I can of it, and so I'll start with one of my favorite memories.

That's Connie Nix, wearing a silk slip and nothing else and then pulling it up over her head and standing there naked in the late afternoon sun.

We were in her room at the Chelsea. I was in bed. The light came through the gap in the blackout curtains and hit her just right, tinting her brown skin pink and shining on her black hair. Boy, did she look good. She saw me smiling, and she was quick to pull the heavy curtains closed and hurry under the covers with me.

She said, "I took a chill walking back here. You've got to warm me up."

I was ready to oblige. You see, this was the winter of '33, and Prohibition was about to end. For five years, I'd been peacefully running a neighborhood speak. Well, mostly peaceful. Things got interesting from time to time. Like everybody else in the business, I paid off the local cops and my alderman and a few other guys, and life went on. But now I was going to have to go legit for the first time in my young life or find another line of work. I'd greased a guy who worked for the State Alcoholic Beverage Control Board, and he had my name on a list for one of the first licenses. But getting everything else signed and approved and examined and tested turned out to be more complicated than I thought. I'd spent the whole day

1

at City Hall trying to chase down the right Sanitary Inspector. Then I had to slip him a fin to get him to promise to get to my place next week, and then he said there were two other guys who'd have to sign off on his work. I'd have to take care of them, too.

I walked away feeling like I'd wasted my time, and I was no closer to getting what I wanted than I'd been that morning. I needed something to cheer me up, so I found a nickel and called the speak. Frenchy answered. He said business was slow. I asked him to put Connie on. I told her I had an important job for her and she should meet me in her room at the Chelsea, PDQ.

Thus, I came to be in bed warming her up.

By then we'd known each other for about a year and a half and we were getting along fine as I saw it. We still had two rooms at the hotel, hers on the fifth floor, mine on the third, to keep from scandalizing the neighbors. Fat chance of that in the Chelsea.

That afternoon, her hands really were cold, not that I minded for the moment, considering what she was doing with them.

Then she said, "The strangest thing happened today. Just after you called, we got another call from a fellow who said he was Willie Seabrook and he had to see you right away..." The name startled me.

"What's wrong?" she said, looking up at me. "You don't know William Seabrook."

I pulled her close. "Sure I do, but he can wait."

She pushed me away. "What do you mean? You can't just leave it at that. We're talking about William Seabrook, **the** William Seabrook. If it wasn't for him, I probably wouldn't be here."

Then I was confused. "Willie got you here?"

She twisted away, switched on a bedside light and pulled out a drawer on her nightstand. I wrapped my arms around her and tried to pull her back.

She held up a battered green book for me to see. There is was, stamped on the cover, "*Adventures in Arabia, W.B. Seabrook.*"

She opened it and read, "'Adventures in Arabia among the Bedouins, Druses, Whirling Dervishes and Yesidee Devil Worshipers.' I guess I was about thirteen when I read this. It changed everything." She sounded excited by the memory of it. "This book showed me that there was a part of the world that wasn't Browns Valley, California. The places he wrote about were magical and brutal like fairy tales but they were *real*. He had been there." She stared at the book. "I could go there."

Yeah, that was Willie, all right.

"What did he want?" I asked but I wasn't really interested. I had other things in mind and pulled her closer.

"He said he was at Doctors Hospital." Where the rich drunks dried out. So the booze got to him. "He needs to see you. He said it's important, life and death. You aren't kidding, are you? You really do know William Seabrook?"

I said I knew him, all right, and tried to scoot lower in the bed. She pulled me back up. "Stop that. Not now. We've got to go there." She saw how much I didn't like that idea. "Don't worry, honey, we've got all night."

"No, we don't. I wasted a day downtown so I'm going in tonight."

She rolled on top of me and kissed me hard. "Then we'll make time later," she whispered. "Now we're going to go." She slipped out of bed, put on her underwear and got dressed. She started talking and laughing a little, mostly to herself. "I thought it was a joke. Didn't even mention it to Marie Therese or Frenchy. This is just unbelievable. William Seabrook!"

I strapped my brace on my knee and put my clothes back on. She said, "This isn't a joke, is?"

I said, no, damn it, it's not, and we caught a cab uptown.

On the way, Connie fretted about how she looked. She even said we'd been in too much of a hurry before and we had to go back to the Chelsea so she could put on a better dress and fix her hair. I told her not to worry.

"Willie's going to love you. He's going to be so charming you'll want to stay and listen to him all night and then he'll try to sweet talk you right into his bed."

The way she smiled, I figured maybe she wouldn't mind that.

Doctors Hospital was up on East End Avenue at Eighty-seventh, just across that little park from the East River. Inside, you didn't see a lot of people in white, doctors, nurses and orderlies, like you did in a regular hospital. This was a smaller place, meant for well-heeled swells. There were two smiling guys in suits at the Admissions desk. I told them who I was and said that Willie Seabrook wanted to see us. They checked a list and pointed us to the elevator. The nurse at the station on the fifth floor said Willie was in the penthouse, right behind us. The door was open.

It looked like the penthouse took up half the floor. Willie had a suite of rooms and a terrace overlooking the park. With shaky knees, he got up from an armchair when he saw us. I won't say he looked terrible but he sure looked worse than I remembered. It had been more than two years since I'd seen him.

The quick smile, the round cheeks, the little mustache, and the messy hair were the same, but his face was puffy and yellow and his hand trembled when he shook mine. He wore a dress shirt with a collar but no tie, the rough denim pants he favored and bedroom slippers. He still towered over me.

"My god, it's good to see you. You've filled out. It suits you." He took a step back, looked closer and said, "You're different, more serious."

"Things change. You've changed."

"And not for the better. I know that. It's why I'm here. The last two years have been…" He noticed Connie and his face brightened. "You haven't introduced us."

"This is Connie Nix. Connie, Willie Seabrook. She works at my place, and she reads your stuff."

She gave him a cool look. "I didn't believe you were you when you called."

I couldn't tell if he measured up to whatever she expected. She didn't sound very impressed for somebody who'd dragged his book across the country.

Willie ran true to form. He took her hand in both of his. "You know, it's always a pleasure for a writer to meet a reader. I try to tell stories that like-minded men and women want to experience, and I feel a real responsibility to give my best with each book. I don't always succeed."

"Nobody does," she said, smiling. That wasn't what he wanted to hear. "I've been carrying a copy of *Adventures in Arabia* around with me for five years. It's beaten up and dog-eared but I hope you'll sign it for me."

"With pleasure. But what kind of host am I? What can I offer you to drink? I've got whatever you want as long as it's Scotch."

There was a bottle of Black and White and a soda siphon on a sideboard. I asked for seltzer. So did Connie, and I explained that we had to work that night. Willie fixed the drinks, added a small drop of whiskey to his, and lit a cigarette.

"Why are you here, Willie? Not in a hotel or the place downtown?"

He tried to laugh but didn't mean it. "It's all a mistake, really. I thought I'd gone off the rails but it's not that serious." He settled back in his armchair and went into his story.

"Mink and I went back to France—"

"Mink's his wife," I said to Connie.

"Oh, no, we're not married," he said, taking a measured sip. "We might as well be, I suppose, but we both like the situation the way it is."

Connie wasn't buying that. "And where is… Mink?"

"She'll be here soon. She had to close up the villa. I traveled first."

As Willie told it, when he and Mink left America, he had a contract to write two books, and he had to fly to Timbuctoo to gather material. After that, they lived in Toulon for more than a year. But he couldn't get the book started. Hoping a change would help, he rented the Villa des Roseaux in La Gorguette. While they were living there, he had dozens of famous neighbors and houseguests, and he started dropping names, like he always did. He talked about Aldous Huxley and Thomas Mann and Gertrude Stein and Malcolm Cowley and other people. It looked to me like Connie knew who they were. I didn't, except for Gertrude Stein. She and I had a lot of fun together one time, but that's another story. Anyhow, the point is that while Willie was in his villa, he hobnobbed and drank but he still didn't write.

He lit another cigarette. "I wrecked the car one day after lunch. They thought I was dead, but it turned out to be a concussion. For a time, I feared it had so damaged my vision that I couldn't work, but that cleared up soon enough. Still, I couldn't get involved with the book. I wrote a hundred pages, read them, threw them away, and opened another bottle of brandy. That, I think, was my lowest point."

When he couldn't write, he drank. The longer he couldn't write, the more he drank.

"I'm not sure how I did it, but I managed to get the first book done. That's *Air Adventure*. But the drinking got worse. I was putting away a fifth of the Five Star before lunch and another afterward. About a month ago, I cabled Alfred Harcourt and told him I needed help. He told me to return immediately and arranged for me to be admitted here. I booked passage on *Europa* from Cherbourg. Four days later, I was here. But something changed during the course of the voyage."

He paused then and sounded like he wasn't sure about what he was saying. "It certainly wasn't a 'sea change' in the conventional or classic sense, but I gained some perspective on the problem and saw it with more clarity."

He said Harcourt met him at the dock and brought him straight to Dr. Lambert there at the hospital. The sawbones looked Willie over and said he didn't need to worry. Sure, Willie was drinking too much, but if he just cut back to say, three drinks a day, rested, changed his diet and got a little exercise, he'd shape right up.

"As you can imagine, I was relieved to hear that."

Looking at him that night, I couldn't tell if Willie believed what the doctor said. I sure didn't. In my line of work, I ran across more than my share of drunks. Yes, I've sold some of them drinks when I probably shouldn't have. Other times, I've told them to go home or go someplace else to drink themselves to death. As Arch Malloy says, we have to balance our concern for our fellow man with common greed.

Willie still needed a lot of help and I think he knew it, even if he wasn't admitting it to himself yet.

I said, "It's too bad you had to go through something like that, but it's good to see you again."

"It's good to be back. Or, that's what I thought until the mail arrived this afternoon. Does this look familiar?"

With a shaky hand, he gave me a heavy envelope with gold foil lining. There was a card inside.

Please join Mrs. Victoria Garner and Brother Emmanuel
December 2 at 6:00pm
Couffignal House, Collier's Neck, Long Island
For a demonstration of advanced psychical powers.
We humbly request that you bring an earthly treasure.

I remembered it all right. "Victoria Garner. She's the widow?"
Willie nodded.

"And Brother Emmanuel is Manny the Dip. You think the Abbé is in on it?"

Willie nodded again. "Yes, I'm sure of it. He's back."

I turned to Connie. "The Abbé is a fellow Willie used to know. He changed names more often than some guys change their socks. We had some trouble with him and Manny when Willie was here before, those two and another guy named Xeno Pool."

All the color disappeared from her face, and she swayed like she was losing her balance. I grabbed her arms. "What is it?"

It took a second for her to steady herself. "Xeno Pool. Describe him."

"Five ten, maybe. Dark hair, dark eyes. Flashy dresser. Cocky. Can't control his temper." I remembered then that Pool knew who Willie was.

Frowning, she looked from Willie to me and back. "Is this some kind of trick the two of you are pulling on me? Did you see my copy of *Adventures in Arabia* and cook this up?"

"No, what are you talking about?"

She grabbed my lapels and got in my face. "Swear to me that this is not a joke, that you don't know about me and Xeno."

"Wait a minute. How the hell could you know Xeno Pool?"

She let go of me. "It's hard to explain and it goes back a long way. The simplest part is this. He gave me the book."

We would have said more then but a crowd of Willie's friends showed up. Two men and four women who acted like they were three couples. Willie started to make introductions but I said we had to go to work. As we were leaving, Willie caught me and lowered his voice.

"You know I can't let this rest. Whatever he's up to, I have to see it. Will you come with me?"

"We made a mistake letting them go. We didn't finish it."

Willie shook his head and there was something in his eyes I hadn't seen before. He was afraid.

It was a little after eight when we got out of the cab on Twenty-Second Street.

Jimmy Quinn's was in a narrow brownstone around the corner from the Chelsea. The speak was a few steps down from the sidewalk. We had booths along one side, a mahogany bar on the other, tables and a little dance floor in between. The Cruzon Grill was upstairs. I owned the building.

Fat Joe Beddoes was working the door. He grumbled and cursed when he let us in. Fat Joe cursed at everything. Arch Malloy, Frenchy and Marie Therese were behind the bar. Frenchy and Marie Therese were with the place when I bought it from Carl Spinoza back before the Crash. They handled most of the day-to-day running of it. I stayed out of their way and paid the bills. Arch had joined us a year or so before when I got into some dicey business with a bunch of Nazi bastards. He handled the inventory and worked behind the bar. Connie hurried over to talk to Marie Therese. I told the guys the same thing she was telling Marie Therese. "Willie Seabrook's back in town."

Frenchy, remembering what happened before, looked worried and muttered something in French. He didn't do that very often.

Malloy smiled behind his soup strainer mustache and said, "You know that mad bastard, Seabrook? Isn't this a day full of surprises?" Then he spouted something in French back to Frenchy.

I asked Arch if we had any of the Hennessy Five-Star. He said we did, and the two of us went down to the cellar. That evening, it brought back the strange times that Willie spent down there in the room with the white sheets covering the walls. Arch said he'd stashed the Five-Star behind the false door. "The damned stuff is so expensive that we never sell it, toothsome as it is, and I knew you wouldn't want it to be included in the inventory that we'll have to present to those government thieves."

I said, "I need a fifth and if Willie's going to stick around, we'll have to order more."

He pushed the door to click it open and came back with a dusty bottle. "Over the years I've heard many strange stories about Seabrook. I've found him difficult to pin down. I've read his books, of course." Of course. That Mick had read everything.

I wrapped the bottle in brown paper. "'Difficult to pin down.' Nobody could argue with that."

"How do you know him?"

"It's a long story. I'll explain it later."

Upstairs, I put the Five-Star behind the bar and told Frenchy to start a new tab for Willie.

Business was slow and so we decided to close up before midnight. Connie took the day's cash and receipts up to my office to count while I helped Frenchy, Marie Therese and Arch lock up. Connie had finished by the time I got to the office. She'd also been up to the kitchen of the Cruzon Grill and fixed up a plate of sandwiches—cheese, ham, and ham and cheese—and a thermos of coffee.

We settled on the divan and dug in.

Between bites, she said, "Now we've got time. Tell me about Xeno and Willie."

"It was two years ago, before I met you..."

Chapter Two

1931
NEW YORK CITY

"Mr. Seabrook is... unusual. You'll see what I mean when you get there."

I was on the phone talking to Klaus Cassell, the head waiter at Longchamps restaurant. It was about six o'clock on a Wednesday evening. I remember it was a Wednesday because I was so damned worried about Thursday. Cassell had a customer who needed a lot of good hooch PDQ. That's why he called me.

"It's a simple dinner party. I need more than enough for about a dozen people. Let's say Gordon, Dewar's, Bacardi's. Three cases of wine, one red, one white, and champagne. Some brandy. What do you have that's on the sweet side and expensive?"

"I've got a Courvoisier Napoleon that fits the bill."

"I need it by 8:30."

"At the restaurant."

"No, across the street, at 66 Fifth Avenue."

I knew the address. "That's Dauber & Pine's bookstore, or the theater, the one that shows the French pictures."

"Yes. Mr. Seabrook's rooms are above them the top floor front. As I said, this engagement presents us with some difficulties, but nothing that affects your part in it."

I didn't really know Cassell but Longchamps was a swanky chain of beaneries so I figured he could pay the freight. It averaged out to about twenty bucks a bottle. Add in the carrying charge and it came to seven hundred and fifty, but only half of it was profit. You see, when I said I had Courvoisier and Gordon and French champagne, I was talking about the real stuff, not some junk that claimed to be Benedictine and came with a fancy red wax seal but when you looked close, you saw that it said "In God We Trust" and had a picture of George Washington stamped in the middle.

Business at my speak was built on serving the best imported booze but in the two years since the Crash, that kind of high class trade had been on the thin side. Cassell called me because he knew that I had the best product and I wouldn't show up with it looking like some thug who scared and embarrassed his customers.

So, the Longchamps order meant it was going to be a profitable night. But there was also the other matter I'd got myself involved in, the one that had my stomach churning. At least this took my mind off it. I went down to the bar and told Frenchy to move his truck into the courtyard behind the place. Then I loaded up the wooden cases in the cellar and nailed the tops on.

When French was ready, I stacked them onto the little hand truck and lugged it up the back stairs to his truck. We tied it all down on the flatbed. The truck was an old Chevrolet with a wooden cab and bed that French built himself.

I had time to go back to the Chelsea to wash up and put on a better suit, a new navy worsted from De Pinna, a clean white shirt and a wine red tie. You see, when I was a kid working for Arnold Rothstein, I learned that you had to dress right. You make your living breaking the law with booze or gambling, you've got to look respectable. It's even more important for me because I'm short. The men I deal with wouldn't take me seriously if I schlepped around looking like a bum. But if they see a guy in a well-cut suit, nicely pressed shirt and the right tie, they know he takes care of himself. They probably also think I'm a simple thug, but it never hurts to be underestimated.

That night, after strapping on my knee brace, I thought about carrying a pistol. There had been trouble over the past few weeks with booze trucks being hijacked—that's part of the reason I was worrying about Thursday—but it was happening out on Long Island and down in Jersey with shipments coming off the boats. There was no reason to expect any trouble in the city heading downtown. So I left the .38 in the safe and figured the brass knucks and my stick would do.

I parked in front of the address on Fifth at quarter after eight. A couple of guys in tuxedos were wheeling steam trays on carts across the street from the restaurant. I loaded my cases onto the hand truck and followed them inside to an elevator in the back. The smell of the food filled the car and made me hungry. We went up to the fifth floor. The doors opened onto a wide studio or dancehall, not an apartment like I'd been expecting. I found out later it had been a ballet school. The guys from Longchamps were setting up on one side, spreading white tablecloths and setting out silverware. The room had some nice carpets, a few pieces of furniture, and a Steinway on a raised stage.

I asked one of the guys if Cassell was around. He said Herr Cassell would be there soon and showed me where the bar was going to be.

I pushed the hand truck over to that corner and waited. A few minutes later, a lanky blond came out of the elevator along with two more waiters pushing steam trays that made the place smell even better. The blond noticed me and the booze, parked his steam tray and hurried over.

"Mr. Quinn, a pleasure to meet you. There are the ice buckets for the champagne and white wines."

"First there's the matter of the bill." I handed it to him.

He tucked it into a pocket. "I'll see that Mr. Seabrook gets this first thing tomorrow." Then he saw I wasn't buying it, and said, "Mr. Seabrook is one of our very best customers. We wouldn't be going to this trouble if he were not. I assure you he's good for it."

I shook my head.

"Very well then, shall we split the difference? Put the wine on ice. If there is any question after Mr. Seabrook arrives, I'll see that you're... Ah, here he is now."

Cassell headed for the elevator as a crowd got out. That's when I understood why he wasn't hosting this affair in his restaurant.

She was the tallest colored woman I ever saw. The guy standing next to her, I guessed it was this Seabrook character, looked to be a shade over six feet in a comfortably rumpled, bespoke tweed suit. But she was almost a head taller than him and everybody else in the room. She wore a jeweled turban and a high-collared red dress that looked like a Russian military uniform with gold braid and fringe on her wide shoulders, and high-heeled red leather boots. She carried a jockey's riding crop under one arm.

I'd never met her. Never seen her picture either but I figured she had to be A'Lelia Walker, probably the richest colored woman in the world. Her mother had invented some kind of stuff that relaxed kinky hair. It was so popular she turned it into a cosmetics empire. When she died, this lady inherited a fortune.

She and Seabrook were arm in arm, and talking intently. Maybe half a dozen colored men and women, all dressed to the nines, came out of the elevator behind them. They appeared to be as surprised at the place as I had been, giving the eye to the high ceiling and the fancy layout of food and booze. As they strolled around and took it all in, I noticed that they held themselves proudly, acting like it was the most normal thing in the world for a bunch of white waiters to be attending to them. I hadn't seen that before, but then, I didn't often get up to Harlem. In my part of town, just about all the colored people you saw were doing the jobs nobody else wanted.

Cassell waited until there was a break in the conversation and spoke to Seabrook. He pulled a hefty roll from his pants pocket, peeled off a good part of it and gave the cash to Cassell without counting. Then he went back to his talk with Miss Walker.

Cassell gave me my share and said his guys would take care of the rest of the set-up. I drove back to the speak. Seabrook called two hours later. By the sound of it, the party was going full throttle. I could barely hear him over loud voices and the piano.

"We need more," he yelled. "More of the Chateauneuf du Pape and that Napoleon, let's have more of that. I didn't really believe Cassell when he told me that he could get the genuine article. You must bring more, right away."

"What do you want, and how much?"

"You wouldn't happen to have any of the Hennessy Five Star, would you?"

"No, only the Courvoisier, but I can get the Hennessy for you. What do you want now?"

"Rum. Barbancourt if you have it. The Haitian consul-general will be joining us soon and he'll want to see some of the local product. Come to think of it, forget about the wine and the cognac for now. Just bring the rum. A case."

He hung up without saying anything more.

It was close to eleven by then, and business was slow, so I told Frenchy to call a cab. He and Marie Therese could close up without me and they'd need the truck to get home. Out on the street, Frenchy and I loaded the rum into the trunk of the cab. I asked him if he was ready for Thursday.

Looking grim, he nodded his head.

"I'll see you and Fat Joe at eleven. Tell Marie Therese not to come in until six."

He nodded again and said, "She knows and she's not happy about this."

"Nobody is."

I got in the cab and told the driver to take me downtown. When I got out, I could hear the music and laughter through the open fifth floor windows. Upstairs, it was loud and happy.

Seabrook was dancing with A'Lelia Walker. She'd taken off her boots so they were about the same height. I recognized the guy noodling on the Steinway as Noel Coward. His picture was in the papers all the time. Most of the other people were dancing, too, in just about any combination you could come up with. Colored people and white people, men with men, women with women, and some that I couldn't tell. You saw that often enough down in the Village—the lilting lavender part, anyway—but not much in this neighborhood, and not the black and white together, that was rare in my book.

I schlepped the rum over to the bartender. By and by, Seabrook broke away from Miss Walker and came over. Without asking, the bartender refilled his glass with Scotch and I got my first good look at the guy.

He had rosy round cheeks, dark hair that he hadn't paid much attention to, and a little mustache right under his nose, but the first thing you noticed about him was the way he was so curious and interested in what was going on around him. He gestured with his drink and said, "Let's go over here where we can talk."

We went to a corner by one of the open windows and he held out a hand. "We haven't really been introduced. I'm Willie Seabrook."

I knew the name but couldn't place it. I said I was Jimmy Quinn and gave him one of my cards. "My place is a block off Broadway. Drop by some time. Just show this to Fat Joe at the door, he'll let you in."

"How do you get this stuff? This is the first real drink I've had since we got off the *Berengaria*."

"I know some people. We have an agreement."

"As you can see, this affair was a bit difficult to arrange. Miss Walker had some very kind things to say about a book that I wrote and I wanted to do something special to thank her. Van Vechten was able to set it up, but when I told Karl at Longchamps who was on the guest list, he said that they simply couldn't manage it in the restaurant. Then he suggested catering. Of course, no one would raise an eyebrow in France, but here..."

"I wish I could tell you that you could book my place, but the neighbors would raise hell."

"You do rent it out though?"

"Sure." I tried not to sound eager. This guy was loaded. "Now, about the rum." I handed him the second invoice. He glanced at it, pulled out his roll and peeled off five bills.

He leaned close so I could hear him. "As it happens, I'm soon going to need a place for another little party I'm planning. Do you think—"

He was interrupted by a plump smiling colored man who clapped him on the back and said, in a big booming bass voice, "My friend William, so very good to see you again." Trailing behind him was a nervous looking young white woman with a long face and a fan of thick black hair.

Seabrook turned to her. "Mink, this is the man I was telling you about, the consul-general. He's here to tell us about Haitian pineapples." The three of them headed for the stage and before long, the plump guy was talking about pineapples.

I got into the elevator and worried about Thursday.

Chapter Three

1931
NEW YORK CITY

The Thursday business had to do with Meyer Lansky.

You see, in those days, besides running my speak, I worked for him. Not every day but two, three times a week, I'd pick something up or deliver something. This and that. I didn't ask what it was. We did our business face to face. Meyer didn't trust telephones since he heard that the feds were listening in, and he didn't like to put anything on paper either.

One evening I'd stopped by the office he shared with Charlie Luciano in the Barbizon-Plaza Hotel. I don't remember exactly what I was there for but that's not important. Meyer told me to pour myself a drink and wait until he'd finished what he was doing. He had something he wanted to talk over with me in private.

So I had a short scoot and read the papers until it was just Meyer and Charlie and me in the office. Then Meyer poured himself a scoot. That was unusual. He was not one to drink when work was at hand.

"You know a truck got hit coming in from Long Island a couple of weeks ago? One of Schultz's."

I nodded.

Charlie said, "Somebody knocked over one of ours last night."

Back in the first days of Prohibition, that kind of hijacking happened all the time. That was when the ships full of booze were first anchoring off the coast of Long Island and New Jersey. They transferred the product onto speedboats and then into trucks to ship it back to warehouses where they'd cut the stuff. Things weren't very well organized then, and guys ambushed other guys' trucks all the time. I did it myself once. Well, I helped. It was Meyer and Charlie's operation. I scouted the route to Egg Harbor City and went back with them and the others when we knocked over a really big shipment. Shot a guy, too. It was a hell of a night for a twelve-year-old.

By and by, business settled down as guys found more reliable ways to get booze and divided up the pie. Nobody had been hijacking trucks for years, at least not among the guys I knew. Until now.

"The guy that was driving the first truck, Izzy Stern, they killed him. They beat up the two guys who were driving our load, but they got the truck. Now, here's where it gets strange." Meyer hitched forward in his chair and explained.

He got a call that morning. There in the office at his private number, a number that not many people knew. The guy on the other end didn't introduce himself or even say Meyer's name. He just said that he understood some merchandize had been misplaced. Said he was new in town and he'd "taken possession" of the merchandize and sold it without knowing whose property it really was. He just learned who that owner was, and now he wanted to apologize and to make things right. If they could arrange a place to meet, he'd be there with fifteen, meaning fifteen thousand dollars. Alone.

I said, "That's nuts."

Meyer and Charlie agreed.

"So what does he really want?" I asked.

"We don't know," Charlie said, "But for fifteen, we're going to find out."

That made sense. "What are you going to do?"

Meyer said, "I'm going to tell him that I'll meet him. At your place."

"But you won't be there."

"Of course not."

For a while, we didn't say anything, all of us thinking about the ways this could go bad.

I asked how much. Meyer said a hundred if it turned out to that the guy didn't really have the fifteen, or five percent of it if he did. I said ten percent and Meyer and Charlie took care of any damages that might occur. And I wanted some of their guys there if there was any rough stuff. Meyer said ten and no damages, because it was damned unlikely that the guy was really going to bring the fifteen, and he was going to be alone, so he probably couldn't bust things up much.

"I don't care. I want extra hands."

Charlie said, "We could send the Rosens, the guys that got their truck stolen."

Meyer thought it over and said, "Yeah, we could use them for that. And we'll do something else."

He set it up for Thursday.

A little before noon Thursday, Fat Joe opened the door to three guys. The Rosens were younger than I'd thought, still teenagers. It was hard to tell at first because both of them had taken a pretty good pounding. Yellow bruises, split lip still not healed. They wore suits shiny at the elbows, poorly knotted short ties and battered hats. They were brothers. The third guy was Slappy Strauss. Him, I knew. Slappy was a driver for Meyer and when I had a lot of distance to cover, Meyer usually sent him with me. He was better dressed than the other two. All three of them were edgy, almost as edgy as I was.

Fat Joe put out the CLOSED sign. He knew we were expecting one more guy.

Inside, I offered drinks. Slappy said no. The young guys asked for beer. Frenchy drew two glasses. They said they were Pep and Irving Rosen. I asked if anybody told them what was happening. They shook their heads.

"A guy's supposed to come here to make a payment. He's expecting to meet Mr. Lansky, so he might not take it too well when he doesn't see him. He'll be alone. You and Slappy are going to make sure he behaves himself."

They looked at each other like they were confused and one of them said, "I thought we was going to get the guys what stole our truck."

"This guy's their boss," I said. They looked even more confused. "I just want you to take care of him if he makes trouble. What're you carrying?"

One of them produced a length of pipe wrapped in friction tape. The other had a sawed-off baseball bat under his coat.

"Guns?"

They shook their heads.

"Good. I don't want you putting holes in the walls."

I knew Slappy carried a Browning automatic in a shoulder holster, and I was happy to make an exception to the "no guns in Jimmy Quinn's" rule that afternoon. Frenchy kept a big Webley that he called a "hogleg" under the bar. Fat Joe preferred beating people with his fists.

I told the Rosens to stay with Frenchy at the bar. Slappy took a booth near the front. I sat at my two-top in back with my newspapers, and worried. I kept slipping my knucks on and off my fingers, and tried to figure what was going on. I mean, nobody steals fifteen thousand dollars of quality hooch and then tries to give the money back. What did the guy really want? We waited for an hour.

The guy who showed up was about my age. He had a cocky smile and dark hair slicked back with pomade. His topcoat was unbuttoned over a glen plaid suit with wide lapels and a nipped waist, and black and white two-tone shoes—too flashy to my taste. He was smoking a thin cigar, hardly bigger than a cigarette. He surveyed the place, and as he walked over to my table, he added a little skip to his step, like a dancer. His walk was as cocky as his smile. I didn't like him.

He stopped in front of the table and said, "First thing, Mr. Lansky, I got to apologize. If I'd known it was your liquor, I wouldn't never have touched it. I mean, I heard a lot about you from the first day I moved here and I sincerely hope you will forget about this and we can work together. I could be a useful part of your organization."

That part, I understood. Anybody who knew anything about the way the booze business worked in New York wanted to work with Lansky. He paid off the right pols and handled the most product. You didn't see his name in the papers, but nobody made any more money year after year.

It also figured that this guy hadn't met Lansky, but he knew Lansky was short, good looking and well dressed, and so he assumed I was Lansky. I set him straight. "Mr. Lansky couldn't make it. I'm Jimmy Quinn. I'm here for him. Who're you?"

"Xeno Pool. Maybe you heard of me." He pulled out a chair and sat across from me. Then he put his hat on the table, just so, like it had to be in the right place, and said again, "So, you heard of me?"

I just looked at him. That was too stupid to answer.

"But I still need to explain this to Mr. Lansky personally so he'll understand it was an honest mistake."

"Explain it to me."

He blew smoke at me. "How do I know you represent Mr. Lansky?"

"He told you to come here, didn't he? Anything you give to me, you give to him."

"But I need to explain it to him, so he'll understand it was an honest mistake."

"You said that already. Explain it to me."

He opened his mouth to speak but stopped, like he didn't know what to say if I wasn't Meyer Lansky. That didn't make sense. If he knew how important Meyer was, then he knew a man in that position would never agree to meet a schmuck like him, not even for fifteen grand.

"But I gotta give this to Mr. Lansky personally." He took an envelope out of his breast pocket and opened it just enough for me to see that it was stuffed with bills. I can't say it was fifteen Gs, but it was a lot of green. He put it back in his coat.

"Suit yourself. You can give it to me or you can leave."

He sat there and didn't say anything more, and I could tell he was getting mad. His fingers drummed on the table like he was trying to make up his mind. Then his shoulders bunched as he grabbed the edge of the table. He muttered, "To hell with this," and yelled, "Now!"

He flipped the two-top into my chest. I was already pushing away and my chair toppled backward as the table landed on me, hard. I tried to push it off as he came around and kicked at my stomach. I could tell something else was going on but didn't know what it was. Turned out to be the two young Rosen guys going after Frenchy and Slappy.

Pool shoved the table away as I was getting to my feet. He kicked at my stomach again and knocked the wind out of me. I doubled over helpless and tried to keep my head away from that ugly two-tone shoe. I twisted around, and he got me on the point of my left hip. My leg went numb. I managed to pull a chair between us but he threw it off and kicked me again on the hip. The pain exploded.

He had an easier time with me than the young guys had with Frenchy and Slappy, but I didn't see any of that. I was trying to cover up.

Fat Joe weighed in to help Frenchy, but even though the Rosen kid was outnumbered, he was fast and kept them away by swinging the pipe. The other one broke off from Slappy after he smacked him once with the bat. There was a lot of yelling and somebody threw a chair that shattered the mirror behind the bar. Fat Joe went down after one of the Rosens gave him a solid smack. As Frenchy tried to help him, the three bastards managed to get out the front door. Slappy ran after them and saw them pile into a car and drive away.

By the time he got back inside, Frenchy had Fat Joe sitting in a chair, and Fat Joe was saying that the fucking kid didn't knock him down, he just slipped. That got them started rehashing the fight. I couldn't join in.

I couldn't even stand up.

Chapter Four

1931
NEW YORK CITY

Frenchy and Fat Joe carried me upstairs to my office while Slappy went back to tell Meyer what happened. I've never been shot in the hip, but it couldn't hurt much more than that did. I mean, when I tried to put any weight on the joint, it just buckled. Even lying on the divan, it was hell. It hurt so damn bad I was sweating. I treated it with the Napoleon brandy. All right, I was not as completely and helplessly miserable as I was when I ruined my knee and Arnold Rothstein was killed and Mother Moon died within a couple of days of each other. But that's only because I was three years older and you can learn a lot in three years. With the hip though, the pain was a hundred times worse and I'm not exaggerating when I say that. It was like a drill right through the joint every time I moved. I didn't even want to eat.

A few hours later, a doctor showed up, Dr. Strieber. He said Meyer sent him. When he saw what I was drinking, he poured a double for himself, fired up a cigarette and told me to pull down my pants. My hip was already bruising up. He poked at it. I yelled and he knew how bad it was.

"Roll over on your other side," he said.

I couldn't. That made it hurt even more, a sharp flaring pain. He said if it was broken, it would hurt a lot worse, so it was probably just torn tendons and muscles and the only thing to be done was to stay off it, and ease back into my regular life when it got better.

As I was tugging my trousers back up, he noticed the brace on my knee and asked what it was.

"I busted something inside it three years ago. The guy who looked at it said there was nothing to be done about it either." I didn't tell him that the guy was a hophead who wasn't a real doctor.

"And the brace, where did you get that? I've never seen anything quite like it."

"Guy down in Chinatown made it for me."

He lit another cigarette. "Interesting design. Is it comfortable?"

"I wear it almost every day. I can't run but I can do just about anything else. As long as I've got my stick."

"Good, you're going to need it," he said and knocked back the last of his Napoleon. He gave me a bottle of pills and told me not to mix them with the brandy.

Meyer came by the next afternoon—Friday, while the glaziers he hired were putting in the new mirror. Yeah, he sprung for that, too. If you worked for him long enough, he treated you right.

I was still on the divan. Marie Therese had found me some crutches and with those, I could hobble to the office bathroom. Looked like I was going to be living in my office for a while. Even though I took naps on the divan when I was normal, somehow I couldn't find a position that was comfortable for more than a few minutes before the pain shot through my hip again.

Meyer sat down and said, "Tell me everything that happened." He looked like he was angry, almost as angry as I was. He didn't say anything until I finished.

"Xeno Pool? What kind of name is that? Any accent?"

"I don't know. Yeah, I guess so. At least he didn't sound like he was from around here."

"And you're sure you didn't recognize him?"

"Never saw him before. Never saw those Rosen kids, either. You know them?"

He frowned and nodded. "Yeah, they're from the neighborhood. Brothers. But I didn't work with them until a year ago. Until now, everybody said they were reliable. Had their own truck."

He stopped and thought on it for a time. "Then it figures it was them and Pool that knocked over Izzy Stern's load, and then they were in on it with Pool hijacking my shipment from their own truck. Hell, they probably beat each other up."

"They were ready. As soon as Pool said 'now,' they laid into Frenchy and Slappy."

Meyer shook his head and stood up. "It's a stupid play. If he's still in town, I'm going to find this Pool character. Same for the Rosens."

"They wouldn't be dumb enough to stick around after pulling something like this."

"You never know," Meyer said, and it turned out he was right. "Sorry as hell about your place. There'll be something extra for you next week."

"If you find Pool, I want to be in on it."

"You bet."

That was Friday. Willie Seabrook showed up Saturday night.

I was still stretched out and miserable on the divan. The pills weren't doing anything and the Napoleon wasn't either. I hadn't slept worth a damn for two nights when Marie Therese knocked on the office door and came in. "Someone's here to see you. He—"

Willie was just outside the door and when he saw me, he didn't wait to be invited in. He just stepped past Marie Therese and said, "My god, man, what's happened to you?"

Before I could answer, Marie Therese started speaking French to him. The only word I could understand was 'Willie.' He answered in French and it sounded like he was asking for something. It ended with Marie Therese saying "oui" and scurrying out. Willie pulled up a chair.

"They certainly got you good. What is it, the hip? Butt?"

"Yeah."

"Madam Reneau says you can't sleep."

"Damn, you two hit it off quick."

He shrugged. "She's concerned about you and I think I can help. When I lived with the Beduw, we dealt with this kind of injury and—"

"Beduw?"

"Bedouins. In Arabia, I lived with a group of them in the desert and when we treated hip problems, we rearranged the bedding."

He said that like he was explaining that he had to stop and pick up his laundry on the way over. It was just a minor detail that explained things.

"But we'll get to that when Madam Reneau comes back. Actually, I came here for the case of the Hennessy Five Star. And there's another matter."

"Right, the brandy. There's an open bottle of the Napoleon over there. Pour a couple of knocks. The Five Star will be here Monday"

He did. We drank.

He sat back and closed his eyes, and I could tell he was savoring the smooth heat. "This is superb," he said and gestured toward my hip with his snifter. "What happened?"

"Some business that didn't work out."

"Of course." He understood and never asked about it again. Then he said he wanted to rent my place for an evening. "It's perfect for another group of friends, and there's a separate matter that's more difficult to describe and requires some discretion."

"What do you mean?"

"Do you have a cellar? Might I have a look at it? There's no point in my trying to explain if it's not suitable."

That sounded as mysterious as he meant it to be. "Sure, we've got a cellar. Normally, I'd take you downstairs myself, but why don't we wait for Marie Therese."

"Excellent. Now, tell me how in the world you manage to deal in this kind of brandy, and the wine and whisky you delivered. In restaurants that claim to be the very best, I've paid as much for alcoholized red ink in a phony Chateauneuf du Pape bottle."

Even in my condition, I was pleased to be flattered like that. I said, "Without going into boring details…"

"Oh, no," he interrupted and poured two more knocks. "I want the details."

And I wound up telling him about working as a runner for Arnold Rothstein when I was a pup and the World Series we fixed and how I met Meyer and stole trucks and cars for him and Charlie to move hooch, and that led somehow to Mother Moon and my growing up in her place in Hell's Kitchen. And he told me about his time in Maryland and Kansas, and how he'd loved his Mother so helplessly when he was a boy but now he wanted to kill her as often as not for the way she treated him and his brother.

Now, I never—and I mean *never*—open up like that around guys I don't know, and not even around the few guys I do know pretty well. But, Willie, well, that's just the way he was, particularly when he'd had just the right amount to drink and had persuaded you to do the same.

We were still talking when Marie Therese and Frenchy came in carrying armloads of cushions and rugs and pillows. Don't ask me where they got them.

Willie said, "Yes, these are perfect. When I was with the Bedouins we reclined on the sand but our bedding was made of rugs, German mattresses and camel saddles, and it was as comfortable as any hotel. Your problem, Jimmy, is that because your hip hurts so much and you can't turn over, you're trying to stay completely flat. You need to bend."

He took folded rugs and stacked a pillow on top of them and put them under my knees. I raised up and he put more behind my back. Right away, the stabbing pain faded, just a little. They adjusted things this way and that until Frenchy handed Willie an ugly brownish gray wool blanket. Willie stopped, rubbed the rough texture of it and spoke to him in French. Frenchy answered, and whatever they were saying made him look serious.

When they finished, Willie said, "I apologize. That was rude. It's just that I've spent so much time in France that the language seems as natural as English to me now, and this blanket, it's been a long time since I saw one. Not since the war."

He folded the blanket and put it under my feet. "How's that? Good? Yes. Then perhaps Madam Reneau could show me the cellar?"

They went downstairs and came back ten minutes later. Then we worked out the details. First, he arranged to rent the place in two weeks, on a Friday night. He expected between twenty and forty guests, all white this time, or close enough that the neighbors wouldn't notice. He said they were friends from years ago when his wife Katie ran a coffee house down in Greenwich Village.

"Is that the woman who was with you the other night?" I asked.

"No, that's Mink… Marjorie. Katie got fed up and we divorced years ago. God knows, I put her through enough. She deserved better and all of our friends knew it. I guess that's part of the reason for this party. I want to show them I managed to make something of myself on my own. And now I'll give the bastards a taste of some decent liquor for a change." He drained the brandy.

"Now, about the little room in the cellar. I'd like to rent that, too, and I'm going to want to use it for two or three hours a day. Alone. Probably for a week, maybe more. I'll want a table, a chair and a lamp."

"Sure, we can provide that."

"Some others will be joining me from time to time, a friend who's a photographer and a detective. I've engaged one from the Continental Agency. Can you make sure that the thick-necked thug who guards the door knows about them?"

Marie Therese, who didn't have the highest opinion of Fat Joe to begin with, said she'd make sure. Willie had charmed her, too.

So, after a little more talk and another Napoleon, we agreed on a price. Willie pulled out his bankroll and peeled off bills. As he counted, Marie Therese smiled. So did I. It was going to be a profitable month.

Marie Therese went back to work. Willie poured two more brandies. He said, "I'm making this sound more mysterious than it really is. You'll understand soon enough. A couple of young women have gotten themselves into something that's hard to describe. When women delve into criminal matters, it's always difficult, and women are completely capable of them. Blackmail, murder, even bank robbery—"

That's when it came to me. "That's how I know your name. The newspapers. You did that stuff with that girl. What did they call her, the girl who robbed the banks?"

Willie laughed. "The Bobbed-Haired Bandit. Little Cecilia. She and I certainly sold a lot of newspapers for Mr. Hearst."

"For a while, she was all you saw in any of the papers."

That was back in '24. The girl we were talking about was Cecilia Cooney. She and her husband lived in Brooklyn. They were having trouble making ends meet and she was pregnant, so they decided to stick up neighborhood grocery stores. They didn't even shoot anybody, as I remember it, but to read about her in the papers, you'd think she was a one-woman crime wave. When they finally caught her, Willie bribed his way into the jail and got her full confession.

"I loved all that," I said. "I've been reading the papers since I was a kid. That's where I learned to read and it was stories like that, and the funnies that really got to me."

"How did newspapers teach you to read?"

"I told you about working for Rothstein. Sometimes he'd get into these pool games and poker games that lasted for more than a day, and he'd want me to be there in case he had to conduct some business but didn't want to leave the table. That left me with a lot of time on my hands, and there was always a stack of papers around. Hell, in those days, there must have been a dozen dailies. At first, I'd just look at the pictures. Then I started keeping a little notebook with me to write down the words I didn't know. I still keep one. Here."

I reached over and found my current notebook under a stack of newsprint on the table by the divan.

Willie gave me a funny look. "It's curious. That's how I've thought of my readers. Whether it was crime stories like that or the latest Nostradamus prophecy that's come true—no matter how slight the piece, I imagined a man picking up a paper that someone had left on a subway car or at a lunch counter, and then seeing something of mine that catches his interest. If I'm able to entertain him for a few minutes, and maybe make him think about something he hasn't thought of before, then I've done my job."

He frowned into his brandy. "I wish it was that simple now."

Chapter Five

1918
NAPA, CALIFORNIA

You can't understand what happened with Willie and me if you don't know about Connie and how she came to New York.

She was born on a farm in Arkansas, but she didn't remember it. It flooded for the third time when she was little. She had an older brother and an older sister. Later she had two much younger sisters and one younger brother, the baby of the bunch. Her being the middle kid, nobody paid much attention to her except when she didn't want them to. In the end, that's why she left.

After that last flood, her mother and father sent word out to everyone in their families that they were ready to move. Did anyone have a suggestion? One of her mother's cousins wrote that grapes and prunes just about grew themselves in Napa, California, and the weather was perfect for drying fruit. They scraped together enough money for her father to take a train and see what it was like. Two weeks later, he wrote that Connie's mother should sell what she could, pack the rest in their Model T and bring the kids to California. He'd found the perfect place for them in Browns Valley. Connie said that her first real memories were of riding in that car. Hot wind, rain and sleeping on the floor when they couldn't stay with family.

In California, the first place they lived in was an auto camp on the Napa River. After that they moved into a rented farm house in Browns Valley in the middle of a prune orchard that seemed to go on for miles. I've got to admit when she described it to me, I couldn't picture it. So many trees, no buildings. Who could live in a place like that? Her parents got help from the local farm center. They worked the prunes on the land they'd rented. Whenever they had any extra time, they worked for other farmers.

When Connie was old enough, she worked in the orchards, too, and went to a one-room school. She hated the orchards and loved school. But that didn't matter. Girls were supposed to work and get married. Her father said school was a waste of time for her. By the time Connie was old enough to argue against that, she was smart enough to keep her mouth shut. She knew she couldn't change her father's mind about anything.

He was one of those guys who just knew he was smarter than everybody else. That's why he could see opportunities and ideas that other guys ignored. That's why he was willing to take risks that everybody else said were foolish. It seemed to Connie that whenever they got ahead, he came up with a new technique or a better product. If walnuts did so well in Browns Valley, why not Brazil nuts? That one never got any farther than some seeds he bought from a traveling salesman, but there were others. Connie's mother, a willful woman, tried to keep her husband in line but it was a full-time job. The kids cleared the room when they fought.

On Sunday mornings, her father fired up the Ford, and took them to church. They never stayed with a church for very long, but the churches were all the same to Connie. Small buildings or basements or barns or back rooms filled with loud people and loud ugly music. Sometimes the places were too cold but most of the time they were too hot and crowded. Connie's father found churches with names like the First Tabernacle of Full Gospel Holiness or the Church of the Blessed Trinity. They would go there until he got into an argument with one of the other men about something Connie didn't understand. It usually had to do with the end of the world. Then they'd stay at home on Sundays until he found the Temple of Illuminated Emancipation and Connie would suffer through Sunday mornings there. She never took any of it seriously. Even when she was little, she could tell the adults were trying to convince themselves.

Connie's mother and her older brother and older sister kept working for other farmers. One year, her father bought a horse-drawn spraying wagon. It carried a tank full of a foul liquid that killed bugs on pear trees. It also burned her nose. They had to wear hoods, masks, raincoats, and gloves when they used it on the orchards. Connie hated it. It smelled as bad as the tannery by the river.

When the next kid came along, Connie spent more time looking after him. That's when they had to move to a larger place with electricity and hot running water. They got a mortgage on a five-acre farm near the railroad tracks closer to Napa. It had a two-bedroom house and four small redwood outbuildings that her parents planned to fix up and rent out as tourist cottages. There was also a garage, a shop building, a chicken coop and rabbit house, and a feed shed. And trees, prune trees and cherry trees.

By then, Connie was old enough to take care of her younger sisters and baby brother while her parents and her older sister and older brother worked on the tourist cabins. She hated that almost as much as she hated spraying the pear orchards. No, she told me once, that wasn't true. She didn't hate the kids. She just wasn't that interested in them. They bored her.

When the tourist cabins were ready, Connie's older sister demanded one for herself and her parents gave it to her. It was easier than trying to fight with her about it because Connie's older sister took after her mother. She had ideas about how things should be done. If she had power over anybody smaller or weaker or younger to make them do what she wanted, she let them know, and backed it up with slaps, pinches and threats. She got her way.

Connie thought it was pretty terrific when she moved into the cabin. More room for her. She took the better bed by the window. At night, even when it was cold and the window was closed, she could hear the sound of the trains on the tracks and the whistles. Most of them were freight trains. But some of them, she knew were passenger trains. The whistles sounded sharper and faster, and those trains were carrying people, travelers heading to the cities in the East, the places she'd only heard about.

Chapter Six

1931
NEW YORK CITY

I spent the next three weeks in the speak. They brought some of my clothes from the Chelsea, and I was able to wash up at the sink in the office bathroom. Using a crutch and my stick, I could move around well enough. When my appetite came back, the guys in the Cruzon Grill made my meals on a tray. I spent most of my time dreaming up violent ways to fix Xeno Pool's wagon the next time I saw him, but I knew that that wasn't likely. Only a crazy man would screw around with Lansky and then stay in the city.

As it turned out, Willie Seabrook gave me a lot to think about.

I sold him a case of the Hennessy Five Star but he still dropped by to drink and talk. He also wanted to check on the room in the cellar they were getting ready for him. He explained it one afternoon by asking if I remembered seeing a very pale young white woman at the party he gave for Miss A'Lelia Walker. I said no. Willie settled into a chair and told the story.

"She's an actress who's had some success. Her name is Lily White. At the party, I noticed that she refused to sample any of the food, though I could tell how much she wanted to eat. You remember how it smelled. How could anyone not be tempted? But she was pale and thin and somehow frightened, I thought. She made a point of speaking to me and said that she wanted to see me again privately. When we met for lunch at her apartment, she served me a proper meal but had nothing but gruel herself and she ate it with a wooden spoon. I asked if she'd salted the gruel and when she said no, I knew what was going on. She thinks she has been bewitched by Haitian voodoo, and everyone who knows me knows that I have made a study of black magic."

He said that with the same off-hand ease he said all the other screwball stuff, like living with the Arabs. To him, there was nothing unusual about it.

"She told me that another actress has put a curse on her. I know this woman almost as well as I know Miss White and I don't particularly care for her. Though Miss White tells herself rationally that there is nothing to the curse, she cannot force herself to disbelieve in its power."

I must have let something show.

"I can see you don't believe this either. Well, let me explain it to you. Miss White admitted to me that this actress, one Ruby Rose, has a very good reason to wish her ill."

He said that the women had been in a risqué revue together, quite scandalous at the time. Oh yeah, I remembered it well, Ruby Rose most of all.

As Willie put it, the show was nothing special but it attracted more than its share of Stagedoor Johnnies. Miss Lily White connived to steal one of the richest ones away from Ruby Rose. She did it because she could, for fun, and she thought that after her little escapade with the young man was over, it would all be forgotten. It was not. Miss Ruby Rose stewed over it and when she decided to do something, she proved to be particularly vindictive and imaginative.

"The stories and rumors started right away. Since they're actresses of roughly the same age, these women travel in the same circles. Even in a city as large as this, within certain groups everyone knows everyone and they don't keep secrets. I'm sure it's the same for you. That being the case, three of these mutual acquaintances went out with Miss Rose and the four of them got wobbly on the Upper West Side at the Fitzroy Tavern."

The Fitzroy was a fair speak, I suppose. Nothing special.

"At the end of the evening, she insisted that they come up to her apartment because she had something to show them. It was a doll."

According to Willie, this wasn't just any doll, not something that a little girl would play with. It was more realistic than a department store dummy with carefully detailed hair, eyes and facial features. It was a perfect representation of Miss White, even down to the mole on her lip, and the dress. The dress was a replica of a Chanel gown, gray and pink, that had been made for her. It was unmistakable. Miss White had worn it publicly, and so it was something that everyone in her circle would know immediately and they would not associate it with anyone else.

"Ruby Rose told them that she takes the doll out of her closet every evening, if she isn't working, and stabs hatpins into the stomach. They could see that the middle of the gown had been shredded. Miss Rose's sadistic joy in mutilating it thrilled and horrified all of them. Word spread quickly after that, as Miss Rose knew it would. There had been rumors of her voodoo curse before, but now it became common knowledge that Miss Rose was trying to kill Miss White."

Miss White told Willie that her stomach problems and her inability to eat had begun before the rumors reached her. She could afford the best doctors and she'd been to see all of them. To a man, they told her that they could find nothing wrong, but still she had the stabbing cramps, the vomiting, the weight loss.

"And, I tell you, she looks dreadful. She was always slender and graceful but now she looks like she's been starving. When we talked over lunch, she claimed not to be superstitious, not to believe in any of this nonsense. But, I asked, if that were true, why was she using the wooden spoon and why was she refusing salt? She couldn't answer, so I did. 'Because you know that if a powerful spell has been cast, salt turns to poison in the victim's body, and eating from silverware is just as dangerous.'

"It's all rubbish, of course, but not if the intended victim believes in its power. She broke down then and said that yes, I was right and she was at the end. I was her last hope and she didn't see how I could do anything. I assured her I could and that's why I'm here. I'm going to stop this because if I don't, I truly believe that young woman may die."

"Wait a minute. Are you saying you believe that some dame can hurt another dame just by sticking hatpins in a doll?"

I've got to admit that if I hadn't heard how sincere his voice was and seen how grim he looked, I'd have thought he was trying to put one over on me.

He said, "I have seen many things I can't explain by conventional means. Fakirs and charlatans of every stripe have tried to trick me. What I'm saying is that I try to be careful with what I believe, what I disbelieve and what I suspect. For example, I doubt that anyone could hurt you, Jimmy, by damaging a doll. You believe in what you can see and touch. Any sort of spiritualism is so much foolishness. But if you were predisposed, as Miss White is, to believe in such things, then, yes, another person could hurt you. It's psychology, not magic, and it works both ways. To save Miss White, we are going to fight fire with fire. No, we are going to fight a small fire with a big fire."

He paused to drink. "The important thing to remember here is that Miss Rose believes this too, just as much as Miss White does. She may think that she's only playing at it but she wouldn't be doing it if she didn't accept at least the possibility that the business with the doll would be effective. Do you understand that?"

"Sure."

"We're going to let her know that we believe it, too."

"How?"

"We should find out this evening."

Around six o'clock we were having a couple of Five Stars in my office—I still wasn't going anywhere—when Marie Therese came in with a short fat woman and said she was there to see Willie.

He introduced us. "Jimmy, this is Theodora Opperman of the Continental Detective Agency. Mrs. Opperman, Jimmy Quinn. He owns this establishment."

I guessed her age at around thirty. She wasn't much taller than me but she was twice as wide around the middle. She wore a black coat and skirt over a white blouse. She had short brown hair and a face that was hard to remember. She gave me a long once-over and said "Quinn?" like she was trying to bring something to mind. I didn't recognize her, but I could think of three or four occasions when the Continental Agency might have been interested in me, and we could have crossed paths professionally. There was no need to bring those up.

She asked Willie if he wanted her report then, meaning did he want her to talk in front of me.

Willie said, "Of course."

She took out a pack of Fatimas and fired one up. Willie asked if she'd like a drink. She took a brandy and opened a small notebook.

She said she and her partners started, as Willie suggested, in the toy departments of the big stores. Those places handled a few special orders but no one recognized the photograph they had of Miss White. After that, they went to the more expensive shops that sold nothing but dolls. Again, they came up dry. Those places handled special orders every week, but nothing like the detectives described. No luck at the places that built mannequins, either. The two men she was working with were ready to give it up as a bad job by then. She didn't say as much but you could tell that the guys thought it was damn silly for a couple of detectives to be chasing after a doll in the first place.

Then she thought of an angle they'd missed, a place that wasn't on their list.

"I found it in a little shop down off of Mulberry Street, where an old Italian works. He makes puppets."

When she showed him the picture of Miss White, the Italian said right away that he knew it. The gentleman came in with the same rotogravure of the beautiful lady in the elegant gown. The gentleman said she was his fiancée and he wanted to surprise her. He described the colors of the dress and the materials and he came back to the shop twice to check on the facial features as the Italian was carving the head. And he insisted that the body be filled with kapok. A traditional wooden body would not do.

When the puppet was finished, the customer was happy, and the old man said it was one of his finest creations. He hoped there was nothing wrong with it now.

Willie jumped out of his armchair and said she was brilliant. "That's exactly what we need. Did you learn anything about the man who placed the order?"

"No, only that he paid in cash."

"Perhaps I can get something out of the Italian. Let's go." They left.

When Willie came back the next evening, he was really jazzed. He poured a double Five Star and said that he had everything lined up. He just needed to finish the invitations to his party.

I sipped my coffee. "Does this party have anything to do with the business involving the doll?"

He said, "Yes. Originally I hadn't intended it, but it will suit my purposes nicely. I've given Madam Reneau a list of food and drink to be laid in, and my special requirements." He gave me a curious look. "I'm afraid some of them may offend her."

"Offend Marie Therese? You gotta be kidding me. Plenty goes on here that folks in polite society don't talk about and she's worked joints a lot gamier than this."

He cocked an eyebrow and one corner of his mouth ticked up. "We'll see. But right now, I will bet you one dollar that when my party is over, you'll admit that you've never seen anything like it in this place."

He held out his hand and I shook it, knowing that I was going to lose. He could tell what I was thinking and said, "Don't worry. It'll be worth it."

He drained the brandy. "We should have the room in the basement ready tonight and I'll start to work. If you're up to it, come down and take a look."

I was still mostly lame but I was also bored. After reading eight daily papers, the words were blurring together and the radio was no better. So, around ten o'clock, I put on a clean starched shirt and the vest that went with my slacks. I tried to get my feet into a pair of shoes but I couldn't reach down to tie them, so I had to settle for slippers. Then I went down the stairs one step at a time. With one hand on my stick and the other on the railing. It took less than half an hour to get to the basement.

I can't say exactly what I expected to find but it sure wasn't what I saw. That's the way it always was with Willie.

We kept our stock in the cellar—the booze, the beer, the wine, mixers, cigarettes, cigars, ice, glasses. Most of it was in one large room with a rough plank floor and a low ceiling. It smelled of dirt and spilled hooch and was lit by bare bulbs. We had a dumb waiter to move things up to the bar and the kitchen at the Cruzon Grill where we washed glasses. Willie wasn't interested in any of those. He wanted to use our junk room, a little place not much bigger than a closet. Willie had cleared everything out. He'd even washed the floor.

That night, Brenda and Dorothy, our waitresses, were fluttering around Willie, ready to do anything he might want. Marie Therese was there, too, and she kept shooing the girls away. They ignored her.

I could tell that something wasn't right about the place and I saw that three of the bulbs in the main room had been unscrewed and electrical cords were running from the sockets into the junk room. It glowed with bright white light like it never had before.

I edged in between Dorothy and Brenda and saw that lamps had been set up inside. Willie and a guy with a Rolleiflex camera were moving the lamps around. There was a table in the middle of the room. It was covered with a white sheet and there were more white sheets on the walls. Mrs. Opperman was behind Willie. She had a long cardboard box under her arm.

A puppet was propped up on the table, and the guy with the camera was adjusting the lights to show its face. It had hennaed hair and a black and white striped dress. The face looked like it had been carefully carved, but I don't know beans about dolls or puppets.

The guy looking down into the camera said, "This will probably work, at least for the first pictures but I'll use the flash. We may have to bring in more lights for the rest of them."

Willie said, "Where should I be?"

The guy said, "That's fine. You just want your hand in the shot, right? That's easy. I can crop it."

Willie knocked back his Five Star and said, "Then let's get on with it."

The guy took a few pictures of the doll from different angles. When he said he was ready for the next set, Willie nodded to the detective.

She stubbed out her smoke and opened the long box and handed a miniature wooden coffin to Willie. They spent another twenty minutes working with the puppet in the coffin. They moved the lights around to throw heavy shadows on different parts of it. The photographer opened a bag of paints and powders, and he and the detective went to work on the puppet's face. I don't know what they did but by the time they were finished, the puppet's eyes looked like they were wide open in fright and her mouth seemed to be screaming.

The photographer took more pictures, the flash crunching with each one, all of the doll in the coffin. It was pretty damn creepy, I can tell you. As the guy was packing up his equipment, Willie said, "As soon as they're ready, give the prints and the negatives to Mrs. Opperman, and don't breathe a word of this to anyone. I promise there will be nothing that can be traced back to you. No one will know you helped me."

The photographer cut his eyes at me and Mrs. Opperman.

Willie said, "They're professionals."

Once everyone cleared out, Willie explained his plan. At first, I thought it was pure malarkey, but I gotta admit, the way it worked out, Willie knew what he was doing and he was more right than wrong.

"Remember that I told you Ruby Rose invited those friends who knew Miss White to see how she tortured the puppet. She did that because she had to be absolutely certain that Miss White knew she was being attacked in that manner. I propose to do the same thing to her."

He said that he let it be known among the same group of theater people that he was up to something. Then he handed me a piece of yellow foolscap and said this item was going to run in Ed Sullivan's next *Daily News* column.

"Author William Seabrook is in town. As he prepares for his next book about Africa, he is said to be involved in a secretive personal project for a friend. Who could the lady be?"

"Ruby Rose is sure to see it," he said. "She'll read it in the morning and when she opens her mail, she'll find a photograph of this puppet. Mrs. Opperman is sending it."

"I don't get it."

"I'm going to do to her what she is doing to Miss White."

"But it's horseshit."

He started to say something but stopped and thought about it for a moment. "You think it's horseshit. I think it's horseshit, but Miss Rose doesn't think it's horseshit, or she wouldn't be doing it to Miss White. Agreed?"

"Yeah."

"And if Ruby Rose believes that this kind of magic can work *for* her, she will also believe..."

"That it can work against her."

"Exactly, and she knows that I am much more well versed in these dark studies than she is. That is why Miss White came to me in the first place."

"So, you let her know that you're putting the hex on her, and she sees a picture of the puppet—"

He nodded his head. "The black and white dress isn't as closely associated with her as the Chanel is with Lily, but it's based on one that she wore in publicity photos."

"And then she stops the business with the pins and Miss White feels better and everything is hunky-dory."

"No, I'm afraid not. It's a little more complicated."

"How?"

"I cannot simply pretend to curse her with this magic. You don't idly stab a pin in a doll and get any results. You must concentrate on the doll, imagine the person you're trying to influence and focus every ounce of your mental and spiritual being on that target while seeking one specific result. That's what I'll be doing every day."

"Wait a minute. You just said this is horseshit."

He shrugged. "Maybe it's not."

Willie was as good as his word. He came to the speak every day and spent three or four hours down in the cellar room with the puppet and the coffin. I saw how exhausted he was after each visit. Some days he'd go to the bar, attracted by a happy crowd and a pretty girl. Some days, he came up to the office and drank with me. His face was always sweaty and his hands shook when he lit his smokes and poured his brandy.

"What the hell are you doing down there?" I asked the first time he came in looking like that.

"I told you. I'm putting a curse on Ruby Rose. By now, she knows that I am involved. Word is getting back to her, second and third hand. I'm told she is asking questions about what I'm doing. Wonderful! That's the reaction I was hoping to get. I'll reinforce those fears at my party which she has been invited to. I strongly suspect that sometime soon, she will let me know that she no longer cares what Miss White does, and it will all be finished. But until then, I must take it seriously. I must sit at that table and stare at the puppet and I must let the white walls become my entire universe, and I must focus my mind to saturate the doll with sickness and evil."

"You stick pins in it?"

"Yes, but I'm convinced that if there is any reality to this, my concentration and my will are more important. The pins are merely a prop."

He could tell I wasn't buying it and went on. "There's a man down at Duke University who's conducting carefully controlled scientific experiments on these matters. His name's Rhine. He uses cards with symbols printed on them. One man studies a randomly chosen card and tries to transfer that symbol with his mind to another man. Rhine has some promising results but I doubt that anything will ever come of it. If this sort of magic, or whatever it is, works at all, you'll never find it in a cold, sterile laboratory. It comes from the more powerful emotions—lust, passion, hatred. Believe me, I know." He frowned when he said that last part and I figured he was speaking from experience, but I still didn't buy it.

I mean, ever since I was a kid, I've known people who believed all sorts of screwy things, like old Mrs. Harsbeck who lived upstairs at Mother Moon's place and thought she could put the evil eye on you. She wouldn't let her kids go outside without some bit of color on their clothes to keep other people from putting the evil eye on them. And there were the guys who thought they could make a living betting on horses, or people who pray to a statue to make something happen. But Willie didn't seem like any of those. I'd only known him for a few days and I hadn't figured him out yet, so I asked him again.

"Do you believe it? Can you make that girl sick by thinking about it?"

"When I'm sitting here talking to you, maybe I don't believe it. But in the cellar, it's different. Sometimes, I swear, the puppet becomes her, Ruby Rose. I can see her face, her real face and it's different when I turn off the light. Darkness and blindness change things in another way. You see..."

His thought trailed off and he started again. "I can't give you a simple yes or no answer. As I said before, I believe this particular form of witchcraft is psychology, not magic, and that's what I'm practicing against her, too. But at the same time, I believe..., no, I don't believe, I *know* there are many aspects of the physical and metaphysical worlds I do not understand. No one does. But I will. In time, I will."

"But why are you doing this? I thought you wrote books."

Willie waved that off. "I write books about things and places that interest me, and they always come back to magic, the things I can't explain. And sex, because that's what drives everything."

Chapter Seven

1925
NAPA, CALIFORNIA

Connie's older brother was one of those guys who figured out early what adults wanted to hear from him. As soon as he was out of knee pants, he started talking about how he was going to go to divinity school and spread the word of god as his life's work. Then when the grownups weren't paying attention to him, he was stealing candy, then cigarettes, then cigars, then liquor. Connie didn't care. She thought he was wonderful. Once he started getting caught doing the stuff he wasn't supposed to be doing, Connie watched her father and mother squaring off with him. Sometimes they yelled. Sometimes they fought. It always ended with Connie's older brother claiming that he understood he'd done wrong and promising that he wouldn't do it again, and Connie's father and mother forgiving him again.

Like most of the other kids, when there wasn't work to be done in the orchards, Connie worked in Sawyer's Tannery making baseball gloves. That's where she learned, just like I did, that a kid could sneak a few nickels and dimes, maybe even a dollar from a pay envelope without a grownup catching on. The trick was not to spend it. You showed up with a new magazine or pocketknife and you were sunk. But if you found a place to hide it and keep it, then maybe you could do something with it someday.

And there were things to do in Napa. Besides the orchards, the town had a busy waterfront of wharves, warehouses and lumberyards. Steamers came up the river to ship goods down to the docks in Vallejo and San Francisco. The waterfront was always interesting. You didn't know what you might see there. Once, Connie and her older sister were there when a steamer came in and unloaded. Most of the cargo was the usual boxes, crates and bales, but there were also two big wicker cages on the deck.

Connie could see a woman inside each cage as the workers lifted them off the boat and put them on wagons. The women were in straitjackets. One lay on her side. The other tried to stand but fell when the workers tilted the cage. They had matted hair and frightened faces. Connie's older sister whispered that the women were crazy and they were being taken to the Farm. That's what everyone called the Asylum. It was a huge spooky old madhouse that looked like a castle with stone walls, turrets, and towers. Connie thought it was wonderful, mysterious and frightening.

Connie's older sister pinched her arm and said that they'd take Connie to the Farm if she didn't do what she was told. Connie tried not to believe her.

Alta Heights, the Italian part of town, was another forbidden place. Connie's mother and father told the kids never to go there. Connie's older brother and older sister snuck off to it whenever they could.

But the place Connie loved was downtown Napa. That's where she discovered the Goodman Library and the Free Library, a clapboard building that reminded her of school. She went inside by herself, and a woman behind the deck explained how it worked. The next time her mother took her into town, Connie made her go inside and sign the form—the form Connie filled out—so she could have a library card.

Like me, Connie couldn't remember not knowing how to read or how she learned. All she knew was that she was the only person in her family who cared about it. Her mother and father and her older brother and older sister were always telling her to "get her nose out of that book" and do something else. They didn't understand. She once told me, "The libraries and the books showed me that there were places outside Napa, Yountville, and Browns Valley, and the books made me want to know more about them, more about everything. You just can't explain that to some people."

Chapter Eight

1931
NEW YORK CITY

They brought the column in on Friday afternoon. Willie's party was that night. Marie Therese had been working with Vittorio, the Cruzon maître d', to arrange the food. Frenchy took care of the booze, wine and beer. I hobbled around my office and said yes when they asked about anything.

The column was eight or nine feet tall. I don't know what it was made of but it took four guys to get it down the steps from the street and through the door. It was painted white and had a square base. At first, they wanted to nail it to the bar but we scotched that in short order. The bar was mahogany. They wound up using metal straps to attach it to the wall at the end of the bar near the coat room. I didn't know what the hell Willie wanted it for.

It looked like Dorothy and Brenda knew. They'd been making eyes at Willie every time he came in, and they made sure his glass was never empty. When they saw the column, they blushed and started giggling and whispering to each other like a couple of kids. Marie Therese told them to get back to work.

I gimped back up to my office. An hour or so later, Meyer Lansky and Slappy Strauss showed up. Since the business with Pool, Slappy had been driving him, and he kept another guy with a gun close by. Meyer was always careful.

He said he had a line on Xeno Pool. "Word is he hasn't left town."

"What the hell was he trying to do here anyway? He flashed a wad of cash like he really meant to pay up."

Meyer chewed on that one. "Yeah, if he just wanted to poke a thumb in my eye, why would he risk bringing money with him? Well, hell, we'll ask him about it when we nail the son of a bitch. Those little cocksuckers that were in it with him, the Rosens, they've been around their old neighborhood in Brooklyn, bragging about what tough guys they are. Pool's going to show up, too, I know it."

"Don't go after him without me."

"Then get better. I'm not going to let him get away again. Can you walk?"

"If I have to. If you find Pool, I'll walk." It wasn't a complete lie. I'd healed enough to bend over and tie my shoes.

I was pretty damn stir crazy, too, so after they left I put on my hat and coat and went out of the speak for the first time in more than a week. It took me twice as long as it usually did to go up the street and around the corner and down the street to the Chelsea Hotel, and when I got there, my hip was throbbing so hot that I had to sit down in one of the chairs in the lobby before I got in the elevator. Yeah, I was ready to go after Pool. I couldn't have whipped a determined kitten.

Up in my room, I knocked back a couple of the doctor's pills and sat down again until the pain eased back and I could stand up long enough to take a shower. It felt good to wash off the stink of smoke and booze but I still couldn't stay on my feet long enough to enjoy it. Getting dressed took a long time, too, since I still had to stop and sit when the hip spoke up. I managed to make myself presentable in a medium-weight slate worsted, a pin striped shirt and a dark tie. If Willie's guests were the same kind of rich famous folk as Miss A'Lelia Walker, I needed to look sharp.

I debated shoes with myself. I had a nicely polished pair of wingtips. But they had leather soles. And since I wouldn't be walking much, I was planning not to wear my knee brace. That meant I had an unsteady knee and a bum hip, so I needed the best shoes I had. Those were the crepe-soled brogans. They wouldn't take a good shine but they wouldn't slip out from under me, either.

Besides, there was Rule Number Two. Always wear comfortable shoes.

That settled it. I took my time lacing them up—hell, I couldn't hurry—and sat back in my chair and enjoyed the view over the balcony down Twenty-Third Street to Seventh Avenue. There wasn't much to my place. Just a couple of rooms and a bath, but after a week in the speak and not seeing the outside except for the alley in back, I wanted to sit with the window open and listen to the noise and watch the afternoon traffic and the sidewalk parade, and smell the exhaust fumes. It was great.

Around nine thirty or ten, I hobbled back and went upstairs to the Cruzon. Friday night being what it was, the place was busy so I told Vittorio I'd eat in the kitchen. The guys threw a chop on the grill and fixed up some hash browns and commiserated with me over my hip and the state of the world.

After I finished, I gimped back out the front door and went down the steps from the sidewalk to the speak. Fat Joe opened the door. He had a funny look on his face.

"You're not gonna believe what these fucking guys are doing."

I saw what he meant right away. There was a naked girl chained to the column.

A lot of noisy talk and smoke was floating out from the bar, and at first I thought she might be a mannequin or a statue, but as I got closer I saw that she was real, all right. She had a big mop of wild copper-colored hair and she wasn't completely naked. She had about a dozen silver bracelets on each arm, and she was wearing a black leather blindfold. Her hands were up by her head and her wrists were cuffed to a chain that went up to the top of the column. She was chewing gum and from what I could see of her face under the blindfold, she was pretty and bored. And though she was a redhead, she wasn't Ruby Rose.

I said, "Good evening, are you part of Willie's entertainment?"

Her head snapped toward me. "I'm not supposed to converse with guests."

"I'm not a guest. I'm Jimmy Quinn. I own the place."

She smiled a little. "Deborah Luris. Pleased to meet you, and I guess it's o.k. to talk to you. The funny thing is, just between you and me and the wall, Willie went on and on about how I wasn't supposed to talk because he wanted to see how his pals reacted to me. But you're the first person who's said anything."

"I guess they're surprised and don't know what to do."

"Yeah," she said. "It's a little unusual. Most times we just do this at Willie's place."

"He chains you up?"

"Oh, yeah, and the blindfold, too. That's to see if I can detach my mind from the sensory envelope of my objective body and experience other realms of perception."

"What other realms?"

She shrugged nicely. "I don't know but I'm not complaining. The pay is great, better than my day job and Willie likes it when I tell him stories about what I see behind the blindfold."

"You see anything now?"

"Nah, too noisy. You gotta have quiet to detach yourself from the sensory envelope."

"Sure you do. Need anything?"

From across the bar, Willie yelled for me.

Her head turned toward him. She stopped chewing her gum and her expression turned serious. "Back to work," she whispered.

Willie lumbered over, threw an arm across my shoulders and almost knocked me down. Still roaring, he said, "These silly bastards didn't believe me when I told them you had the best liquor in town."

"They must not know how much you're paying for it."

There were about fifteen or twenty guys in Willie's party and about half as many women. "Body and Soul" was playing on an Electrola somebody had set up on my table, but you couldn't really hear it for all the yakking. Most of the men seemed to be arguing about writers. I didn't know any of them. Willie introduced me to a lot of people and told me that this one had written this thing and that one something else, but none of it cut any ice with me, either. Not that it mattered. Willie was past caring about that.

Dorothy and Brenda were still taking care of him, and it looked to me like he'd reached that happy level where the world glows with a rosy haze and everything you say is brilliant and funny. For the next hour, he and his friends soaked up the booze at a rate that made me smile, and I was hoping that Willie's bad girl, Ruby Rose, would show up soon. By then, the good doctor's pills had taken hold and I felt like everything was a step farther away than normal.

I remember that Willie and two other guys were having an argument about a "golden sofa," whatever the hell that was, when the room went quiet, starting at the end near the bar. I looked over, and there was one of the strangest looking men I've ever seen. Everybody stopped talking to look at him. Willie was the last to pipe down.

The guy had a bare bald head. It looked like he'd shaved it that morning when he shaved his face, and by that time of night, both his heavy jaw and his head were blue with stubble. He was wearing a bright red priest's cassock that came down to the floor. His hands were folded across his chest and he kept them stuck into the sleeves like a Chinaman. The skirt of his cassock swinging, he clomped across the room on heavy hobnails, and stared at Willie with a funny look on his face, friendly and threatening at the same time.

I reached into my pocket and slipped my fingers into my knucks.

"So, the hunter is home from the hill." He had a deep, rumbling actor's voice, and when he pulled his hands out of his sleeves, I saw that they were wide mitts with long bony fingers. He grabbed Willie and lifted him up in a bear hug that was the same kind of friendly threat. Willie seemed not to notice.

"Put me down, you silly bastard," he said, laughing, "Your breath is still as foul as ever." The laugh sounded forced to me, but Willie had a snootful. It was hard to say what he was thinking.

The other people in the room were whispering to each other like some of them knew who the bald stranger was and the rest of them wanted to know. He and Willie paid no attention to them.

Willie pulled away. "Are you still beating your women?"

Nobody said anything until Willie went on, trying to make his friends laugh, "With some men, that's the beginning of a bad joke, but not with Sidney—oh, excuse me, your holiness, I see by your robes that you're the Abbé this evening. The Abbé believes that women were created to serve him. He says that they are 'impure vessels.' Isn't that the term you used?"

By then, nobody else was talking. The bald guy said, "You were so close, Seabrook, and now, look at you." He punched Willie in the shoulder, one of those punches that looks friendly but isn't. Willie didn't feel it.

"Crowley was right," Willie said. "Nothing changes with you."

The Abbé snarled, "Damned charlatan. He understands nothing. But what about you? I heard that you went to Haiti. That's a start."

"You still believe that drugs are the key, then."

"What I'm doing now is nothing like what we talked about and experienced. I'm so far past it that it's a distant memory. But I didn't come here to argue about the past, and I can't stay. I just heard about this and stopped by to congratulate you on your literary *success*."

The way he said *success*, you knew he was lying.

"None of us thought you'd ever be anything more than Katie's husband. Congratulations."

The insults didn't bother Willie. He shrugged. It was like watching two boxers, one sober.

The Abbé shook his big head. "You still don't understand," he sighed. "No matter, I wish you well, but…" He moved closer and lowered his voice, "Stay out of my business."

Willie laughed. "What on earth are you talking about?"

The Abbé turned to leave and said over his shoulder, "By the way… Deborah—that's a nice touch. Send her around when you're finished with her."

On the way out, as he passed the girl, he whispered something to her and gave one nipple an evil twist. She didn't react.

It must have been close to four in the morning when Willie stumbled into my office. He was gassed.

I was on the divan with my knee propped up. By then, the day had caught up with me. I'd spent too much time on my feet and the hip was on fire. The doctor's pills and the brandy weren't doing any good.

Willie shrugged off his tweed jacket and rolled it up. He said, "I'm too drunk to go home. D'you mind if I…" Without finishing, he stretched out on the carpet and used the jacket as a pillow. "Jesus, what a night."

"Who was that guy?"

Willie rolled over onto his side. "Sidney Abbey. He calls himself the Abbé. He claims to be the prelate of the High Church of Sexual Magick—that's *magic* with a *k*—or some such nonsense. Sometimes he wears that clerical drag he had on tonight. He stole that part of his act from Crowley."

"Crowley?"

"Aleister Crowley, a wonderful, ridiculous genius. In our younger days, Crowley and I and the Abbé spent our afternoons together discussing various aspects of metaphysics and witchcraft and other related subjects. God, we were green then, just back from the war. It seems like another life now."

Willie sat up straighter. "Crowley's basic belief is that other heightened states of consciousness can be reached through the sexual act and specific rituals. Many of those rituals also involve drugs, particularly cocaine. That led him to the Abbé. Sidney believes that cocaine, peyote, and other drugs can give us glimpses of those higher states, but only a glimpse. With more sophisticated compounds, he believes that deeper insights are possible."

By then, Willie had forgot I was there and was talking to his memories.

"They argued that point but they agreed on another one and that's where I finally parted company with them. Sidney says that women are lesser beings than men. They are receptacles that exist only to serve his pleasure. He makes no bones about it, and his appetites are insatiable. He mistreats his women horribly, but he seems to have no trouble finding women who want to be mistreated. Neither does Crowley. I don't understand it. I put up with it—we all did—until he was beastly toward my wife Katie. Everyone witnessed it and after that, no one in our circle would have anything to do with him.

"That was the worst of him, but some of his ideas are sound. The search for a higher truth is something he takes seriously. At least, he did at one time."

Willie paused and was quiet for so long I thought he'd fallen asleep. Then he said, "And there was that one day, the day that he and Crowley argued. I saw them do things in broad daylight on a New York street that I still cannot explain."

Chapter Nine

1926
NAPA, CALIFORNIA

Connie's father and older brother worked the orchards. When the prunes were ready, the whole family picked them. It was dirty and sweaty. After the prunes were picked, Connie had to dip them in a lye solution, and then put them out to dry on trays in the sun. If it rained at night, they had to get up and stack the trays in the barn. She worked in the family vegetable garden, pulled weeds, and shot rabbits with her father's .22 rifle.

Connie was also in charge of collecting the eggs from the chickens and taking them into town to sell at a grocery store. That was another place where she could pocket the odd nickel. Her parents came to figure that she was a smart kid who understood money. They gave Connie a cast iron coin bank that looked like a piñata. (She had to explain to me what a piñata was.) The bank was where she kept the money they knew about. The rest went into a Di Nobili Toscani cigar box that fit into the space underneath the bottom drawer of her dresser.

The family stopped going to the strange little churches when her father bought a radio. Until then, the wonderful talking music box was something that Connie only heard in a store downtown. She knew that most of the other girls her age had a radio at home. When she asked her father about it, he said that radios were the devil's tool and they couldn't afford one.

But one evening, he and Connie's older brother came back from town with a heavy, beautifully polished wooden box in the Ford. It took both of them to get it up on the porch and into the house. Then they spent an hour on a ladder putting a wire antenna under the eave, and adjusting it to pick up the Oakland station. That night, for the first time, Connie heard dance band music in her house. The man introducing the show said that it was coming from the High-Ho Club in New York City. Connie could hardly believe it.

But that wasn't the reason for the radio. Connie's father bought it so they could listen to Sister Aimee Semple McPherson. She broadcast from the Angelus Temple of the Foursquare Gospel Church. She preached about the evils of alcohol and evolution, and the transformative power of Jesus and how true Christians had to band together. Connie's father loved it. They gathered around the radio every Sunday and every night when she was on.

For Connie, the thing that was so amazing about the radio was the idea that there was a man and an orchestra playing music in New York, on the other side of the continent, and she was able to listen to it. She asked the librarians for books about New York.

Connie's mother and older sister became harvest captains at one of the larger farms in the valley. They made more money bossing crews of pickers than the family made with their own place. When Connie was eleven she started riding the Napa Interurban train into town by herself. She was supposed to be selling eggs and buying the few items that they didn't provide for themselves. She also told her mother she needed to go to the library for school work. That was true sometimes. She also went to the book and magazine counter at the stationery store.

She was at the corner of Pearl and Main Streets when she first saw the nurses.

There were three of them in the front seat of a Ford Model-A sedan. The driver was an older woman with silver hair. She sat up straight, chin high, with her hands gripping the wheel near the top. All three of them had nurse's caps pinned to their hair and their hair was neatly fixed up to go with their starched uniforms and capes. Connie knew where they were going. They worked at the Asylum. By then, she had outgrown the fears that her older sister had planted, or she told herself she had. The place was still mysterious but it wasn't as frightening. The three women sparked something new in Connie.

She'd seen pictures of nurses in magazines and read about them in books, but these three were not like any other women she'd seen in person. Not like the women at the farm center, or the teachers she'd had, not like the other wives at the little churches, certainly not like her mother. No, these women were doing what they wanted to do. Maybe the woman driving the car owned it. Was that possible? They sat up there proudly, like it was the most normal thing for three women to be out on their own, going to work or out for a drive.

One of them noticed Connie's wide-eyed stare and waved to her. Connie said she thought she waved back but she wasn't sure. That afternoon, she started pestering her father to teach her to drive. She could do more work around the place, she said, and it would save time from taking the train. Her father knew that farm kids younger than Connie drove trucks every day, and he told Connie's older brother to teach her. Her older brother complained but agreed.

When Connie tried to tell her older sister about the nurses, her older sister shut her up. She sniffed and said they were just spinsters who couldn't get a husband, and Connie was such an ugly little monkeyface, she'd probably end up just like them. Connie's older sister's eyes got hot. She thumped Connie's head, and said she already knew who she was going to marry. Xeno Pool.

Chapter Ten

1931
NEW YORK CITY

Willie was still asleep on the floor when I found the article on page twelve of the *Times*. It was between a story about a motorcycle cop who was fined for beating up a stock broker who tore up a speeding ticket, and a story about a New Jersey veteran who was killed in a head-on automobile accident when the pipe he was smoking was driven into the back of his head. This was the headline of the story I was interested in:

RACKETEERS SLAIN
BY AUTO GUNMEN

Two Brothers
Shot Dead in Their Car

Speed Away Through West 93rd
Street – Victims Had Been
Arrested Several Times

Irving and Schmuel Rosen drove to
west 93rd Street early Thursday night in
a late model Lincoln coupe, to pay a
regular Friday night call on Carol
Schwartz and Miriam Richardson, with
whom they had been keeping company
for several months. Another car was
parked before the house in which the

young women live at 132 West 93rd Street.
So the brothers selected a parking space a few
doors further on, drove their car to it, and
stopped. At that moment another car which
had been following pulled up abreast of
the coupe. A fusillade of shots rang out. Both
brothers slumped in their seats. Irving, the
driver had four bullets through the body.
Schmuel also had four. They were killed
instantly. The other car drove away.

As soon as word of the shooting
reached the police a squad of detectives
was sent to the scene. They found Miss
Schwartz and Miss Richardson beside
the coupe. They had heard the shots and
raced downstairs to find that the Rosen
brothers had been killed.

Detectives questioned witnesses to
the shooting but were able to learn only
that the other machine had carried a New
York license and that it sped away after
the murders. No one was able to say how
many men were in it.

Neither could Miss Schwartz or Miss
Richardson give the detectives any assistance.
They seemed dazed by the deaths of the Rosen
brothers. About $300 in bills were found in
Irving's pockets. Schmuel carried $120 in bills.
Although they had never been convicted
both had long police records dating back to 1925.
They were first arrested in Hoboken charged with
assault. Subsequently, Irving was arrested five
times in New York and New Jersey on charges
of grand larceny. Schmuel was charged with
robbery in New Jersey.

The police say the shooting undoubtedly
was the result of a feud among racketeers and

that the Rosens' assailants, apparently well
acquainted with their habit of visiting on
Thursday nights, lay in wait for them.

So, the guys who helped Xeno Pool bust up my place weren't going
to bother anybody else. I chewed over it and called Meyer Lansky. It was
about noon. Without mentioning the piece, he said he'd already seen the
paper and he wanted to talk in person.

I nudged Willie with my stick and told him to wake up, I had business.

Meyer and Slappy sat in front of my desk. Meyer stubbed out a cigarette
and fired up another one. He was frowning. "We gotta make it snappy. I
gotta see another goddamn doctor about the kid."

The kid was his son Buddy. They knew that something wasn't right
with him, but back then, in '31, nobody could tell him and his wife what it
was. The boy wasn't a year old yet.

Meyer said, "Tell me again exactly what happened with Pool."

"Slappy brought the Rosens over. They said they didn't know what was
going on and they thought they were going to get a shot at the guys who
stole their truck and your booze. Hour or so later, Pool showed up."

"Any indication they knew him?"

I shook my head. "They were drinking beer at the bar. Pool didn't pay
any attention to them when he came in. I wasn't paying attention to them
either. I was worried about Pool. Frenchy told me later they acted nervous
but, hell, we were all keyed up."

Meyer said to Slappy, "You notice anything when you picked them up?"

"No, like Jimmy said, they was acting a little hopped up, like kids their
age do."

"I don't think Pool was acting when he thought I was you. At first,
he was showing respect. 'I want to apologize, Mr. Lansky... I've always
wanted to work for you' and like that."

Meyer said, "So it was Pool and the Rosens that knocked over Schultz's
truck and killed Izzy Stern. The Rosens did odd jobs for a lot of guys in the
business."

Slappy said, "I know they was driving for Waxey Gordon."

Meyer said, "That's right," and thought about it for a few seconds.

You see, Meyer hated Waxey Gordon. It went back to the Egg Harbor business. It was Gordon's shipment we took and Gordon knew Meyer was behind it. That was ten years ago and they hated each other ever since.

"Then maybe they were still working for Gordon. They sell him the beer they stole from Schultz's truck. They tell him they're going to deliver a truckload of booze for me, and they offer to fake a knock over and sell it to him. They beat each other up to make it look good. Then Pool collects from Gordon, calls me and brings the money with him when he comes here … No that doesn't make sense."

"He had an envelope stuffed with bills in his coat pocket. Maybe he was telling the truth. Maybe he was hoping he'd give you the cash and you'd offer him a job."

"You think it was Waxey who capped the Rosens? Or Pool? Schultz?"

Meyer shrugged. "Doesn't matter but I'd put money on Pool. The booze they stole was mine. Waxey didn't have a reason to go after them. That we know of."

Slappy said, "Word's out that we're looking for Pool and we're paying for good information. Dopey Steenberg claimed he seen Pool in a Buick Marquette on Twentieth Street. But you know Dopey. He'll tell you whatever you want to hear for a buck. Dopey also said he heard it was Lulu Rosenkrantz and Bo Weinberg who did the Rosens on account of Schultz's beer truck."

Rosenkrantz and Weinberg worked for Dutch Schultz. Schultz hated Waxey Gordon almost as much as Meyer did.

Meyer stood up. "Don't worry. If Pool's here we're going to find the son of a bitch. Something like this, him knocking over our shipment, I can't let that go."

Now, I don't know for a fact that anything Slappy or Dopey said was true. It's just what guys were saying, and it doesn't matter because nobody was ever charged with killing the Rosens. That's just the way things were done then. The men who ran things, like Meyer and Schultz, were always testing each other, trying to get a leg up. Guys like the Rosens and Xeno Pool found work wherever they could. They'd hire out with anybody who'd pay them from one day to the next, and when somebody showed up dead, it was hard to say who to pin it on. I mean, Dutch Schultz and Chink Sherman damn near killed each other one night at a club while Sherman was working for Waxey Gordon. At the same time the Italians who worked for Joe "the Boss" Masseria and Salvatore Maranzano were knocking each other off whenever they could. Two more dead racketeers wasn't much of a story. That's why it was on page twelve and I never saw anything else about it.

The important part of this is that Pool was still around. Where he was staying, I don't know. Later, I figured he was spending some of his time watching my speak and the rest watching the Barbizon Plaza waiting for Lansky. Before it was over, he found both of us.

Chapter Eleven

1928
NAPA, CALIFORNIA

Connie knew that Xeno Pool was trouble. Everybody said so. He lived with his uncle up in Alta Heights, the Italian section, but he claimed his family was Greek. Nobody seemed to know if he really had a family. His uncle was in jail as often as he was out, and Xeno Pool always seemed to have money in his pockets. He bragged that he was so handsome the girls in the houses on Clinton Street paid him to come visit them. Connie thought he was wonderful. He and Connie's older brother were plas. They sliced their fingers open and became blood brothers. She didn't see Pool much because while he and her older brother were catting around, she was working.

Connie tried to get on at the Asylum, but she learned that they didn't hire kids for anything there, and most of the staff lived on the grounds. She took work at the tannery and the Cameron Shirt Company. Then she pitted maraschino cherries at the cannery. That was as boring and dull as her own farm. For a time, she was an assistant cashier at the Hippodrome Theater. That was interesting work, but she couldn't understand why the regular customers liked moving pictures so much. They seemed silly to her. People couldn't dance on the wings of airplanes. That wasn't real, and there was so much she wanted to know that was real.

School was more important to her. She liked the books and the writing assignments. She wasn't so good at the social side. She felt like the girls from town were richer, smarter and prettier than the "orchard girls." That's what she called herself, and she didn't fit with those girls, either. They hated school.

Then in the summer after her first year in high school, they hired her to work as a maid at Stag's Leap Manor. It was the classiest resort in the valley. At first, Connie's mother and father refused but when she told them how much she'd make, they changed their minds. This was after the Crash. By then, it had hit California farms as hard as New York streets. Just about any job was a good job.

Despite what Connie's hot-eyed older sister said, Connie wasn't ugly. She knew that. Men and boys looked at her different, and that was part of the reason she'd been hired at the Manor. She couldn't say that she loved the work, but she picked it up quick and did what she was told. She kept her mouth closed, listened, watched what the other girls did, and was careful not to let herself be alone with the male guests.

The Manor attracted the carriage trade, the real carriage trade. Most of the swells took the ferry up from San Francisco to Vallejo, and hopped a train to Yountville where a horse-drawn carriage picked them up and took them the rest of the way. They played tennis and golf, rode horses, went to concerts, and paid about as much attention to Prohibition as I did. Connie said that before Prohibition, they grew grapes in Napa and actually produced good wine, but nobody could make a go of it after 1920 and they tore out the grape vines and planted more prunes. After she'd been at the Manor two weeks, she applied to be a waitress in the restaurant where the tips were better. It also meant that she had to work late, and so she had to move into a dormitory with the other girls and women who worked at the Manor. That led to another argument with her mother and father, and Connie won it the same way she won the first one, by arguing that it meant more money.

Her pay, added to the money that her mother and older sister brought in as harvest captains meant that, for once, they were doing all right. Connie was too green to know it couldn't last.

Now, I should explain here that most of this is what Connie told me that night after we left Willie at Doctors Hospital, when I learned that she knew Xeno Pool. Some of it, I learned later. The rest of it, I guessed. I'm a good guesser.

First thing that happened the summer she worked at the Manor, Connie's hot-eyed older sister got knocked up—not by Xeno Pool. It was one of his friends, another guy who ran around with Connie's older brother. As soon as the guy found out about Connie's older sister, he took a powder to Wyoming.

There was a lot of yelling every night at her house that summer. Connie was glad to be away from it. Nights in the dormitory were an education. Most of the other girls were older. They called her "kiddo," and some of them cursed like she'd never heard, even from her older brother's friends. At first, she'd been unsure, even a little afraid, about what it would be like to be away from home, on her own—well, on her own a little. Would the other girls like her? Tease her? Make fun of her orchard girl ways? They did all that, but she got along with most of them, and the ones she didn't get along with were the ones that nobody got along with. Connie did o.k. because she worked hard.

There were only two other local girls working in the dining room. The rest were from San Francisco and two more were from Seattle. When Connie talked to them, she learned that the city girls had come to the Manor from a special employment agency in San Francisco. It charged a fee but it got results for them. If Connie was interested in finding work anywhere else, she should look it up.

That night before she went to sleep, Connie wrote down the name and address of the agency.

Connie found that the girls she worked with were a lot like her, no matter where they came from. Some were from big families. Some were orphans. A couple had children who were living with their grandmothers. A few had dreams of meeting and marrying a rich man they met at the Manor. The other girls laughed and joked whenever that came up, but Connie could tell that they'd thought the same thing. Once upon a time. Given what she experienced of rich men at the Manor, she didn't think she wanted one. The pats, the pinches, the squeezes, the boozy gropes.

The woman who supervised them told her on the first day that the letchers came with the territory and there was no use complaining about it. Connie didn't. Still, she didn't like it, and her anger burned.

At the end of the summer, her supervisor slipped Connie a pay envelope that felt thicker than usual. She said there was a place for Connie at the Manor next June if she wanted it. Connie didn't say how much she dreaded going back to her farm.

Chapter Twelve

1931
NEW YORK CITY

Willie came back on the Monday after his party. He went down to his room in the cellar where he stared at the puppet. About an hour later, Marie Therese came into my office and said there was a girl in the bar who wanted to see Willie.

"An actress," she sniffed. Marie Therese knew a lot of actresses and didn't have a particularly high opinion of them.

"She pretty?"

"Of course."

"Send her up here."

By then, I'd moved back into my room at the Chelsea. I still had a lot of trouble getting around. It was a toss-up whether it hurt more to walk over to the hotel or to struggle in and out of a cab. It was easier to get a ride with Frenchy in his truck.

As I recall, that night I was wearing a medium weight, double-breasted navy suit and a shirt with a light blue pinstripe. I don't remember the tie but I'm sure it looked good with the suit. The girl Marie Therese brought in was a blonde with pale skin and big dark eyes in a narrow face. She wore a tailored ivory-colored suit over a high-necked white silk blouse, and low-heeled black shoes with bows. She had a small black hat pinned to one side of her hair. She carried a black leather purse under one arm. I thought I knew who she was.

I said, "I'm Jimmy Quinn. This is my place. Willie is conducting experiments, you might say, downstairs, but I bet he's told you all about those. Have a seat."

She sat, facing the desk and touching as little of the chair as she could, still unsure about me.

"And you are…"

"Lily White." She looked to me to be on the skinny side, but you can say that about a lot of actresses. She sure didn't look like she was wasting away.

"Willie ought to be finished any time now. Can I offer you a drink?"

She shook her head.

"Don't mind me," I said and gimped over to the little bar to pour a Five Star.

I read the papers. Willie showed up about twenty minutes later, tie loose, hair a mess the way it was after one of his sessions with the puppet.

She popped up out of the chair as soon as she saw him and ran over to hug him. He was surprised to see her.

"Willie, it's worse than I told you. There's someone else now." She started crying.

He moved her over to the divan and tried to calm her down. He poured two more Five Stars. She accepted the brandy from him and coughed after the first sip. She said, "I saw Helen Stiles this—" She stopped and glanced at me.

Willie said, "It's all right. Jimmy knows what we're doing. He's helping."

She still looked suspicious but went on, "You remember her, don't you? She was a regular at the coffee house with Ruby's crowd."

"Only vaguely. The plump brunette?" Willie said.

"Yes, she's… 'plain.' She called this morning and asked if she could come around to see me right away. She said it was urgent. Of course, I agreed and when I saw her, I was shocked."

As Lily White told it, she met Ruby Rose and this Helen Stiles when the three of them lived together in a place for women called the Studio Club up on West Fifty-seventh. It was a particular favorite of young actresses who'd moved to the city to make it big in show business. The first break they had was when the three of them landed roles as the Gay Greek Chorus Girls in *Scandals of the Great Gay Way*, a revue where all the girls sang bawdy songs, danced like they hadn't been taught in school and didn't wear too many clothes.

The Gay Greek Chorus Girls were the most popular part of the show. Ruby Rose wrote the bawdy songs and vamped around the stage in a red silk dress with next to nothing under it. Lily White wore a white choir robe and sang with a light angelic soprano voice that made the songs funnier and sexier. To the tune of "Button Up Your Overcoat," she sang "Stiffen Up

Your Underpants." The third girl was Helen Stiles who was billed as Bertha de Blues. She had the best pipes of the three. She could belt out the big numbers and cool it down for the slow songs.

The three of them were, as they say, the toast of the town. The producers put their pictures on the posters and plastered them all over the city. You couldn't get away from them. I remember thinking at the time that if the redhead was half as racy as she looked on that poster, I had to see the show. But I waited too long and the Legion of Decency closed it down.

Any other revue would have found a place for the girls, and Ruby tried to talk them into keeping their act together. But Lily White wanted to do more serious dramatic material, and Helen Stiles knew that she was wasting her voice with novelty songs. The Gay Greek Chorus Girls may have been over, but the three of them were hot properties. Invitations to sing at parties, offers of other jobs, guys lined up every night. They enjoyed the ride while it lasted and all of them got parts in other shows before long. Lily White worked steadily in smaller parts in better productions. Ruby Rose became a real Broadway baby who came home with the milkman every morning.

Helen Stiles, aka Bertha de Blues, the plump brunette, did better. She may have been plain, but she still had that voice. She recorded some songs and was in another show that had a great torch song, "Meet Me in the Shadows." Seemed like every band was recording it for a while but once you heard her version, that's the one you remembered and wanted to hear again. Before she sang it, you always saw "Bertha de Blues" in quotation marks under her real name on records, so people would remember how they knew her, like Cab Calloway was "The Hi-De-Ho Man." But after "Meet Me in the Shadows," people knew who Helen Stiles was.

She toured with a few big bands and had numbers in a couple of movies. She moved to Hollywood while Lily and Ruby stayed in New York. The two of them were friendly until they got into it over the rich Stagedoor Johnny and the puppet business got started. By then Helen had moved back east to a Park Avenue apartment, but they didn't see her anymore. Until that morning.

"She looked good," Lily White said. "In fact, she's lost some weight and she's positively svelte."

I found my notepad and wrote down *savelt?*

"But when she opened her mouth, she could barely speak. Her voice has become a most hideous stammering croak."

Helen Stiles told Lily White that her voice began to fail a few months ago. At first, she ignored it, thinking it was just part of the total body redevelopment program she'd been following to lose weight. She was completely enthralled by the plan. It was the only thing she'd tried that worked and she had tried absolutely everything else. Now she was harnessing her seven energies and focusing them on her true self.

The seven energies, she said, formed a fan-shaped pattern spreading upward and outward. For one to reach her true purpose, one had to refocus those energies and bring them to bear on that purpose. Only then would one become the woman she wanted and needed to be.

A frown crossed Willie's face when she said that.

But, as her seven energies were reshaping her physical body, her voice was becoming harsh. Her throat burned. She lost her breath control. She didn't know what to do until she learned that her friend was fighting off a curse that sounded similar.

"That's why she came to see me this morning. She said that—"

Willie interrupted, "I think it would be better if I heard this from her."

"You don't understand how difficult it is for her to speak."

"I don't care. It's more important that I see her as soon as possible. Do you have her number?"

Forty minutes later, he let Helen Stiles into my office.

She seemed pretty svelte to me. Yeah, I'd looked it up. I'd seen one of the moving pictures she was in and she did look thinner that night than she had on screen. She wore a dark dress and coat, and a hat with a veil over her eyes. She had an uneasy expression on her face until she saw Lily White and hurried next to her on the divan. She whispered something, and Lily White asked if we could get a teapot, hot water and cups. I said sure and called the kitchen of the Cruzon Grill.

One of the waiters brought it right down. Helen Stiles produced a silk teabag out of her purse and dropped it into the pot. Before long, a musty smell filled the office. I couldn't decide whether it was good or bad, but it was strong. Willie went straight to the teapot and sniffed several times.

Again, the singer whispered to Lily White and she said, "This tea helps her throat. Without it, it's almost impossible for her to speak."

Willie said, "By all means," and poured a cup for her. After she finished it, he said, "Now, please, tell us what's been going on."

She cut her eyes at me. Willie said, "He's helping us." I don't know what it was about me that made all of Willie's women so nervous.

She started talking, but her voice was a scratchy whisper. The truth is, Lily White did most of the talking with Helen Stiles correcting her here and there.

It boiled down to this. The singer knew she had to slim down if she wanted to do any more work in the movies, but she was afraid to do anything that might hurt her voice. Then she heard about this new teacher who conducted classes in the Meditative Spiritual Arts. They were quite exclusive. You had to go through a psychological interview before you were invited to join, and she'd heard that some of the wealthiest women on the Upper East Side had been refused. The Instructor—that's what he was called, the Instructor—preferred to limit his classes to less than ten. He also did individual consultations. Still, she was Helen Stiles. It was worth a telephone call.

A woman answered. Helen Stiles gave the woman her name and said she wished to know more about the Instructor's classes. The woman said the Instructor knew who Helen was and what she wanted. Then she gave the singer an address in Tudor City, told her to be there at ten o'clock that night.

Helen Stiles followed her orders.

Now, at that time, Tudor City was a new development off Forty-Second Street by the East River. Before then, it had been a shanty town where wild goats wandered around, but they got rid of those and built a bunch of red brick apartment houses, hotels and parks, all meant for regular people, the hoi polloi, not the Wall Street crowd. You didn't faint when you saw the rent.

The address turned out to be in The Cloister, an apartment building on the north side of Tudor City. A young woman wearing a simple brown shift with a cloth belt at the waist opened the door. She smiled and said, "Good evening, Miss Stiles, I love your music. Please come in."

A short hallway led to a larger room that smelled of fresh paint. There was one floor lamp turned low, and two love seats facing each other.

They sat. The young woman said, "I am the Assistant. You're here because you wish to lose weight."

Helen Stiles nodded.

"Is there anything else?"

"Well, I mean… What exactly do you do? How expensive…"

The Assistant smiled. "There is no charge for the classes. The wholesome supplements that many of our clients choose to take are quite reasonable. No one pays more than five dollars a month for them."

"I don't understand. It's so difficult to contact you. How—"

"The Instructor will explain everything to you. However, first I need to understand all of your concerns. We must know everything about you before we can help you. People seek out the Instructor for many reasons, but inevitably they discover that the concerns that brought them to us are not their real problems."

Helen Stiles told the young woman about her short time in Hollywood. How hurt she'd felt when the men there told her that she would never do anything more than sing in front of a big band unless she became slender. They didn't understand that her voice was part of her body. When she'd tried to starve herself before, she simply couldn't sing.

The young woman asked what Helen thought of the people in her apartment building, her parents, the president, how much alcohol she drank, her boyfriends, her dogs, her first love, her career, and on and on. The young woman didn't write down anything, simply sat, smiling at her. After Helen had been talking for almost an hour, she heard a faint "bong." The young woman stood and said, "Very well, he's ready for you." They went through a door to another room.

Heavy curtains covered the windows, making the second room even dimmer than the first. She heard melodic Oriental music but couldn't tell where it was coming from.

Helen Stiles could see that a man sat in a wheelchair near the far end. He had long tangled dark hair and a stringy beard down to his chest. She couldn't make out anything more of his shapeless clothes or his face. There was a candle on the floor before him and an incense burner beside him. The Assistant moved a chair behind her and left the room.

The man said, "Please sit. I hope you are not put off by this unusual introduction and our brief time together this evening. This is my hour of personal meditation but I sensed it was important we meet. Sometimes I understand things without knowing why I understand them. Can you accept that?"

"Oh, yes."

"Good. Now, you will come to see me again tomorrow night. At that time, I want you to be able to describe exactly who you are and who you want to be. I shall do the same. I shall tell you who you are and who you are meant to be."

He also said that the Assistant had prepared a list of foods she should eat. Most of them could be found at Gristedes grocery store, but for some of them, she'd have to go to a market in the Syrian quarter near Washington Street. He had the address.

She did what he told her to. At ten o'clock the next night, she went to the same apartment. The Assistant let her in and led her back to the Instructor's room. The same dim lights, same Oriental music, same wheelchair. The only difference was a folded square of blue paper on the Instructor's lap.

He said, "Tell me who you are, Helen." He bowed his head and folded his hands.

She described herself as a singer first, a good one but not as good as she wanted to be. She was also an actress though she knew that the good roles would always go to the pretty girls. She was from Pittsfield, Massachusetts. Her parents hadn't approved of her moving to New York. At the time she came to the city, she thought she could be friends with the other girls who were trying to succeed like she was, but she'd learned that wasn't easy. There was a lot of jealousy of her success in the business. She tried to stay above it.

When she finished, he paused before he spoke. "Now, tell me who you want to be."

She said she wanted to be a better singer, someone who was offered the best new songs. She hoped to have a radio show of her own one day. She wanted to be slender enough to be in moving pictures. She wanted to marry, of course, but professional success was more important. Those were the things she really wanted.

Again, he paused. Then he raised his head and looked directly at her for the first time. Though the only light came from the candle, his face was somehow illuminated "as if by inner fire," she said, and she saw his dark bright eyes. His face was serious.

"Remember that I told you sometimes I understand things without knowing why I understand them." His voice was strong, more animated.

She nodded. He reached into the folds of his robe, brought out the folded piece of blue paper, and handed it to her with a flourish. "Last night, after you left, I wrote this. Read it please."

She took it and held it near the candle.

"I am a singer first and foremost. I'm also an actress, though I have not seen the success I've hoped for. My hometown in Pittsfield Mass. My parents did not want me to move to New York and warned me that the girls I met would treat me badly. It has been difficult not to do the same to them but I have resolved not to. I want to be a better singer. When I am, I will be the first to see the great new songs and that will lead to a network radio show and success in the movies and in my most intimate relationships."

Her mouth dropped open. She realized then that he was already in her mind. He smiled.

"Now," he said, holding out his hand. "Let us create that woman. First, you must understand that the body contains seven energies—mental, physical, spiritual, vocal, sexual, elemental, and transcendental. When they are properly balanced, we are happy and fulfilled."

Willie glared at her, his face angry and exasperated. "Describe the Instructor to me."

Helen Stiles whispered, "The light is kept low at all times. He is extremely sensitive to it." Willie snorted. "Since he's confined to the chair, I can't say how tall he is. Besides, it's the force of his mind, his personality that's important."

"We'll let that go for now," Willie said. "How long have you been seeing him?"

"Three months… almost three months."

"And at first, the results of his diet regime and the individual consultations were astounding. You lost weight. You gained confidence. You were filled with vitality and energy. Your voice was never better."

"How did you know?" the singer whispered and I could see that Lily White was surprised, too.

Willie ignored the question. "But then the problems with your voice began. When?"

"Two weeks ago."

"First, he changed the diet, didn't he? He eliminated some foods and added others."

"Yes, from his own supplies."

"For a time you felt better but then you worsened."

She nodded, looking a little scared.

Willie said, "Describe your symptoms as precisely as you can."

"Nothing tastes good to me. My stomach is constantly upset. Vomiting, headaches, terrible headaches. A constriction in my throat and sinuses that makes speaking difficult and singing impossible… without this tea. It helps for a short time."

"How much money have you given him?"

She bristled at that. "Very little. I buy the vegetables and teas. He has never asked for anything more. But I have given the Assistant some small donations. The Instructor strives for monastic simplicity."

"I'm sure he does. Did he ever advise you to see a doctor?"

"No, he doesn't believe in Western medicine and our so-called science. Neither do I. And I can't say that I care for your tone. I do not believe you can help me." She had her back up pretty good.

"Don't be so sure about that," Willie said.

Lily White said to the singer, "Hear him out. He's helping me."

Willie backed off. "Helen, I must apologize. I've gotten ahead of myself and if I have insulted you in any way, it was inadvertent. The important thing now, for both of you, is that you have done the right thing by coming to me. I'm sure that I can help. It will simply take a little time. Now, one more thing."

"Yes."

"You said the Instructor is very exclusive. How did you get his telephone number?"

"Ruby gave it to me."

Chapter Thirteen

1931
NEW YORK CITY

Willie told the women to come back to my place the next evening. After they left, he poured himself another brandy and asked me what I thought.

"I'm still not sure about whatever the hell it is that you're doing staring at the puppet, but what Helen Stiles is describing, that's a simple con game."

"How did he work the folded blue paper?"

"Come on, that's easy," I said. "He had somebody under the chair, either the Assistant or a kid who was scribbling down what Helen Stiles said and pushed it up through a slit in his robe while he shoved a blank one down. Hell, a few years back, Danny Two Shoes worked Cooper Square begging on a little wooden tray on roller skate wheels. Looked like his legs had been cut off at the knees. He wore army medals and everything, claiming that he lost his pins in the Great War. Whenever the cops tried to roust him, he'd jump out of that thing like he was on springs and beat it down the sidewalk so fast nobody could catch him."

Willie laughed and asked, "What about the rest of it?"

"You got me there. You said that the other girl, Ruby Rose is trying to put the hex on Lily White because she stole away some rich guy, right?"

"Yes."

"So she's doing that because she's mad or jealous."

He nodded.

"But then she set up Helen Stiles with the Instructor for money?"

Willie said, "We don't know everything that's going on, but I know how to find out."

The next night around eight, Willie came into my office with Theodora Opperman, the Continental detective. He poured a Five Star for himself and offered her one. She said yes and lit up a Fatima. I added two more to his tab. While Willie told her what Helen Stiles had told us, the detective stared at me so hard I had to force myself not to fidget. After Willie finished, she said, "This Instructor is either about to ask Miss Stiles for money, or he'll propose marriage."

"My thoughts exactly," Willie said. "We have to learn more about him. Can you help us?"

She nodded and said she'd have another contract drawn up the next morning. Willie explained that Helen Stiles and Lily White were coming to my place that night and he wanted the detective to talk to her. Mrs. Opperman said, "Since you're a repeat customer, all right. Even though we don't have a contract."

"And for now, I don't want them to know you're a detective."

Two cognacs later, Willie introduced Mrs. Opperman to Helen Stiles and Lily White as an acquaintance.

The detective jumped up and shook the singer's hand. "Miss Stiles, this is such an honor. Mr. Opperman, my late husband, loved 'Meet Me in the Shadows.' If he played your record once, he played it a hundred times. I like it, too, but he… well, he simply loved it and whenever I hear it now, I think fondly of him."

As she spoke, I watched Helen Stiles' face change from a frown to a grateful smile. The detective knew how to warm her up, all right. She didn't let Willie say anything.

Like Willie did the night before, she guided the singer to the divan and they sat together. She said, "Willie has explained your terrible situation to me. I've known other women who've found themselves in the same predicament and I think I can help.

"Gentlemen, could you give us girls a few minutes to ourselves?"

Willie and I headed to the bar.

It was about an hour and a half later that Mrs. Opperman and the two other women came downstairs. Looked like they'd become bosom buddies by then. They talked to each other all the way to the coat check room and the front door.

Willie and I went back to my office. There were three lipstick-stained glasses on the table and the bottle of Five Star was empty. At least one of them had been mixing it with ginger ale and having it over ice. Willie switched to scotch. I stuck to seltzer.

Mrs. Opperman came back in and opened her notebook. "I've got the address to the Tudor City apartment so it won't be any trouble finding out whose name is on the lease. Given what the situation looks like, I'm probably going to find a false name. That means it will take more time."

"I expect you to do whatever it takes," Willie said.

"I understand the similarities between the two cases. Have you made any progress on the matter of Miss White and the puppet?"

"Not yet, and I had hoped to know something by now. On the chance that Ruby Rose missed the mention in Sullivan's column, I'll approach her directly if I don't hear anything soon."

"Miss White looks healthier than I thought she would from the way you described her."

"Of course. Whatever psychological influence or advantage Ruby Rose might have had is gone now that Lily knows we're helping her. Again, even though she has always known intellectually and rationally that the puppet means nothing, our actions with the photographs give her the psychological support she needs. What did you think of her and Helen Stiles?"

Mrs. Opperman put away her notebook. "I don't get paid to have opinions about the agency's clients. I solve their problems. These are interesting cases, though. They'd actually be easier if any demand for money had been made. As it stands, neither of them has really been threatened in a way that would stand up in court."

"They will be," Willie said.

After Mrs. Opperman left, Willie said he was going to spend another hour with the puppet. I asked him why he was doing all this for two women that he didn't really know. "I mean, you're laying out some serious cash for the Continental agency, the puppet, the costume and everything. Why? What's in it for you?"

"I can't really explain it. Part of it is sheer folly on my part. For the first time in my life, I've got more money than I could spend, and this whole story, it… interests me, and when a story catches my attention this way, I follow it. It's a little adventure."

"Fair enough," I said and fished a buck out of my wallet. "Here. Now we're even."

Willie took it, not understanding what it was for.

"The bet. You said your party would be like nothing I'd ever seen in this place, and I gotta admit you were right on that. You also said it'd be worth a dollar. Guess it was. We've never had a naked woman chained to a column."

He smiled, "Yes, you know I did the same thing when I hosted a group of French intellectuals to a dinner in Paris. None of them even mentioned the girl, as if they were somehow above such earthly concerns. The guys from the old crowd were more curious. What did you think?"

"What was her name? Deborah something, Louis, Luris, something like this. Yeah, I asked her how she was doing and she explained how you hired her to detach herself from the sensory envelope. I guess it was a pretty good way to show those gents how well you're doing."

Willie tried to act like he was offended that I'd accuse him of doing something like that just to shake up his old friends. "It was much more than that and the work I do with Deborah has to do with what we were talking about before, the experiments that Rhine is conducting. Under the right circumstances, she can accomplish feats that neither she nor I can explain."

"Whatever you say."

Now, the truth is I'm a pretty good liar when I need to be, but on my best day, I couldn't convince anybody that I understood half the stuff Willie had been telling me—voodoo curses that don't work but they do work, and how his staring at that puppet was going to make this other girl stop sticking pins in *her* puppet and then Miss White would be able to tuck into a tenderloin again. None of that made any sense to me, but it sure was interesting to watch Willie while he made his way through all of it.

I was gimping through the lobby of the Chelsea toward the elevator when a man called my name, making no more noise than he had to. I recognized the voice and turned to see Xeno Pool sitting in a highbacked chair. His topcoat was spread across his lap and his right hand was under the coat. He didn't need to show the pistol. Mine was in the pocket of my suitcoat. It was about three in the morning.

Pool said, "Sit down. I wanna talk. That's all and I'll make it worth your time."

He pulled a creased envelope out of his breast pocket and tossed it onto a low table in front of him. It looked like the same one he flashed that afternoon at my place, but thinner. I unbuttoned my topcoat, sat facing him and put my hand in my pocket. He knew what I was doing.

He said, "Look, first I gotta apologize. Understand, when I came into your place, I thought you were Mr. Lansky and I've been trying to see him ever since I got to this city. That's why I'm here, to meet him. When you said you weren't him, it threw me and I got mad and things got out of hand. This'll take care of the damages. Take it. It's yours."

I didn't move. Didn't touch it. Didn't say anything.

"I understand I made a mistake, but that's all it was, a mistake, and I'm going to make it right. That's what I wanted to do from the beginning. Make it right with Mr. Lansky. But to do that, I gotta see him, I gotta talk to him face to face. I want you to tell him that."

"Why does he want to talk to you?"

"Because I have a solid business proposition to make to him."

I shrugged. "You think I'll tell him that some son of a bitch who tore up my place and stole a truckload of his liquor and got two other guys to screw him over—*that* guy has a business proposition for him?"

"It's not like that. You don't understand. When the Rosens got in touch with me, I had no idea they were working for Mr. Lansky. If I'd known that, none of this would've happened."

"Did you kill 'em?"

That seemed to surprise him. "What? Who?"

"The Rosen brothers. Somebody capped them while they were visiting their girlfriends uptown. It was in all the papers."

He sat there looking confused for several seconds. Then he shook his head and said, "It doesn't matter anymore, not them. They weren't important. I still need to see Mr. Lansky. You take this money. Tell him that I've got every penny I owe him and more, and I want to make things right. If he agrees to see me, he'll never regret it. Tell him that. He'll never regret it. I'll call your speak day after tomorrow to set up a meet any time, any place that he wants. Will you tell him that?"

I nodded.

"Good," he said as he stood up, pocketing a little automatic. "And here's something else so you know I'm on the up and up. There's a guy watching your place. Big guy wearing a watch cap. I think he's shadowing that other guy who's spending so much time there."

"He's following Willie Seabrook?"

"That guy is Willie Seabrook?... Well, what do you know." He turned around and hurried out of the lobby.

Chapter Fourteen

1929
NAPA, CALIFORNIA

For Connie, the nine months after that first summer at Stag's Leap Manor were hell. Her mother and her knocked-up older sister yelled and fought and made up with each other and cried together and fought again.

Then, just when the harvest was about to begin, Connie's older brother blew up at their father. They yelled and fought, bloodying lips, noses, and knuckles. Connie's older brother stormed out. Connie kept her head down.

A few days later, her older brother came back to pick up some clothes, and said that he and Xeno Pool had a room at a boarding house in town. After more threats and shouts and tears and curses, Connie's mother and father realized they couldn't stop him. Xeno Pool was outside smoking a cigarette and leaning against a red Indian motorcycle with a sidecar. He wore a leather jacket and his cap backward to accommodate big goggles. When he saw Connie looking at him through the screen door, he winked at her. He was the most handsome and exciting thing she'd ever seen and he made her blush. She'd have been more tempted to do something with him, if her older sister's situation had been different. Still, she watched him and her older brother from inside the house until they'd ridden out of sight.

Connie had another problem to deal with. The cash she had been skimming for years was adding up. The De Nobili cigar box as stuffed so full she had to wrap rubber bands around it. She waited until she was alone to count it. It came to ninety-six dollars in coins and small bills. She pulled out about half the paper money and put it in a manila envelope that she hid in the chicken coop. Then it was back to work, picking and drying prunes.

Connie's mother and older sister still worked as harvest captains, but when that was over, her older sister went to Texas to be with Connie's mother's maiden aunt. Her mother and father continued to fight, and her father started to drink. He'd always been one to pick up a pint from the local bootlegger on a weekend. But that autumn, he had two or three belts every night after dinner, if he ate dinner. If he didn't feel like eating, he drank more. He never hit Connie's mother or any of the kids, but his mood became sour and he listened to preachers on the radio without speaking or answering Connie's mother if she asked him a question. Connie and her younger sisters and baby brother were afraid of him.

School and the library were the places that saved her. Connie read everything. She also wrote to the San Francisco employment agency. The response came a week later. It was a short, typed letter thanking her for her interest in the Fulton Agency, and there was a form to fill out with her background, work experience and references. But that day, Connie's father got to the mail before she did. He read the letter and gave it to Connie's mother. She said that Connie was much too young to be thinking about such things and tore the letter up. Connie was ready to argue. Did her mother want her to wind up like her hot-eyed older sister? Then she remembered the fights and how they always ended, and she knuckled under. Connie agreed with her mother and kept her head down. The next time she was in town, she wrote another letter to the agency with a General Delivery, Napa, California return address. She also wrote to her supervisor at Stag's Leap Manor, and asked for a letter of recommendation.

Connie's older brother and Xeno Pool showed up at her parents' farm from time to time that year. On their first visit, her brother was behind the wheel of a shiny new Chevrolet convertible. He also had a new blue suit that was too small for him. A couple of real sports, he and Xeno Pool had money for his mother, whiskey for his father and two roast chickens from a restaurant in town for dinner. Xeno Pool had his own new tight-waisted suit, and was as charming as he could be to everyone. He told Connie's mother she looked wonderful, flattered her father and let the little kids climb all over him. It was like his being there was enough to make everybody forget the angry scene with Connie's older brother.

Over dinner, Connie's older brother said they were "engaged in certain enterprises," like he and Xeno Pool were big shots. Connie didn't pay any attention to him, not while Xeno Pool was sitting next to her at the table.

He asked her how she liked working at the Manor. In his experience, he said, it was quite an interesting place. He'd heard from some of the other girls who worked there that Connie was really popular, and he could certainly understand that. His attention was kind of overpowering.

Now, if I sound a little jealous and angry about all of this—even though it happened before I met Connie and she didn't know who I was—well, yes. Hell, yes, it still burns my ass that he tried to make time with her the way he did. And there's more to say about that, but not now.

Connie's older brother and Xeno Pool were in the car ready to leave that night when he motioned her over and said he'd heard she was a real bookworm. He wanted her to know that he was a bookworm, too. Then he looked around to see if anybody else was nearby, and motioned for her to come closer. He lowered his voice and said, "Really, the only reason we're coming back here is so I can see you."

She had trouble going to sleep that night. The train whistle was sadder and sweeter than ever.

Chapter Fifteen

1931
NEW YORK CITY

The next afternoon, Wednesday, I considered what Pool had said about Meyer Lansky. I called his office at the Barbizon-Plaza. Slappy Strauss answered. I said we needed to talk, and they came over that afternoon.

I told Meyer about seeing Pool. "Funny, isn't it. He keeps saying the same thing—that he wants to talk to you."

Meyer lit a cigarette. "Do you have any idea how many guys try to talk to me every week with these great ideas? Too damn many, and Charlie and me, we've got as much as we can handle going on now. I'm sure as hell not about to throw in with some mug I don't know on anything, but…" He stopped and thought. "He's still saying he'll bring the money he owes me from the stolen shipment?"

I nodded. Meyer asked how much Pool gave me and I told him there was a hundred bucks in the envelope. Then he said that when Pool called back, I should tell him that Mr. Lansky would accept payment in full for his merchandize and he might entertain a business proposition.

"You're not going to do this *here*," I said and Meyer said he had someplace better in mind. He told me about it. I agreed.

Willie came in that evening and went straight to the new bottle of Five Star. Without going into anything Pool said about Lansky's business, I told him that I heard a big guy had been tailing him.

"Probably a reader who's too shy to speak to me. It's happened before. Often."

"The guy who told me this didn't know who you were. When I mentioned your name, then he knew. Guess he reads your books or something. But what's important here is that he said this other guy was wearing a watch cap."

Willie shrugged. "It's cold outside."

"Or maybe he's covering up a bald head like your Abbé."

Willie chewed on that while he poured another. Finally, he said, "If that's the case, then we've got to reconsider our options."

He went downstairs to stare at the puppet. Mrs. Opperman showed up at eleven. After she and Willie had settled down with two more brandies, she opened her notebook and read her first report.

She said she started at the offices of the Fred French Management Companies on Madison Avenue. That was the outfit that bankrolled and ran Tudor City. She was able to get a gander at the tenant files of The Cloister. The apartment was leased to one Robert Haldorn. Mr. Haldorn paid sixty dollars a month for a two-bedroom. He'd been there since April, 1930 and was usually about two weeks late with his rent money. Mrs. Opperman had his previous address and the names on his letters of recommendation but she hadn't checked them.

From the French office, she went over to Tudor City and found The Cloister. For two bucks, the super admitted that he couldn't tell her much about Haldorn. Nobody really knew him. Haldorn and a woman that the super assumed was his wife kept odd hours. They had a lot of visitors, all women. Every time the super saw Haldorn, day or night, he was wearing a hat and sunglasses, and he used two canes to get around. The neighbors hadn't complained about noise but one neighbor—the lady on the floor who knew everything that everybody was doing—told the super that women were in and out of the place all night long. And, the super said, Haldorn and his wife weren't there so much during the day.

For a fiver, he went up to the fourth floor with Mrs. Opperman and knocked on the door. He was ready to say to Haldorn that other tenants had complained of flickering lights and he needed to know if they'd been bothered by it. But there was no answer.

They went in and found the place that Helen Stiles described. The kitchenette was empty. No ice in the icebox, nothing in the cabinets. Two love seats in the main room. The larger bedroom smelled of incense. The chair Helen Stiles sat on was in the middle of the room. The back wall was curtained off. Behind the curtains, she found a door to a bathroom filled with cosmetics. The bathroom connected to a smaller bedroom. That's where the wheelchair was. Brown robes were hanging over it. The chair rode on four small wheels and the frame had been enlarged. It was deeper and taller, and there was a long slit in the leather seat.

They also found a crystal ball on a round table, the incense burner, two more wooden chairs, an Electrola and five records with labels written in a language that didn't use normal letters. Mrs. Opperman thought it was Indian writing and figured it to be the source of the Oriental music Helen Stiles heard. There was also an open steamer trunk. In it was a magician's black suit with extra pockets inside. Mrs. Opperman opened the drawers in the trunk and found an assortment of unmarked powders and liquids in small jars.

By the time they'd seen all that, the super was nervous and ready to leave. Mrs. Opperman made him stop in the larger bedroom. At the edge of one of the window curtains, she found a small spotlight mounted on the wall. It had a blue gel filter in front of the bulb.

On the way out, they met the lady who knew everything that everybody did. The super introduced Mrs. Opperman as the new Facilities Inspector.

"So," the detective said in my office, "I can continue to check this Haldorn's background, or we could assign men to shadow him and the woman, or we could do both." She reached into her bag. "I've got the contract here. Once you sign, we can decide."

She handed him two copies of the contract. As he signed, Willie said, "I want you to do both. Earlier tonight, Jimmy told me that he's learned a man may be following me. I've tried to convince myself it's someone who's read the books, but I'm finding that more and more difficult to believe."

She told him she could put a man on him. Willie said he thought that would be for the best.

Just when I should've kept my mouth shut, I piped up. "O.K., Mrs. Opperman is going to look into this character's bona fides, and two more guys are going to tail him and his woman, and another operative is going to keep an eye on you. Do you have any idea how much money you're talking about? These people are expensive. I know. They chased me often enough."

Mrs. Opperman snapped her fingers, pointed at me and said, "That's it! Now I remember your file. 'Jimmy Quinn, juvenile. Height five feet. Weight ninety pounds. Hair, black. Eyes, black. Complexion, fair. Known associate of Mary Frances Quinn, aka Mother Moon, and Arnold

Rothstein. Suspected involvement in 1919 World Series. Multiple arrests for theft, interfering with a police officer, carrying a concealed—"

"No convictions," I said, cutting her off. "My record's clean."

She shook her head. "So?" Both of us knew we'd always be on opposite sides of the fence. She was the law and I wasn't. In her eyes, I'd never be much good.

Willie looked like he wanted to know more but he went back to his business, "Expense doesn't matter. One detective, three, four. I told you, money is unimportant. I suspect that two women's lives may be in danger, or at least their livelihoods and their reputations. Besides I'm much too deeply involved in this to leave it now."

Xeno Pool called on Tuesday. I said that Lansky had agreed to a meeting, if Pool brought the cash. His voice got excited then and he said he could have it within five days. I told him to call back then. Truth is, I figured that would be the last time I heard from him. Fat chance.

Mrs. Opperman came in later and told Willie that, as she suspected, all of the Robert Haldorn information was phony. She said that the detective who was shadowing Willie had not seen anyone else showing an interest in him. She didn't have much to report on the Instructor and the Assistant either. Two men were watching the entrance to The Cloister. They saw the man and the woman come into the building around eight o'clock. Like the super said, the Instructor was wearing a raincoat, wide-brimmed hat and sunglasses. He walked with two canes. The Continental men said they'd describe him as fat, not particularly tall, and slow-moving. One of them went up the elevator with them and saw that they got off on the fourth floor.

Foot traffic was constant for the next two hours. They could not say who might have gone into 431. The Instructor and the Assistant came out, dressed as they'd been when they went in, after two in the morning. They entered another building in Tudor City, only a few hundred yards away, where the operatives lost them. The second building had two other doors they could have used or they might have gone upstairs. The operatives were sure they had not been spotted.

When Mrs. Opperman finished the report, Willie asked her what she thought of it.

"Hacken and Begg are good experienced men. If they say the

suspects did not identify them, I'll accept that." Willie nodded and poured another brandy.

Mrs. Opperman said the same thing the next night. The night after that, she said that her men saw Helen Stiles go into the apartment in The Cloister at ten. She came back out at midnight. Mrs. Opperman hadn't come up with anything on Robert Haldorn, so she was going to join the men watching the apartment. She got results.

First, she went back to the super. She told him it was possible that Mr. Haldorn and his wife might have another place in Tudor City. Maybe he could ask around and find out if that was the case. She'd make it worth his time. Then she arranged a meeting with the woman who knew everything about everybody on the fourth floor.

The woman who knew everything about everybody was Florence Pruskaya. When Mrs. Opperman asked if she had a moment to talk about any unusual activities she might have noticed in the building, the woman beamed and invited her in for tea. Within the hour, Mrs. Opperman knew that Florence was unmarried. Her parents fled Russia when the communists took over. She lived with them in Belgium before they moved to New York. Her father worked as a waiter at the Samarkand restaurant. After he and her mother died, Florence was lucky to find a place as nice and economical as Tudor City. Her neighbors were mostly cold fish but wasn't it always like that in the city?

It wasn't hard to get Florence to talk about the people in 431. Someone else, someone Mrs. Opperman couldn't name, had told her that she thought they were Reds. Florence scoffed. She knew Reds and those two weren't Reds. Reds had meetings at all hours of the day and night, and they had loud arguments. These two were so quiet during the day that she wasn't even sure they were in the apartment. No, it was worse than that. They were Hindoos, she thought, from the incense she sometimes smelled in the hall when she was near their door, but it was hard to say because of Mr. Boringer in 408 and his stogies. When he was smoking one of those, she couldn't smell anything else. And sometimes, faintly faintly, she could hear what she was sure was heathen Hindoo devil music when she put a glass up to the wall in her bathroom.

What about the visitors, Mrs. Opperman asked.

It's three women, Florence said with a sly look in her eye. They're never together. They always come separately and on different nights, and all of them wear some kind of veil.

The first woman had dark blonde hair. That was Helen Stiles, Mrs. Opperman figured. She was Tuesday and Thursday.

The second, Saturday and Wednesday, was a widow who wore black and a heavy full veil.

The third was a fat woman—"even heftier than you, dear"—who wore a smaller veil, like Helen Stiles, and a shiny blonde wig. She was Monday and Friday.

The next night, a Saturday, the detectives spotted the woman in widow's weeds when she went in, and they followed her when she left. At two in the morning a hired car was waiting for her on Forty-Second Street. That's what Mrs. Opperman told them they'd find. She figured a woman out that late by herself would have arranged for a ride. The car let her out at an apartment building on West Eighty-Second. One of the detectives was able to see through the front door that she went to the second floor in the elevator.

On Monday night, they saw the plump woman in the shiny blonde wig. Like the others, she came in around ten. The detectives were outside where they could watch the lobby. About one o'clock, the doorman answered the house telephone and then placed a call on another telephone. When the woman in the wig came out fifteen minutes later, a yellow cab was waiting for her. They followed it downtown to an apartment in Murray Hill.

Helen Stiles came again on Tuesday.

Mrs. Opperman had her preliminary report ready when she showed up at my place that night. Working with the information she had, she had learned that the first woman really was a widow, Mrs. Victoria Garner, age fifty-seven.

The woman in the wig was Mrs. Cassandra Hickey, thirty-two, wife of Gus Hickey who owned a sweat shop in the garment district.

"Given what I saw in the apartment," Mrs. Opperman said, "I'd guess this Instructor is running a spiritualist confidence racket on Mrs. Garner. She still hasn't gotten over the death of her husband, and her friends are worried about her. With Mrs. Hickey, I think it's the same weight-loss scheme he's using on Miss Stiles. We can assume, despite what Miss Stiles said, that she and the other two women are giving him money. If you want to ascertain exactly how much money, that will involve getting into their bank records. It will take longer and cost more."

I wrote down *ascertain?* In my notebook.

"And there's something else that's more important about this case. Mrs. Hickey's husband lives for his work. He seems to spend every waking hour either at his factory or talking about his work on the telephone or sending and answering telegrams. In short, even when he is at home, he isn't at home. Mrs. Garner is a widow. Miss Stiles is unmarried."

Willie interrupted, "Like Ruby Rose, they're alone, they're more vulnerable than they realize."

Mrs. Opperman's tone sharpened. "No, they know exactly how vulnerable they are. Every woman in this city knows that every time she sets foot on the street. But for the moment, they've forgotten it and they've put their trust in a man who means them harm."

"They're all so easy to lead," Willie said.

"Not all of us," she muttered. By then he was pouring another Five Star and didn't hear her.

Chapter Sixteen

1929
NAPA, CALIFORNIA

Connie knew something was wrong one Tuesday after school. She was walking up the gravel road toward her house, staying to one side to avoid the puddles in the ruts when she saw her mother and father standing on the front porch. From twenty yards away, she could tell they were angry. Angry at her. There was only one possible reason. They'd found out. Yes, Connie's father was holding the Di Nobili cigar box. Her mother had the money. Connie's money.

"Where did you get this?" Connie's mother demanded.

Connie's father, booze in hand, said, "She stole it. Where did you steal it from?"

She stepped up onto the porch. "I didn't steal it. I saved it."

Her mother slapped her open-handed, scorching her face. "Don't lie. There's forty-three dollars here. You couldn't save that much."

Connie staggered back and couldn't keep the tears out of her eyes. They blurred her vision and her cheek burned hot. She could have said you can save forty-three dollars if you start when you're seven years old, but she stayed silent.

They yelled at her for a long time and when they got tired of yelling, she explained how long she'd been at it. In the end, they believed that Connie hadn't stolen the money, but, they said, at the same time, she had stolen it. She'd stolen it from her family and that was worse, much worse. Hadn't they agreed that she would contribute what she earned? Share and share alike. So, now, Connie was going to do what she should have done all along and give this money to the family. Give it cheerfully and with love. Connie stared at the floor so they couldn't see her face and said yes.

When it ended, hours later, Connie's cheek was red and swollen. Her mother, still storming, asked Connie if she'd learned a lesson. Family before everyone else. Conni agreed and thought the real lesson was to find a better hiding place.

That night, as she listened to the train, she knew she'd be on one before long. She'd been lucky. They hadn't found the manila envelope in the chicken coop. It had another eighty or more, and a letter from the Fulton Employment Agency inviting her to an interview.

A week later, Connie told the nurse at school she had terrible cramps and had to go home. She'd never played hooky before and had such a good reputation as a serious student that the nurse gave her a pass without thinking twice. But instead of heading home, Connie caught a train to Vallejo and from there, took the ferry to San Francisco.

She'd been to the city before. It still scared her but she'd looked at a map in the library. Then she'd written down the streets and turns from the ferry docks to the agency. According to the scale on the map, it was about than two miles. She wasn't sure about the streetcar and bus routes but she had good shoes.

Foot traffic moved faster than it did in downtown Napa. The morning crowd, mostly men but some young women, all seemed to walk quickly. Connie picked up her pace down Market Street to Eddy, and arrived at the agency thirty minutes early, breathing hard and patting her face dry with a handkerchief. She signed in and sat on a wooden bench in a large room with about twenty other girls, some young, some old, all looking somehow more qualified for anything than she was. It seemed like she sat for hours before a girl called her name. As she followed, Connie noticed that almost all of the people they walked past were women. The girl led Connie to a small, smoky room in the basement, and a severe older woman behind a battered wooden desk. Connie sat in a chair that was wedged between the desk and the wall.

The woman told Connie that the agency was part of a charity group, not exactly official, but the group let them use a little space in their building. Most of their work was with orphans, destitute women and the like, but they had been able to help several girls who worked for Connie's supervisor at Stag's Leap Manor, and they made exceptions. What was Connie looking for?

Connie said she planned to work at least another summer at Stag's

Leap, and with the money she made, she should have enough for her travel expenses. Then she wanted to go east and see a big city. New York was her first choice, but she would take a job in Boston or Philadelphia.

The agency woman lit a cigarette and looked over the form Connie had filled out. First, she noticed the strong, clear penmanship. All letters level with the lines. No misspellings or words crossed out. Connie meant for it to look good. She'd practiced enough times on notebook paper before she wrote on the form. Then there was the recommendation from the woman at Stag's Leap saying that Connie could handle all household duties and knew enough kitchen work to serve as a cook's assistant. Connie had added two years to her age on the form, but the woman didn't say anything about that.

Instead, she said, "Contact us in the fall. We might be able to help you. Jobs in service aren't as easy to come by as they were a couple of years ago, but there are still a few families with enough wealth to hire staff and some of them contact us. You're not Irish or an Eye-tie, that's good. What kind of name is Nix?"

"The people on my father's side of the family are English."

The woman squinted at her face through the smoke. "Your complexion's on the dark side."

Connie said quick, "I've been working in the sun." She didn't mention the Mexican part of her mother's family.

The woman said, "The really rich ones tend to be particular about such matters, so let me give you one piece of advice. You're too pretty. Women, even older women, don't like pretty young girls in their home. Cut your hair, no makeup, no nice clothes. Believe me, I'm telling you this for your own good."

Connie remembered the men at Stag's Leap and believed the agency woman.

"One more thing," the woman said, and Connie could tell by the look on the woman's face that she wouldn't like it. "If we find someplace for you, we charge a fee."

"How much?"

"It depends on the position. Don't worry about it now."

Connie worried.

Chapter Seventeen

1931
NEW YORK CITY

The next afternoon, Willie came to my office, not to the room with the puppet. After he poured his Five Star, he asked what Tudor City was. I told him it was a big development on Prospect Hill over by the East River between Fortieth and Forty-Third. About a dozen apartment buildings and a hotel with a park.

Willie frowned. "Fortieth by the river? That's where the slaughterhouses and glue factory are."

"They cleaned it up some," I said. "but I understand it's still pretty rank. This place was built after Grand Central Terminal opened. The idea is that normal people can live there and walk to work. Never been there myself but you can't miss the ads in the papers."

He frowned some more and thought. Then he said, "I need to take a look at it."

"Mind if I join you? I'm ready to get out of this joint for a while."

"Capital idea," Willie said. "I'll have Fat Joe get a cab."

"No need. Frenchy drove his truck. It's got room for three."

Remember that I said Frenchy's truck was a Chevy with a homemade wooden cab and flatbed. No sooner had we got into it and pulled out of the alley than Frenchy and Willie were gabbing away in French. I could tell they were discussing the work that Frenchy had done on the thing. After a bit, Willie realized I didn't understand. He said, "I was just telling Monsieur Reneau that I drove a French ambulance in the war. When we got to France, the first thing they did was send us to George Kellner's Carrosserie where we built our own cars. They had wooden bodies, just

89

like this. All the men were in the army, of course, so the factory was filled with women. They were shorthanded and it was up to us to construct the bodies, bolt them to the frames and paint them. Took us more than a week to build twenty cars. Funny, we hadn't thought of anything like that, but it made perfect sense. No reason to equip a bunch of uninvited Americans if they couldn't prove they were up to some hard work."

Afternoon traffic was building by then so it took some time to get across town and then up town. When Frenchy turned on Forty-first, we saw the sign on top of one of the tallest buildings, TUDOR CITY in big neon capital letters. After we went under the Second Avenue el and climbed the hill, we came to a place where there were grassy parks on both sides of the street. They were surrounded by buildings, looming ten stories or more, all red brick and white stone.

Willie looked around and said, "By God, it's grim."

I didn't argue. Neither did Frenchy. Willie wanted to walk around to get a better feel for it. He and I got out. Frenchy said he'd find a place to park and come back. Willie went off to find The Cloister apartment building. I walked back the way we'd come to the Hotel Tudor. The cocktail lounge was down the stairs from the lobby. The doorman was leery of letting me in until I showed him a card for Jimmy Quinn's place and explained that I was the owner. He didn't know me but he knew the name. The lounge was on the small side for a hotel but the furnishings were good, newer than mine, and the place was packed. I didn't even try to get a drink. I could tell from the bottles behind the bar that their stock was second rate.

I gimped back to the little park and took a seat on a bench when my hip started complaining. It was a busy time of afternoon with men in suits coming home from work and women in dresses and coats going out to dinner. It seemed to me to be a fair cross section of a city neighborhood, better off than some but not close to the best. Maybe a cut above Chelsea, but not really.

I hadn't been on the bench for long when I saw the Instructor and the Assistant across the street. It had to be them, a man with a wide hat, long coat and two canes, and a woman in a coat and hat. I could tell right away that the guy didn't need the sticks. They were for show. He was hunched over but that looked phony to me, too. They walked slowly on the sidewalk, heading north, and crossed Forty-Second. I followed on the other side of the street. They took their time. I couldn't see their faces but it didn't look like they were saying anything to each other.

On the other side of Forty-Second, they cut in front of me. I slowed and let them get ahead as we walked past the second little park. They took a left on Forty-Third.

Willie was half a short block in front of them. I was close enough to see the way he reacted when he recognized them walking toward him. Then he saw me and turned around and walked in the other direction. I followed the Instructor and the Assistant until they went into The Cloister apartment building, then turned and headed back to the park. Willie caught up with me before I got there.

"What a stroke of luck to see them like that," he said. "Now we're getting somewhere."

I shook my head. "They made you."

"What do you mean?"

"You were surprised when you spotted them. I saw it. They saw it."

Willie was offended. "Don't be ridiculous. They have no idea who I am."

"If they're pulling a professional confidence job on those women, they notice when anybody pays extra attention to them. They've got to if they want to stay in business. So, figure they made you and figure they'll do something about it."

Theodora Opperman agreed with me. She showed up again around eleven. When Willie told her what we'd done at Tudor City, she cursed.

"It's never good when a client tries to play amateur detective. You hired us. Leave the work to professionals."

Willie said, "What neither of you understand is that these are not conventional criminals. Yes, they're probably trying to fleece these foolish women out of a few dollars, but as soon as someone shows them up for what they are, they'll run like rabbits. I've seen it before."

I said, "Do you think your Abbé would run like a rabbit? I don't."

Theodora Opperman asked what I was talking about. Willie was confused, too. "The Abbé is this character Willie knew years ago," I said. "Big bastard. Showed up here the other night when Willie threw a party. I didn't get the whole story but he sure acted like there was bad blood between them."

Willie shook his head.

"Did you invite him?" I asked.

"No, but he was part of that crowd. Word got around."

"You think it's just a coincidence he showed up right after you sent the pictures of the puppet to Ruby Rose?"

The detective said, "What does he have to do with my case?"

Willie sighed like he thought we were both nuts. He poured a Five Star and told us a story.

Back in the mid '20s, when he lived down in the Village and his wife Katie ran the most popular coffee shop in that part of town, Willie and the Abbé and Aleister Crowley got together regularly at Crowley's ratty rented house to discuss the mystic arts and spiritualist hocus pocus. They had the idea that magic and miracles were real. They thought there was another "level of reality" that was more powerful than the world we live in, and if they just figured out the right words and rituals, they could get to it. Like Willie told me, Crowley thought that sex was the key. The Abbé said it was drugs. He'd learned about peyote from Indians, used cocaine daily, and he was organizing a series of experiments with synthetic mescaline from Austria. Willie thought they both might be onto something and if they combined their efforts, they could reach that higher level. To hear Willie tell it, they spent a lot of time and effort trying to work that out.

Theodora Opperman looked like she'd heard that one before.

The long and the short of it is that after they'd been trying to outdo each other with their search for the right circumstances for a month or so, Crowley shut the rest of them up by claiming that he had attained a degree of supernatural power and he could prove it. Willie and the Abbé called his hand. Crowley took them outside and said that the three of them would walk down the sidewalk until they'd reached any point that Willie chose. Then he'd show them his proof. They agreed and followed him up Fifth Avenue to Thirtieth.

Willie paused then, letting us know that he was getting to the important part. "I decided to stop him then. Crowley looked about, spotted a man who was approaching us and said, 'Watch him.' The man passed and Crowley fell in step right behind him but not touching him in any way. After they'd taken four or five paces, Crowley abruptly stopped and bent his knees. The man in front of him did the same. His knees buckled and he fell to the sidewalk, as if someone had cut his legs out from under him. When the Abbé and I rushed to help the man to his feet, we saw the bewildered look on his face. Remember, I was close enough to see everything that went on and I swear to you that Crowley never touched the man. It was one of the most astonishing and inexplicable things I have ever seen. But the Abbé was not impressed.

"He told us to follow him and headed back toward Crowley's hovel. Crowley asked us smugly what we thought of what we'd just witnessed. Before I could answer, the Abbé said, 'Not very much, really,' and that, of course, infuriated Crowley. He demanded that the Abbé demonstrate equal magic right there on the spot. Even though there was absolute blind fury behind Crowley's words, the Abbé remained completely placid. He turned to me and said, 'Seabrook, how many people do you estimate are within the range of our vision at this moment. Be quick.'

"It was early afternoon. We were standing at a moderately busy corner. A policeman with a whistle was directing traffic and signaling pedestrians. I said that there might be thirty or fifty people that I could see. The Abbé told me to choose one who could see us. I was to whisper to Crowley who it was but not to let the Abbé know and nod when I'd made my decision. I scanned the crowd and chose a young woman in a white hat on the other side of the street who was about to cross. I told Crowley and nodded toward the Abbé.

"The Abbé closed his eyes briefly and opened them when the policeman in the intersection blew his whistle and the crowd crossed Fifth. I could see that he focused on the girl in the white hat. He muttered a guttural incantation, clasped his hands together and thrust them forward. The girl immediately swooned. If Crowley's man looked like his legs had been cut out from under him, she acted like she'd fainted. Her muscles gave way and she collapsed in the middle of the street. People around her screamed. Cars stopped. The policeman dashed over. We could see that her head was bleeding where she'd hit it on the pavement. The crowd surged around her and carried her across to our side of the street. I saw how pale she was, how shallow her breathing. The Abbé gave Crowley a condescending sneer and said, 'Are you satisfied?'

"The entire afternoon left me shaken, I can tell you."

Willie shivered at the memory, drained his cognac and went on. "Now, are you willing to accept that what I have just told you is true, that I experienced something inexplicable?"

The detective and I looked at each other. I said, "They whipsawed you."

She nodded. Willie still didn't understand.

Theodore Opperman said, "Maybe they were in on it together or maybe each of them came up with the same idea. Whichever, the man who collapsed and the girl in the white hat were in on it."

I said, "My friend Mr. Runyon says that in New York you can run into a guy who will bet you that he can make the jack of spades jump out of a deck of cards and squirt cider in your ear, and if you take that bet you will wind up with an earful of cider."

Willie said, "No, you don't understand, not about this and not about Ruby Rose. What you're saying would be true if it were about money but it's not. There was no money involved with Crowley and the Abbé. Ruby Rose isn't interested in money either. She's motivated by hatred, envy and lust. We don't know what's going on in Tudor City. It may have nothing to do with Ruby.

"Now, I understand why both of you would reach that conclusion. You live in an underworld of criminals who will do anything for a dollar, but that's not what we're dealing with now."

Theodora Opperman stubbed out her smoke. "Whatever you say, Mr. Seabrook. You're paying the freight." She snapped her handbag shut. "I'll see you tomorrow if I have more to report." Tired of listening to Willie, she left.

He turned to me. "What do you think?"

"About what? Ruby Rose? I don't know. The whole business with the puppet and the photographs still doesn't make much sense to me, but I guess I understand what you're trying to do. About these other guys, Crowley and the Abbé—sounds like they were pulling one over on you. If there wasn't any cash involved, maybe they just wanted to play a joke on you, or to make you look bad."

"I'll accept that the man Crowley chose could have been a confederate, but what about the girl I chose?"

"If they meant business, they had more than one person in the crowd with something you'd notice right away—the girl in the hat, a guy wearing a bright red vest or an odd hat, and they had a different signal for each one of them. Or maybe they figured all they needed was the right girl. If I told you to pick one person out of a group on the street and most of them were men and one of them was a young girl in a bright dress or a big hat, you'd go for the girl nine times out of ten. Ten for ten if she was pretty. That's not magic, it's me knowing you."

Willie shook his head and poured more cognac. "You don't understand. I didn't explain it properly. It's just… oh, hell, I don't know what it is."

He collapsed on the divan.

"Tell me something," I said, wanting to change the subject and remembering him and Frenchy talking in French about the cars, "The first night you came here after I got my hip busted, you said something to Frenchy about one of the blankets he brought. What was that?"

"In the war, Frenchy was poilu, a soldier in the trenches. The one thing they all had discovered was that their sleeping blankets had another purpose. When they were ordered 'over the top,' to advance on the German trenches, they'd roll two or three of their blankets around a heavy canvas knapsack and soak them in water. Then they'd crawl on their bellies in the mud, pushing the rolled-up blankets ahead of them, and somehow, those sodden blankets could absorb bullets, even high velocity German rifle rounds.

"One proud corporal showed me where his blanket had stopped sixteen bullets."

No wonder Frenchy hung onto it.

Chapter Eighteen

1929
NAPA, CALIFORNIA

Connie tried to focus on her plan for the rest of the spring. With her older sister and brother gone, more of the work fell on her. She knuckled under and did it. Her mother spent more hours bossing crews at the larger farm where she was harvest captain.

A blight hit the cherry and prune trees in their orchard. All of them had to be cut down, the roots dug out, and burned. They made a bonfire like she'd never seen near the road one night. Neighbors came to watch but nobody could stand close to it. After that, her father replanted the orchard with grapes, and drank more. Even though Prohibition was still going on, he heard about "Vine-Glo," a miracle process that could legally transform grapes into bricks that anybody could turn into wine in their kitchen. He worked the vineyard while Connie's mother took on even more work with other farms.

When her older brother and Xeno Pool came around, they brought liquor and drank with her father. Pool usually had a book for Connie, and he always found a way to catch her alone in the kitchen or anywhere he could. Connie looked forward to seeing him, and she was afraid of him at the same time. Her older sister's situation was never far away.

If Pool ever managed to corner her that spring, she didn't tell me about it. But given his determination and her fascination with him, it figures that he did. And there was one night that she did tell me about, the night Pool gave her Willie's book.

She was washing dishes when she heard a car pull up outside. She knew who it was. A few minutes later, Pool came into the kitchen looking for glasses. He had a book for her, the same one she showed me, *Adventures in Arabia.* Pool leaned on the counter where she was trying to stack the plates in the rack. She could smell raw alcohol on his breath. He tried to make small talk but she asked him why he kept coming around to see her.

The question threw him. She said he stammered that he wanted to talk about books.

She said, "You bring me plenty of books but you never talk about them. How do I know you read them?"

"Yeah, well, this one, it's about this guy who goes over to the desert, and he lives with this tribe of nomads. They sleep in tents and they raid other tribes. It's pretty exciting, all right. At least the part I read was. It got boring by the end, but…"

He stopped and looked at her sharply, "You know, you're a pretty smart cookie, and I guess that's why I find myself hanging around here. You're not like the other girls. I know what they're after and it ain't what I'm after. There's a big wild world out there and I'm going to see it. You want the same thing, and you know how to get it."

She didn't say so, but I figure she cut her eyes at him then, letting him know that she wasn't buying it. "And how would you know that?"

"I know because your brother told me about how you hid that money from your parents."

She slammed her fists into the dishwater and glared at him.

"Don't be like that," he said. "Hell, I understand. It's what you have to do. If you want to get out of this jerkwater burg, you got to have the cash. That's what it takes, and when you get to a real city, then you need even more money, and you better be willing to do what you have to do to get it. Don't expect anybody to hand it to you because you're so pretty. But you could do something in that area if you were interested and I could help you with it."

Connie said she had other plans.

Pool said, "I want to work with the guys who know what they're doing and make real money at it. They're the ones who can teach me what I need to know. If a guy wants to make anything of himself, he's got to watch the guys who have already been successful and learn to do what they do. Those guys are all back east. Capone gets the headlines, but New York, that's where you need to be. Those guys are the best."

As Connie remembered it, that's as far as he got before her older brother and father yelled that they were thirsty. Pool touched her cheek and told her that he'd see her again. Real soon. After he left the kitchen, she didn't understand why she felt so confused, angry, excited, offended, and flattered all at once.

A week later, she moved back to Stag's Leap Manor for the summer.

Chapter Nineteen

1931
NEW YORK CITY

Xeno Pool called the speak the next day and said he had the money. Something about his voice was different. He sounded more confident than when he surprised me in the lobby of the Chelsea. I say that now but it could be hindsight, considering what happened later. I told Pool to call back at six o'clock and I'd give him the when and where. Then I took a cab over to the Barbizon-Plaza. Meyer Lansky was busy with some other guys and I had to wait to see him. When I told him Pool claimed he had the money, Meyer said, "All right. We'll do it tonight then. Ten o'clock. You remember the details?"

"Yeah, but…"

"What?"

I tapped my hip. "If you could wait a few days I might be able to help. Now, I can get around all right but that's about it."

"You don't have to be there," he said.

"Yeah, I do."

"It's up to you."

"I'll be there."

When Pool called back, I told him to bring the money to a garage at the corner of Broom and Cannon Streets near the Williamsburg Bridge. Lansky would meet him there at ten. Then I went back to the Chelsea to change. The garage was a dirty place. I wasn't going to risk a good suit. Back in the early days of Prohibition, Lansky ran most of his business out of that building. He had a legitimate front there renting cars. But he also used it to fix up and repaint the cars and trucks we stole for him. More than once, I acquired a Model A in the morning and brought it to the garage at lunch. Then came back that night and drove it out to Long Island or New Jersey to pick up a load of hooch from a speedboat. But that had been a long time ago. By 1931, Lansky and Luciano had made arrangements on the New York waterfront. Most of the product was labeled as legal and shipped directly to the docks before they took it to their factories where it was cut and rebottled. Hell, Lansky was already making plans to buy his way into a company called Molaska that made powdered molasses and turned it into booze.

I changed into a pair of old twill pants, work boots and a leather jacket. By the time I finished, the hip hurt so bad that I took two of the doctor's pain pills. Maybe they juiced me up more than I knew. I found my knucks, checked the load in the Detective Special I was carrying then, and gimped back to the speak. The guys at the Cruzon Grill fixed me up a hamburger and some fried potatoes.

Jimmy's Rule Number Four: Make time for a sandwich.

I got to the garage around nine. Meyer Lansky wasn't there. Moe Sedway was. He ran a lot of things for Lansky.

He said, "Hiya, Jimmy. What's going on? Meyer said there'd be trouble."

"Yeah, it's kind of involved. I better let Meyer tell you about it. Who's here?"

"Just these guys Meyer sent over." He hooked a thumb at three guys who were playing cards. They were heavyweights, flat-nosed sluggers who busted up strike-breakers for union guys, and busted union guys for the bosses. They looked disappointed that I wasn't the guy they were going to lay a beating on.

Meyer's place was a big square building with blacked out windows in front. It smelled of gas and oil like all garages. But that night you could smell water and steam, too. Most of the place was dark. The only lights were up front near the part Meyer used as an office. There were curtained-off stalls in the back where they did the painting. I saw that they'd pulled the high-pressure water hoses up to the front. They used those to clean cars, but usually they did that in the back. There were about half a dozen rental cars and trucks in the service bays.

Meyer showed up a few minutes later. He hung his suit coat on his chair and put on a pair of coveralls. He told Moe to tell the guys to move toward the back. "I don't want to scare this bastard off before I get my money."

I was wondering what Pool was going to do. Seemed crazy to me that he wanted to see Meyer after he'd pissed him off twice. But then nothing about Pool made any sense to me. Still, you had to figure he wasn't going to waltz into a strange place by himself without some kind of surprise up his sleeve.

At ten sharp, we heard a rap on the door. Moe opened it. Xeno Pool came in slow and careful. He wore a brown topcoat over a dark suit. Same two-tone shoes. Moe frisked him. I slipped on my knucks. He saw me and looked over toward the desk where Meyer was. He stood straighter and said, "Mr. Lansky, I heard you liked to work on cars. Me too."

Meyer said, "Where's the money you owe me?"

Pool said he'd have it in five minutes and went back out the door. Moe waved for the three sluggers to move closer.

When Pool returned, Moe met him at the door and frisked him again. The only thing he found was a roll of bills in a rubber band. He handed it to Meyer and went behind Pool to stand between him and the door. The sluggers walked out of the shadows and waited by the coiled high-pressure hoses. Pool barely glanced at them. Instead, he went into his pitch. Sounded like the first part, at least, was memorized.

"Mr. Lansky, first, I apologize to you and Mr. Quinn. I know I made a bad first impression and that's the last thing I wanted to do because I came here, here to New York, to meet you. Yeah, I heard about you. Everybody has. When they had me locked up in San Quentin, I talked to guys and they said the best in the business is Meyer Lansky. Sure, everybody reads about Al Capone and you hear that Lucky Luciano runs New York, but the man you want to see is Meyer Lansky if you want to make serious money, and that is exactly what I came here to do. I knew some guys who knew some guys who worked for you. At least, that's what they told me and that's how I came to be in business with the Rosens.

"They told me that they were working for you. That's why I threw in with them in the first place. As I heard it, there's bad blood between you and Waxey Gordon, and they told me that the shipment we diverted was his, not yours. What I'm trying to say is that this was an honest mistake and you'll find more than four thousand dollars there."

Meyer and Moe looked skeptical.

"See, when I first met them, they bragged that they knew you and would introduce me. We did a few jobs together. Then, like I said, they told me that I could help them hijack a load from Waxey and sell it to you. Only it wasn't like that. It was your booze and they wanted to sell it to Waxey."

If what he was saying was true, I wondered, why would the Rosens agree to help him bust up my place?

"But now I've paid you back. With interest. If you tell me to go away, I'll go, but if you let me come to work for you, it will be profitable for both of us."

Meyer stared at him for so long Pool got nervous. Finally Meyer said, "You stole from me. Moe, take care of it."

Moe said, "O.K., boys," and the sluggers moved in fast on Pool. Two of them went to grab his arms while the third twisted the nozzle of the high-pressure hose. It jerked against his grip and the hissing fan of water sprayed across the floor. I'd seen that thing strip paint.

Without a second's hesitation, Pool put his fingers to his lips and let out a loud piercing whistle. At the same time, he pivoted to the closest slugger and landed a vicious chop to the guy's throat. The guy staggered but didn't fall. The second slugger came in more carefully. Pool shuffled backward, turning away from the wall, toward the guy with the hose. The guy aimed the thing at Pool's midsection. The force of the water knocked Pool back and I could see that it shredded his topcoat. The spray hit Pool's right hand and it turned red with blood.

Right then, two cinder blocks crashed through the blacked-out windows near the door. They hit one after the other, real fast, freezing the sluggers. Pool had a moment then when he might have been able to make it through the front door before they got him, but he charged straight at the guy with the hose. The other sluggers waded in and the four of them became one wet hissing mass as the hose sprung free and started whipping around and soaking everything. I backed off. So did Meyer and Moe. For a few seconds, the thing was spraying the ceiling and walls. I was far enough away that it didn't slice skin when it hit me but it hurt like hell and it was cold.

One of the sluggers got hit full in the face by the water. He screamed when it sliced into his eye, and the spray turned into a pink mist around them before he fell. Another one slipped on the wet floor. Pool broke away and ran between the bays toward the paint stalls in back. One of the sluggers tried to grab the hose that was still flying around spraying water everywhere. I could hear Pool's loud running footsteps on the concrete floor and a screech when his shoulder pushed open the metal fire door in back. Light from the street came through the doorway and I saw a man standing outside. He handed Pool something. Pool turned around and ran back through the garage. I ducked behind the biggest car I car I could find—a light green Hudson—and pulled my pistol.

Couldn't see Moe or Meyer. Holding hands over his bleeding eye, the wounded slugger struggled to his feet. Pool closed on the sluggers. I saw the gun in his hand. He fired twice. Two of the guys fell and the roaring hose got loose again.

I leaned across the hood of the Hudson, making myself as small as possible, and shot Pool. He whirled around and put two bullets into the grill of the Hudson. Then he was running back toward the fire door before I could get off another shot. I tried to chase him but something went wrong with my first step. The pain sliced through my hip, and I dropped to my knees. By the time I got up, Pool was out the door.

I ducked between two cars and hobbled to the opposite wall and the valve for the hose. I cranked it shut and the roaring went quiet.

Meyer got on the telephone right away and called some guys to board up the broken windows and get rid of the water on the floor and the broken glass. Then he called the same sawbones who'd looked in on me. The doc took the three wounded sluggers away. They were in bad shape. All of us where wet but Meyer and Moe got it worse than I did. They were soaked. We dried off as best we could with shop rags.

Moe said, "You know, Meyer, maybe you should've hired the son of a bitch."

Meyer was sorting through the sodden bills and spreading them across his desk. He shook his head. "Hell, no. He's too damn ambitious, and he shortchanged me. Four thousand, my ass."

"I don't know where he got the goddamn gun," Moe said. "I didn't miss it when I patted him down."

"Guy gave it to him," I said. "The guy who heaved the cinder blocks through the window. Right after he did that, he ran to the back and was waiting when Pool hit the fire door."

"You saw that?"

"Yeah, and, you know, it's kind of funny that Pool was smart enough to come by this place after I gave him the address. He cased the outside of the building and arranged with this other guy to throw the blocks when he whistled—"

Meyer interrupted, "Because he knew I wasn't going to go along with anything he said."

"Or he figured the odds were that you were still mad about him knocking over your shipment but he thought that he still had a chance of impressing you and talking his way into working for you."

Meyer shook his head. "That's nuts."

I said, "Anything about this business that isn't nuts?"

I gimped out to Delancey Street and caught a cab back to the Chelsea. I cleaned up, put on a fresh shirt and suit, slate gray with a black pinstripe, single breasted from Franklin Simon, and a dark maroon tie. As I was getting dressed, I tried to tell myself that it felt good to pay back Pool for busting up me and my place, but somehow it didn't feel as good as it should have. I didn't regret shooting him, but something just wasn't right and it gnawed at me. I decided it was just my hip and took another pain pill.

It must have been close to midnight when I got back to the speak. Marie Therese stopped me by the coat room. She said that some dame had come in by herself and asked if Willie was around. Another actress, she said. I looked past Marie Therese and spotted the woman right away. The redhead with the martini. She was standing at the bar, one high heel hooked over the footrail. Tight shiny black dress, blood red scarf at her throat.

She turned so that I could see her face and I knew who she was. Ruby Rose. The guy that carved the doll of her had done a hell of a job. She was a looker all right and the rest of her wasn't bad either. While I was watching, a guy came up and said something to her, the way guys in bars will do. She smiled a little bit, and said something to turn him down, but whatever it was, it made him laugh.

I told Marie Therese to tell Willie he had a visitor, and to order another martini for his guest. When I got close, I saw that she had a bright red lipstick and a lot of dark makeup around her eyes.

"Welcome to Jimmy Quinn's, Miss Rose. I'm the owner of this joint. I'll bet you're looking for Willie Seabrook."

She gave me the once-over, almost smiling. When she raised her glass, the gin sloshed onto her hand and I could see that she was half in the bag.

She stuck out a hand. "Jimmy Quinn, yeah, I've heard about you."

"Willie's on his way. Let's have a seat." I gestured with my stick to my two-top. She downed the rest of her martini and ankled over to the table. Every guy in the place was watching her.

I held a chair. She showed a lot of leg as she sat, still enjoying the attention. Brenda brought her drink.

Ruby Rose said, "I was invited to the little party that Willie threw here. Heard it was quite the scandalous evening. Sorry I missed it."

"It was different, all right. You'd've fit right in."

"I dunno. I heard there were a lot of writers and they're not my type."

"Willie's a writer," and about then, I think, the third pain pill hit me.

She grinned wider. "I suppose, but he does a lot of other things that are interesting."

"Ain't that the truth."

"I hear he's been spending a lot of time here."

"And why wouldn't I," Willie said. "It's the best speakeasy in the city."

She looked over my shoulder at him and said. "Hello, doll, long time no see."

Willie had a strange looking smile on his mug and her expression changed, too. They acted chummy as hell for the next few minutes but I knew they wanted to have at it. Willie grabbed a chair and they sat facing each other. Brenda hustled over with his Five Star.

"I heard what you were saying to Jimmy and I'm sorry you couldn't join us. So many of the old crowd were here."

"Yeah, I heard you've been seeing Lily. Was she here? I've just been dying to see her again myself, but I hear she's been feeling poorly."

"No, she wasn't here and whatever it was that was bothering her, it's over. She's almost fully recovered now. Really quite remarkable."

Ruby Rose narrowed those big eyes. "You don't say."

"And even more amazing," Willie said, trying to dig the needle deeper, "Your old friend Helen Stiles seems to have been taken with the same mysterious ailment, but now she's on the mend, too."

Willie didn't try to hide a satisfied smirk. He went on. "It was stomach problems with Lily. Helen had concerns about her voice and her throat, but, well, you know, I've had considerable experience with these matters and though my methods are somewhat unorthodox, they can be effective. Tell me, Ruby, how are you feeling? Someone told me that you weren't able to attend the other night on account of terrible cramps. Please tell me that wasn't the case."

She chewed on her olive and spoke around it. "Right as rain. You know me, healthy as a horse, not a delicate flower like Lily."

And they went on like that. I know Willie was lying every time he opened his mouth and it figured she was too, but something wasn't right. I also thought that maybe there was a hell of a lot more to know about what those three women were to each other, something more than one stolen stage door Johnny.

Willie said, "Oh, yes, Helen's back. Has a place on the Upper East Side. The men in Hollywood told her she needed to lose weight if she wanted a career in the movies and so she's seeing someone she calls the Instructor over in Tudor City. I understand you were the one who recommended him to her."

She said, "Everybody knows about that guy."

"Lily came to me because she got the ridiculous idea that someone was trying to place a curse on her. Had you heard that? No? I did a bit of investigating and learned that a lifelike puppet had been commissioned in her image. It had nothing to do with the ailment that had been bothering her but I still thought it best to see the matter through to a conclusion. It's being settled now. But, tell me about yourself, Ruby. I understand you're doing very well these days. Who's the lucky fella? I remember hearing talk of you and Danny Ogilvy."

Willie turned to me. "That's the Ogilvy of Ogilvy's Ovals cigarettes. Quite a catch."

By the way he said it, I figured Ogilvy was the stagedoor Johnny that Lily had snaked away from Ruby. But when Ruby heard the name, Willie didn't get the reaction he was looking for.

She tossed back the rest of her martini and said, "Hell, Willie, that's ancient history. Danny and I had a few laughs. I heard he took up with Lily but it didn't work out. All the guys go for the big-eyed blondes." She cocked an eyebrow. "And with Danny it's never going to work out with a girl as long as his friend Lewis is in the picture, if you know what I mean."

Willie looked like he wasn't buying it, but if she was talking about the Danny and Lewis who came into my place from time to time, I knew exactly what she was talking about. Of course, that didn't mean that she couldn't be trying to put the screws to Lily White.

Willie was still bobbing and weaving. "Are you sure there haven't been any problems? I must have heard it wrong because someone said you were in agony."

"It was nothing and I'm almost over it."

"Oh, I don't think you are. Almost over it, that is. These things can appear to subside and then return twofold if the proper remedies haven't been taken, and I think I can help you with those remedies, if you'll let me."

Those last words had a threat behind them.

Her smile cooled and she said, "I don't need your help. I'm a big girl." But there was something else in her voice, and I got the idea she was afraid of Willie.

"Everybody needs help sometime. I'm not sure you completely understand what's going on. I do and I'm going to make sure that no harm comes to Lily or Helen."

"I don't understand why you keep talking about Helen, or Lily, really."

"No? Listen, sometimes people get involved in something out of a sense of fun or mischief and then they find that it has become more serious and there are powerful forces at work which they don't comprehend, but there's always an option, a choice that can change everything."

A third martini was in front of Ruby Rose. She leaned on the table and had to speak slowly to keep her words straight, "Jeez, you're talking like it's the end of the world or something."

Willie was about to say something else but I said, "You two could yack all night but I think it's time I saw Miss Rose home."

Willie looked like I'd socked him in the stomach.

She drained the martini, stood up and said, "Hell, yes, let's go, doll."

Chapter Twenty

I can't tell you much about the cab ride uptown. Maybe it was the pain pills or the leftover excitement of shooting Xeno Pool or the foolishness of the business with the puppets. Or maybe it was just being in the back seat with a good looking, unpredictable woman on a spring night in New York. Whatever it was, it had me feeling cocky and horny and more clever than I was.

Her place was on West Ninety-first. It was only a block or two from where the Rosen brothers got clipped, but that was the last thing on my mind. She dug the key to the front door out of her bag. I took it from her, opened the door and invited myself into the little lobby.

Smiling, she said, "You take a hell of a lot for granted, doll."

We rode a self-service elevator up to her floor. Her place was about the size of mine at the Chelsea with fresher paint, better woodwork and more expensive furniture. Lots of chrome tubing, glass and mirrors. Light colored two-ply carpet on the floor.

She snapped on a couple of floor lamps and opened a liquor cabinet. "Let me freshen up and I'll pour you a drink, doll. Fix some ice." She strolled into the bedroom.

I found an icepick and bucket. The icebox was in a kitchen area behind a folding screen. I found a soft block in the top and chipped it in the sink.

I opened her Electrola and found a copy of the Helen Stiles version of "Meet Me in the Shadows" at the back of the bin. It was playing when she came back. She frowned and snapped it off.

"Christ, I've heard that a thousand times. Find something else, doll, something we can dance to."

"I don't dance," I said.

She had changed into a belted gold lamé number and I didn't have to look closely to tell that she wasn't wearing anything underneath it. "What are you drinking?" she asked and opened a built-in cabinet.

"Rye if it's any good."

"It's not," she said and poured a couple of fingers. She gave herself another belt of gin over ice.

We sat on a short sofa. She handed me the drink and said, "What's Willie up to? I hear he's at your place every night and it's not just for the booze."

"It's hard to say. I can tell you that he rented a room in my cellar and locks himself in there every night. He doesn't drink before he goes in and when he comes out, he's covered in sweat. The first thing he does," I lied, "is drink a quart of ice water. Now, we don't know exactly what he's doing in there. Actually, I was hoping you could tell me because we've got a pool of bets going about what he's up to and nobody's won yet."

She sat back and breathed deeply, stretching the lame across her chest. She was trying to distract me from the worried look on her face. It worked.

"And there's something else," I said. I leaned toward her and lowered my voice. "I met Willie when I catered another party he threw at his apartment down on Fifth. He wanted to have it at a restaurant but he couldn't. You know why?"

She shook her head.

"Because he invited a lot of colored people, some really important colored people."

She didn't know what to make of that but it worried her.

"Yeah. You ever heard of Miss A'Lelia Walker?"

"Sure, the cosmetics empire. She's one of the richest women in the city, white or black."

"She was there with a couple dozen of her friends, all of them loaded by the cut of their clothes and the way they paraded around. And the Haitian ambassador, he was there, too. Thick as thieves, him and Willie."

She got more worried when I mentioned Haiti.

"There were a lot of white people but with that many colored people, they weren't getting into a restaurant, so they had it at Willie's place and I brought the booze. Now, you know Willie and you know that he's been over in France. So he's got a taste for good wine, liquor and brandy, and he's not about to stomach the swill you find in most places. So, after his party he pays me a visit. We talk, we get along. He asks to see the rest of the establishment and when I show him the cellar, he asks if he can rent the little storage room we've got down there. Just for a couple of weeks, you understand.

"I say yes on account of he's also ordered the most expensive brandy I sell. By the case, no less. He wants to spend more time down there, I'm not about to say no or to ask any questions. But here's where it gets strange."

"Yeah?" she said, eyes wide and curious. I moved closer to her.

"Willie brings Miss A'Lelia Walker with him. Three in the morning, she shows up in a chauffeured Rolls. She's wearing pants and boots and a shawl and gloves and she hurries in so nobody can see she's colored. Then Willie tells us to let another colored guy in the back door. He's a real tall guy dressed in a black frock coat with a priest's collar and some kind of strange gold necklace with a weird symbol on it. And he's carrying a wooden cage with a chicken in it. Then the three of them spend a couple of hours down in the storage room."

"What were they doing?"

I tried to sound mysterious as I made up more lies. "We don't know. All Willie says is that he's helping a friend. From the way you were talking tonight, I thought maybe it had something to do with you and Helen Stiles and that other woman whose name I don't remember. What do you think?"

She chewed on her thumb. I sidled over and put my arm over the back of the sofa. "Does it have anything to do with you?"

"It's just supposed to be a game. He said she deserved it," she muttered, distracted.

"What kind of game? Who said she deserved it? Willie didn't sound like he's playing a game, and there's something else."

I didn't say any more until she looked at me. "That chicken? When the black guy left, Brenda, one of the waitresses, said the cage was empty, and Willie told her to clean the blood off the walls. Don't know why anybody'd want to kill chickens down there."

"I do." She looked scared. "The Haitians. That's powerful magic."

"That's not all. Brenda said when she went down there to clean, there was bedding on the floor and the place reeked of sex. Now, I'm a guy who minds his own business. People want to do things that other people say they shouldn't do, that's nothing to me even if they're doing it in my storage room."

The belt on her robe looked uncomfortably tight. I tried to loosen the bow. She grabbed my hand.

"When was this?"

"Let's see," I made up a number. "Four days ago."

She stood up and poured more gin. The first slug went down fast. She turned to face me and the belt of the robe came loose. She paid no attention to it as she drank.

"Was Willie right? About your having the same stomach problems as that other girl?"

She nodded her head before she said no. "I mean, it wasn't... It didn't amount to... Oh, hell, he said nothing would happen."

"Who said that? The Abbé?"

"What?" She knew the name but something wasn't right, and by then the gin was catching up with her. She made her unsteady way back to the sofa and sat down with a thump, the slushy ice spilling out of her glass. She put it down and tried to focus on me as she loosened my tie.

"You're not supposed to be asking me questions, doll. You're supposed to be telling me about Willie."

"That's right," I said, and eased the robe open. She smiled and gave me a little slap. "Naughty boy. I know what you want."

"Yes, you do."

She grabbed the sides of my face and kissed me hard. Shrugging out of the robe, she stood up and snapped off a light. The floor lamp in the corner cast a shadow that emphasized the high curve of a breast. She walked slowly back to me, knelt, pulled my tie loose, and unbuttoned my shirt. Then, even more slowly, she toppled over onto the two-ply carpet.

I sat there and watched her until she started to snore. Then I buttoned up my shirt and went into her bedroom.

Unmade bed. A vanity with three mirrors, lots of lights and a table overflowing with cosmetics in front of it. More mirrors on the walls. The smell of spicy perfumes and lotions was strong. A chest was filled with clothes and underwear. I went through it trying not to leave any signs of opened drawers or items that had been moved. Her wardrobe was packed tight with dresses and coats and hats. I looked through it well enough to be sure there wasn't room for a box that would hold the puppet. I stood on a chair to look on top of the wardrobe. Underneath her bed, nothing but dust balls and shoes, but by then, my hip was speaking to me again. It hurt so much to get down on the floor that I stood quickly. More soaps and shampoos and lotions in the bathroom. I went back into the little kitchen and found more clothes and cosmetics in the cabinet.

Clenching my teeth against the bright stabbing pain in my hip, I knelt down, got my elbows under her armpits and managed to lift and drag her to the bedroom without straining my back too much. You own a speak, you learn how to handle limp bodies. Like every one I'd ever dealt with, she was heavier than she looked. I got her onto a bed with a satin spread and about half a dozen pillows. I rolled her over onto her stomach so she wouldn't choke if she threw up and pulled the spread over her.

All right, you're probably thinking that I'm lying. I admitted that I thought she was a hot number ever since I'd seen her picture on the poster for the *Scandals of the Great Gay Way*, and that night in her apartment, she made it clear she was more than willing. Why would I walk away?

To tell you the truth, I've wondered about it myself more than once. Maybe if I'd had more to drink, it would have been different, of if she'd had less. But she was out cold and the leftover excitement of the business at Lansky's garage had worn off and my hip still hurt. And, I don't know, it just wasn't right. Damn it.

I was moving a trash can next to the bed in case she threw up when I heard a key in the front door. It opened and closed. Then there were other sounds I couldn't identify. I took the .38 out of my coat pocket, looked through the doorway and put the pistol back. It was the Abbé.

No red robe. No boots. He wore dark pants and a jacket over a sweat stained shirt, no tie, and a shapeless fedora he hadn't bothered to take off. He'd opened Ruby's purse and taken out a handful of bills.

"Don't mind me," I said. "I'm on my way out."

His head snapped around and he pocketed the money. It took him a second to recognize me.

"You were at Seabrook's little get-together with Deborah."

"It's my place."

That surprised him. "Then that explains it. Ruby finally decided she had to see Seabrook. Silly bitch."

He went to the liquor cabinet and filled a glass with rotten ice and seltzer. He settled in the middle of the sofa and glanced down at Ruby's lamé robe on the floor. "Sorry to interrupt. Or did I?"

"The lady had one too many."

"Lady, Hah! Tell me, did she and Seabrook get things sorted out?"

"I can't say, I know they talked about her health. Didn't mean much to me."

"Don't try to deny it. I know what he's up to and I know how foolish it is. Seabrook's a dabbler." He smiled at me like he knew something I didn't and I was just a common little bootlegger not worth a minute of his time. Pissed me off.

I made another drink. "It seemed to me that you and Willie were hashing out some old scores the other night."

"We have unfinished business—and what is that to you?"

"Willie's a good customer, my best. And a friend."

He pulled a small tube out of his breast pocket and twisted it open. The top was also a small spoon. He filled it with cocaine and sniffed it up. "Alcohol will kill him. He doesn't understand that it deadens the mind. This," he held up the spoon, "opens the mind." He didn't offer to share.

"Willie told me you think the way to heaven is through your nose."

"I wouldn't expect you to understand."

"I understand plenty. I saw you taking money from her purse."

That got him hot. "I pay the rent on this place."

"Sure you do. Look, it's no skin off my ass. You want to live off her, that's your—"

He dropped his glass and came off the sofa at me. I brought the stick up and jabbed him in the chest. It slowed him but he still took a swing at me, a big roundhouse right that would have hurt like hell if he'd connected. The guy didn't know how to brawl. I ducked under it, reversed the stick and cracked him right across his bald head. When he brought a hand up, I jabbed his gut again and he dropped to his knees. With that last lunging move, the pain stabbed deep into my hip again.

He started to get up but stopped when he heard me cock the pistol and backed up to the sofa. He winced and rubbed his stomach where I'd hit him. "Why am I doing this?" he said between groans. "The whore means nothing."

I left, trying not to lean on the stick.

Chapter Twenty-one

1930
NAPA, CALIFORNIA

For Connie, June and July were quiet. The Manor wasn't as busy as it had been the year before. People didn't laugh as much. Almost two years after the Crash and things weren't getting better. The guests still drank and ate and complained and squeezed her butt. Connie knew that maybe she had been a little starry-eyed that first summer, but the other girls felt the difference, too, and they talked about it in the dormitory at night. Connie worried.

The first Saturday in August was the big summer dance. Sammy Sterns and His Rhythm Kings were playing in the ballroom, and, for one weekend at least, the Manor was almost full, and spirits were running high. Connie and the other girls worked double shifts. When the band started up at nine o'clock, Connie was clearing the dinner seating and setting up the back part of the dining room for breakfast. After that, she changed into a clean white apron and served drinks and canapes in the ballroom. When she heard the loud crunch outside, she didn't know what it was.

The Rhythm Kings kept playing. Connie could see that something was going on near the big double doors at the front of the ballroom. At first, she could see that a few guests were leaving. Then they were pouring out the doors. Connie and the other girls were curious but their supervisor told them to stay where they were.

Then one of the girls said there had been an automobile accident at the circle past the entrance. She said there was a car in the fountain and the police were there. Another girl said she'd heard the cops say that the car in the fountain was being chased because it had been used in a robbery. Two boys had been hurt. She didn't know if the boys were going to jail or to a hospital.

For the next hour or so, the Rhythm Kings kept at it and a few couples danced, but there was more activity outside. Business at the bar slowed. Connie took it as a chance to get off her feet for a few minutes while one of the other girls snuck outside to get the scoop.

The scoop was that she'd never seen so many police cars in one place. Yes, a convertible had plowed into the fountain and was stuck there with two wheels in the air. The police didn't have anybody. Two guys, or maybe it was three, had run from the car, and the police thought they were hiding in the woods. They'd stolen the car and then robbed a bank, or a post office. As word got about, all the cops in the area left their jurisdictions and came to the Manor. It must have been a hell of a sight. They even brought in bloodhounds and horses for the cops who went through the orchards and into the woods. Other cops went out to cruise the back roads for the fugitives.

One of the girls said she was sure she'd seen a man right outside the dormitory and that set off a wave of squeals and giggles. Those stopped when two big cops came in. Connie felt the first cold tingle of fear as the men spotted the waitresses and walked over. Then one of them said, "Constance Nix? Come with us."

The other girls went quiet and pulled away. Connie felt like there was a spotlight in the ceiling shining straight down on her.

The two cops took her into the manager's office and closed the door. She sat. They towered over her and fired questions.

"When did you last speak with your brother?"

"Two months ago, I think. Not since—"

"Do you know a Xeno Pool?"

"Yes, he's—"

"Has he been in touch with you tonight?"

"When did you last see him?"

"Did you know that him and your brother were planning to rob the Hippodrome Theater?"

"The theater! Is Mr. Kissoloff all right?" Mr. Kissoloff was the manager. She knew that he was there every Saturday. "And the kids who work there. Was anyone hurt?" They ignored her questions.

"You worked at the Hippodrome."

"Did you make copies of your keys?"

She tried to say she never had any keys but they kept at her.

"Why were they coming to see you tonight?"

"Where's their hideout?"

Connie didn't remember how she answered any of the questions. The cops knew that Xeno Pool and Connie's older brother had beaten the manager of the Hippodrome and pocketed the night's box office. The theater had about a hundred seats, so even figuring in the matinee, double feature, popcorn, drinks and candy, the desperados didn't make off with much. And to beat up Mr. Kissoloff, that was crazy.

But, before they knocked over the Hippodrome, they stole an Essex convertible for their getaway. They stole it from a councilman. Straight off, Connie figured the cops were more worried about the councilman than Mr. Kissoloff and the Hippodrome, and that made her mad. The cops kept after her, asking why her older brother and Pool had come to the Manor. She struggled not to cry, not to let them see how much they scared her. She probably didn't fool them. Until the cops found her older brother and Pool, they'd sweat her. But she didn't know that. She hadn't been grilled by the bastards. Hell, she'd hardly ever spoken to a cop before that night, and she didn't have a mouthpiece to spring her, like I did when I was a kid.

She told them she had no idea why her older brother or Pool had come there. They never had before. The cops could ask her boss or anyone who worked there. And speaking of work, her shift wasn't over. The cops told her to can it. They were going to take her in if she didn't tell them everything she knew. Then they ordered her to stay there and left her alone in the office.

She sat and steamed until her supervisor opened the door and told her they needed her in the ballroom.

The Rhythm Kings were packing up, but a lot of the guests had come back, and they were hungry and thirsty. Connie's supervisor handed her a tray of little sandwiches, and sent her into the crowd. Everybody was talking about the car and the thieves. The cops, they said, were sure that the men were close by. Everyone was to stay inside. The buildings were surrounded by officers. None of it made Connie feel any better. Her stomach churned because she knew something bad was coming.

When she went back to the kitchen for more sandwiches, another waitress, one of the older girls who'd called her "kiddo," grabbed her sleeve and whispered, "Xeno's out back. He needs your help."

Connie's surprise must have been easy to read. The older girl said, "How the hell did you come to know Xeno, anyway? No need to answer that, I guess. I know what he's like. Boy, do I ever."

Connie piled sandwiches onto the tray and tried to figure what to do.

She told me that, thinking back on it, when she first realized that Xeno Pool and her older brother had run to her, she was surprised, even thrilled. They didn't think of her as a kid. They needed her help. Wow. But then she got mad. They did something that stupid, she thought, and then came out to the Manor threatening *her* job. Let 'em rot. But then she thought about the two cops and how they tried to bully her. She was still scared of them but she was also pissed off. It was the pissed off part that made her tell the older girl to cover for her.

Connie slipped out the back door of the kitchen. It opened onto a dim strip of blacktop where the service road for deliveries ended. It separated the main building where the guests stayed from the laundry and dormitory. The trash bins were lined up on one side.

The whisper came out of the dark, "Up here."

Connie looked across and saw two shapes. Xeno Pool and her older brother were clinging to something on the steep red-tiled roof of the laundry.

Xeno Pool hissed, "Get us a ladder."

Too loud, her brother said, "A really big ladder," and they started laughing like it was the funniest thing they'd ever said. Then they tried to shush themselves and that made them laugh harder and they started to slip down toward the gutter. Drunk as lords, both of them.

Flashlights shone on the service road. A deep voice yelled, "This way. I heard something over here."

Connie heard men running, a lot of men, and went back through the kitchen door. She had to squeeze past the rest of the girls who were looking out through the glass in the door.

Three cops lumbered up the service road. At first, they shined their lights on the trash bins, but one of them spotted the boys on the roof and pinned them with his light. Xeno Pool and Connie's older brother tried to scrabble up the steep incline. They broke tiles and the tiles rattled down the roof and onto the cops. More lights hit the boys. The cops drew their pistols and more cops joined in. One of them aimed at Xeno Pool. Everything else happened all together. The first shot shattered a tile, sending sharp chunks into her older brother's face. He let go and slid over the edge. Xeno Pool grabbed for him, and went over headfirst. Other cops opened up. A couple of them pulled their nightsticks and laid into the boys.

Connie yelled, "No." She pushed back through the door and ran at the cops. One of them backhanded her with his flashlight. He caught her high on the head and she went down hard. The back of her head smacked the pavement.

Connie came to on a stretcher. Her head hurt worse than it ever had, and she thought she was going to throw up. The other girls told her that Xeno Pool and her older brother had been cuffed and taken to jail in town. When her supervisor asked if one of those boys really was her brother, Connie tried to answer but she couldn't speak.

Some time later, she woke up a second time in a hospital room. Or, she thought she did. She told me she was never sure whether this part of the story was real or if she dreamed it. She got hit on the head really hard twice that night. You can still see a faint scar on her right temple near her hairline where the cop's flashlight caught her. She remembered waking up in a bright white room in bed under a stiff white sheet and a dark blue blanket. A nurse, the older woman she'd seen driving the car years before, was there holding Connie's wrist and looking at a watch to take her pulse. She smiled at Connie.

Connie knew that if it was the same nurse, then she was at the Farm, the Asylum, and that should have scared her, like it did when she was a kid. But that night, somehow, she wasn't scared and that meant that it couldn't be real. Could it? She asked the nurse if she was at the Asylum. The woman smiled and said yes, but she was there because it was an emergency. Connie would be going home in the morning.

She said she knew Connie had been through a lot that night. She wouldn't be able to go back to work at the Manor. When the nurse saw how bad that made Connie feel, she told her not to worry, she was going to be offered another job. Connie wanted to ask her how she could know any of that, but the nurse just adjusted the blue blanket under her chin and said, "It won't be easy."

The next time Connie opened her eyes, she was in her bed at home. Her two younger sisters and baby brother were staring at her and she could hear her mother and father arguing in another room.

Connie's older brother and Xeno Pool took in less than a hundred bucks from the Hippodrome Theater. The councilman's Essex was a more serious matter. As it happened, Xeno Pool already had one juvenile auto theft on his record. He got a fast ride to San Quentin.

Connie's older brother claimed that he'd given in to the temptation of strong drink and had been led astray. The cops had worked him over good, and his face looked pitiful under the bandages. If the judge could see his way clear to give him another chance, he'd commit his life to a ministry in Sister Aimee's Foursquare Church and sin no more, or some such. The judge bought it and gave him a suspended sentence.

Connie's supervisor delivered the things she'd left at the Manor. She said she was sorry it was ending this way. She wished she could say that there'd be a place for Connie next summer, but… She handed Connie her last pay envelope. Connie's mother grabbed it.

By then, the headaches were tolerable. She worried about Xeno Pool and when she was better, Connie signed on with her mother's harvest crew. She picked prunes, dipped them in the lye baths and hated every minute of it. Whenever she could get into town, she went to the Post Office and checked General Delivery. Nothing from the agency.

After school started, she was able to go by the post office almost every day. The letter arrived in December.

Dear Miss Nix:

The agency has submitted your name for a position on household staff. Please stop by our office at your earliest convenience to complete another application.

Very truly yours,

The letter was typed. The agency woman had written at the bottom in pencil, "Bring $10"

Ten dollars was serious money, but Connie was in too far to back out. She took the bills from her envelope in the chicken coop, and hid them in her shoe. The next day, she told the school nurse she had cramps, and took the train and the ferry into the city. This time, Connie didn't have to wait to see the agency woman in the basement. The first thing the woman said through a haze of cigarette smoke was, "Did you bring the money?"

Connie took off her shoe. She didn't like the way the woman's eyes brightened when she saw the bills. Connie asked what the money was for.

"Agency expenses. Here, fill this out."

She gave Connie another form not much different from the one she'd filled out before. Connie held onto the money.

"You said there would be a fee *after* you found a job for me."

The woman waved it off. "This is just a formality. You've as good as got the job."

Connie was excited and suspicious at the same time. "Tell me about it."

The woman frowned around her cigarette. "Look, honey, you don't want this, I've got plenty of other girls that'll snap it right up."

Connie gave her the money and filled out the form.

The agency woman said, "You'll hear from us soon."

Connie left, worrying that the next time she came to the building on Gough Street, she'd find it empty. After that, she waited.

The next letter from the agency arrived in January.

Dear Miss Nix:

Congratulations! We have secured a position on household staff for you. It will require travel on your part. Please stop by our office at your earliest convenience to sign a contract and arrange your schedule.

Handwritten at the bottom, "Bring $90"

Connie felt a cold shiver down her neck. Ninety dollars would come close to cleaning her out.

Chapter Twenty-two

1931
SAN FRANCISCO, CALIFORNIA

The next day in the basement office, Connie sat down and saw that the agency woman had an open file with her name on it. The woman gave her a letter from the Garden State Employment Agency. It said they were pleased to offer Miss Constance Nix a position on the household staff of Mrs. Catherine Pennyweight of Valley Green, New Jersey.

Connie's mouth fell open. "Catherine Pennyweight?"

The agency woman said, "Pennyweight Petroleum, one and the same."

To Connie, Pennyweight was a name like Rockefeller or Vanderbilt.

"This is quite an opportunity. I hope you appreciate what we've done for you. Did you bring the money? Let's have it."

Connie had to take off both shoes to get it. "What's this for?" she said, holding tight to the bills.

"Your train tickets."

Ninety bucks was more than what Connie had figured she'd have to spend, and she didn't feel good about handing the money over.

Then the woman gave her three copies of a printed contract, two pages of tiny type. "Sign at the bottom of the second page. If you want to read it, take it outside. I haven't got all day. You keep one copy."

"What if I don't sign it?"

"You don't get the job."

Connie took a deep breath and signed.

"I need to tell Mrs. Pennyweight when you will be there. I've spoken to some men about that. Meet me at the Southern Pacific waiting room at the Market Street station, next Monday night at eight thirty. Don't buy any tickets. I've got an arrangement with a man. You're getting a great deal."

At first, Connie didn't know what to say. She'd been wanting this and working for it for so long, and now the mechanics of it seemed impossible. "You mean, I should be at the station ready to leave for good?"

Through a wreath of smoke, the agency woman said, "Isn't that what you want?"

Connie nodded.

"You'll pack a week's underwear and hosiery, ten days if you have it," the woman said. "Traveling clothes for cold weather, and one dress or skirt and jacket for your days off. Two pairs of good shoes. Your uniforms will be provided. Got that?"

As Connie stood up to leave, the woman asked if she had a suitcase. Connie started to say yes, but stopped with her mouth open.

"I thought so. Probably haven't been on a train, either. Stop at the Emporium Department Store on Market Street. It's on your way. They ought to have something you can afford."

Connie had been to the big store before, but not with something seriously in mind. All the choices in the Luggage Department set her on her heels. How to make a decision with so many? She wasn't sure what size to get and she didn't want to spend any more than she needed to. The most expensive ones were just beautiful, with gleaming leather, sturdy straps and locks. Confused and sure she was doing the wrong thing, she picked a green one, not the cheapest in the store but close to it, and a matching train case. She didn't have enough money with her for anything better.

As she rode the ferry across the bay, she looked at the bags at her feet and realized that she'd done it. There was no going back. Now, she had to figure how to tell her mother and father.

When Connie got home, she found her father with his ear to the radio. Her mother came out of the kitchen where she'd been making dinner. Connie shooed the little kids away from her new bags. She explained how her supervisor at the Manor told her about the employment agency, and the agency had found a job for her. With the Pennyweight family, no less. Connie's mother and father looked at each other and laughed.

Connie picked up her bags and stomped into her room.

Later that night, after a chilly meal, Connie went through her clothes and followed the agency woman's advice. Packed tight, the suitcase was heavier than she'd expected. Her mother came in without knocking. When she saw the suitcase on the bed, she asked Connie why she was making up a story like that about the Pennyweights. "You haven't gotten over that rap on your head."

Connie said, "I'm not making this up. The agency has arranged everything. When I'm settled I'll write from…" she stopped to remember the name of the place. "Green Valley New Jersey."

Something changed in her mother's face then, and Connie thought maybe she believed that Connie was telling the truth. But she shook her head like she was disappointed. "First your sister and now this. Your father's right. It's a punishment. If only he had, we did everything…" She turned away to hide tears.

Connie thought, yes, you did everything and you stole my money. But as soon as she had that thought, she cursed herself as a selfish child. The whole idea was crazy. She wasn't ready. She couldn't just take off on her own.

And if her mother had pressed her about it there in her room that night, she might have talked Connie into staying. But she left, and Connie sat on her bed and stopped holding back the tears. She argued with herself about staying and going, and wiped her eyes and changed her mind a dozen times until she heard the train whistle.

On Monday morning, Connie got up before everyone else. She didn't want to see her mother again. Drank a glass of milk, and ate some prunes even though she was too excited to be hungry. She packed four jelly sandwiches and more prunes, and caught the first electric train to the ferry. She wore a warm dress and jacket, her most comfortable shoes and her favorite hat. By nine o'clock she was in the Market Street station with a whole day to kill. She sat for a time. Got up and walked when she couldn't stay still, always keeping her bags close. She'd read stories of pickpockets, thieves, and cadets who would entice girls like her into white slave rings. She didn't see any of those but as she walked from one end of the place to the other and back, she knew that she was being watched. More than once, guys followed her or brushed up close or clamped a hand on her butt.

As the hours passed, her doubts grew and billowed. She'd been fooled, lied to. There was no offer from the Pennyweights. How could she have been so gullible. You idiot! How could you trust the woman? You handed her ninety dollars. You just gave it away, after you studied the train schedules and had worked it out—seventy-four fifty for a day coach ticket from Sacramento to Newark. You fool. Now you can't go home and face them. That's impossible, you don't have a choice.

And then, at eight twenty, there she was, the agency woman, under the clock. She waved Connie over and led her out onto the ferry dock. The woman explained that the first leg of the trip was across the bay to Oakland. When they got there, they went through the station to the gate. The agency woman nodded to the agent at the door and he let them through before anyone else. The people who were waiting glared at her as they left, and she had to trot to keep up. It was the first time Connie had seen the agency woman outside the office standing up. She was taller than Connie thought, and she wore a long heavy dress that came down almost to her shoes.

Outside, Connie could see three trains. The platform smelled of steam, water, smoke and oil. The agency woman led her to a group of men who were talking. One of them noticed her and broke away from the others. He was a compact guy with a dark mustache. He wore a conductor's round hat and a coat with pockets that made him look bigger than he was.

The agency woman said, "Hello, Carl, how they hanging?"

"Properly levitated for full efficiency. This must be the young lady you've been telling me about."

"Her name is Constance Nix and she's going all the way to Newark, New Jersey. Constance, this is Carl Casta."

She said how do you do, and he said pleased to meet'cha, and pulled a ticket book and a wad of papers, and then another wad of papers out of his deep coat pocket. He rifled through them, and then through more papers from the other pocket before he found what he was looking for. It was a slender yellow envelope. He handed it to her.

"This is a through ticket on the *Gold Coast*. I'll be with you to Ogden, Utah. You'll change to the Union Pacific there, and Mr. Vergauwen will take over. His name is there with the ticket. Your car stays the same. It's a change of crew and engine. Vergauwen will take you to Omaha where you'll switch to the Chicago & Northwestern. Here's where it starts to get a little complicated." He saw that she didn't understand.

The agency woman said, "Carl got the tickets for you. Think of it as a... discount."

Now, you've got to remember that Connie was only seventeen. She didn't understand that in regular life, there are different ways to get things done. The people who really run things—the conductors and drivers and inspectors and cops and agency women—they talk to each other and figure ways to keep the system greased. It may not be strictly legal, but it got Connie on the train.

The woman went on, "Part of your salary will go to the agency. We have an arrangement with Carl and men like him. He's going to make sure that you arrive safely. Isn't that right, Carl?"

"Of course. Now, look, in Omaha there's another crew transfer. You could wind up on Mr. Wilson's train or on Mr. Richardson's train. If it's Mr. Wilson you're riding with, nothing to worry about. Richardson, that's another story. Be careful around him. He'll give you very special treatment, but he'll want something in return, if you know what I mean. You can handle it however you want to."

Connie didn't know how she should answer that so she just said thank you.

"In Chicago, you'll have to get off the train and go to another station, Union Station. It's a walk, eight blocks or so, I think. That's where you pick up a Pennsylvania Railroad train to Newark. The man to see there is Mr. Dane. Don't worry if you miss your connection with him. Just ask any of the conductors for Dane. If he's not working your train, he'll have made arrangements."

Seeing Connie's confused look, he said, "This sounds more complicated than it is. It's just a series of simple steps. If you run into any trouble, mention my name. Most of these men know who I am. We get people where they want to go every day. You're booked on a tourist sleeper but this train also has standard Pullman sleepers, and if there's an empty berth, we may be able to get you into it."

The agency woman said, "Think of yourself as Mr. Casta's guest. Don't do anything to embarrass him or the agency. Boys will want to flirt, even the 'good boys.' They're away from home and they think they can get away with anything."

Connie remembered the Manor and knew what she meant.

They checked her suitcase in the baggage car and Mr. Casta led her onto the train. It was then, for the first time, that she understood what she was doing. She was about to go across the country, away from the orchards and farms to a place she'd never seen. She knew that working for the Pennyweights wasn't going to be sophisticated and glamorous the way rich people in moving pictures were sophisticated and glamorous. Two summers at the Manor had shown her what it took to keep rich people from bitching and complaining. But this would be different. It would surprise her, and she would learn something. She felt the first real excitement.

Mr. Casta asked her if she had everything she needed for the night in her train case. She said she did. Her passenger car had double seats that faced each other. Mr. Casta showed her where to sit. He told her that George would come by in a little while to fold the seats down into berths. She'd have the upper. Mr. Casta went about his business, and she was the only person in the car for a few minutes. Then she saw other passengers hurrying along the platform and claiming seats. Mr. Casta came back with an older woman who was dressed in an old-fashioned long skirt and jacket. He introduced them. She was Mrs. Mappen who was traveling back to her family in Ogden. He thought they might enjoy each other's company. They did. Mrs. Mappen had several books.

The *Gold Coast* left Oakland at nine. The car wasn't full, and Connie and Mrs. Mappen had the facing seats to themselves. Connie noticed that she was getting looks from the guys in the aisle. Some of them seemed to have a lot of business that kept them walking back and forth past her and giving her the eye.

Mrs. Mappen said she had been visiting her mother and aunt in Sacramento, and was happy to be going home. Connie told her that she was going to work in New Jersey. She didn't say that it was her first time really away from home, but she figured Mr. Casta knew that and had filled the older woman in. When she said she was going to work for the Pennyweights, Mrs. Mappen's mouth tightened like there was something about them she didn't like. Connie asked her what it was, but the woman just smiled and said she was sure they were lovely people. Connie filed that away.

The train went through Berkeley, past Vallejo and into the farm country she'd left that morning. Later, George, the colored porter, folded the seats down into beds and opened the berths. Mrs. Madden took the lower. Connie climbed up the ladder that the porter had left to the upper, and struggled into her night clothes. The older woman went to sleep right away. Connie didn't for a long time until the rocking of the car did its work. The whistle woke her sometime early in the morning. That close, the sound wasn't the same. It was eerie, and the curtained berth felt strange. It didn't smell right, and the pillow and blanket didn't feel like the ones she was used to. Connie had another moment of doubting herself, thinking she could get off at the next stop and go back home.

It went away and she went to sleep.

The Gold Coast stopped at Reno early Tuesday morning. Connie ran in and bought three hard boiled eggs and a cup of coffee from a counter in the station. She drank the coffee, ate one of the eggs and saved the others. For the rest of the day, they went east along the Humboldt River through Nevada. Connie had trouble paying attention to her book. Mrs. Mappen had lunch and dinner in the dining car while Connie had the other half of the jelly sandwich she'd started in San Francisco.

That evening, the train reached the Great Salt Lake. It looked beautiful, cold and dry. Mrs. Mappen smiled and said she was glad to be home. They pulled in to Ogden around nine o'clock. Mrs. Mappen was the first person out of their car when the train stopped. Connie didn't see if her family was there to meet her. After most of the passengers had left, Mr. Casta came in with another conductor and introduced him to Connie. Mr. Vergauwen. He was younger and better looking than Mr. Casta, and Connie thought she wouldn't mind being looked after by him. Wouldn't mind at all. But his idea of taking care of her was to tell her they were in a new time zone and she had to set her watch ahead an hour.

A girl about Connie's age took Mrs. Mappen's empty seat and asked if she could sit with her. The girl whispered, like she didn't want anybody else to hear, that two boys had been giving her the business, and she didn't want anything to do with them. She made it sound dramatic and dangerous. The girl was slender and kind of pretty with curly brown hair. Her dress was about as old as Connie's.

Connie said of course the girl could sit with her. Right away, the two boys who'd been giving her the business showed up and asked if they could join the ladies. Mr. Vergauwen appeared behind the boys. He told them their tickets weren't good for that car, and led them away. The girl with curly brown hair was disappointed. She sat for a time but they couldn't find anything to talk about, and the girl wandered off.

Another colored porter came by and opened up the berths. By then, Connie had heard other passengers talking and had figured that all of the Pullman porters were colored, and all of them were called George. That struck her as strange, and she wanted to ask someone about it. But she knew she was so ignorant about so many things that she was embarrassed to let anyone know about this one.

The rains came Wednesday morning as the train left Utah, and went into Wyoming. Connie couldn't really see the mountains or any of the country she was riding across, and that frustrated her. As the afternoon darkened, she walked around the train to see the other cars. The train was less than half full. She found that the curly-haired girl had decided she didn't mind the business that one of the boys had been giving her. His friend had found another girl, and the four of them were flirting, kissing and giggling like crazy. The grown-ups in the car were outraged, but that didn't stop most of them from getting an eyeful.

Connie bought a sandwich for lunch and another for dinner at the train station in Cheyenne. The rain continued across Nebraska, and the countryside that had been so new and interesting the day before became flat, wet and boring. And they lost another hour. That night in the upper berth, it was hard for her to go to sleep. She couldn't get the kissing and flirting out of her head. How could girls do that in public? Why wasn't she doing it? Nothing was stopping her.

The train stopped in Omaha to change equipment and crews at two thirty Thursday morning. This was the stop that Mr. Casta had warned her about. Connie got dressed, climbed out of the berth, and checked the yellow envelope he'd given her. Yes, there it was. Mr. Richardson or Mr. Wilson. She had put a question mark beside Richardson's name. Now, she wasn't sure what she should do. A small feeling of dread knotted her stomach. As the Omaha passengers cleared, she could see three conductors talking to each other on the platform. She got up, just wanting to be outside for a while, and went up to the men.

They stopped talking. She asked for Mr. Wilson. A larger man with skin almost the same color as hers said he was Wilson. As she explained her situation, one of the other conductors, a tall number with a look in his eye, stepped up and said he'd be happy to help the little lady. He had to be Richardson. Wilson said, no, he would handle it, making it plain that there was nothing more to say. Richardson didn't like it.

Mr. Wilson took her elbow and led her back onto the train. By then, she was tired but not really sleepy and not sure what she should do. The sensible, safe part of her wanted to stay quiet and not be noticed. Keep your head down. That's how she grew up but maybe the time for that had passed. Maybe it was time to speak up.

"Mr. Casta told me that if I was on Mr. Richardson's train, he'd give me special treatment and he'd expect something for it. I know what that means and I don't want it."

"I'm glad to hear that," Mr. Wilson said. "Let me worry about him. Get back in your berth. I've got another party for the lower. Richardson won't be bothering you."

Connie climbed back into the berth and closed the curtain. Sometime later, she heard Mr. Wilson and a woman's low voice whispering something, but by then she was mostly asleep.

The next morning, she met the new seatmates that Mr. Wilson had found for her, a young mother and her two daughters.

Mrs. Langdon introduced herself, and her girls Matilda and Frances. They were going to visit Mrs. Langdon's sister in Chicago. The girls were three and four. It was their first train trip, and now that they were awake, they were so excited they spent the next twelve hours trying to destroy anything or anyone they could grab, bite, kick, punch or tear. Mrs. Langdon thought it was wonderful that they were so high-spirited. Connie said she understood. Her two younger sisters and baby brother did the same things when they were the same age. She didn't tell Mrs. Langdon that she didn't like high spirits. Still didn't like kids.

She kept her mouth shut and smiled at the right times as Mrs. Langdon went on. It turned out that she was an officer in the Women's Christian Temperance Union. She was eager and happy to spread the organization's word on protective purity, the Americanization of immigrants, the importance of an eight-hour work day, and dozens of other things.

Mrs. Langdon's husband worked for Mutual of Omaha. Even though Connie was single "for the moment, I'm sure," she might want to think about buying a policy.

It was four thirty on a bitter Thursday afternoon when the Gold Coast pulled in to Chicago. Connie said goodbye to Mrs. Langdon, and collected her suitcase from Mr. Wilson in the baggage car. He explained that she had plenty of time before her next train, the Pennsylvania Railroad's Juanita, from Union Station. She could take a cab, but he knew she was watching her money. The walk wasn't bad if she didn't mind the cold. The station was a half block east on Madison Street, turn right on Canal and go down a few blocks. It's a big building. You can't miss it.

Even though it was a ten-minute walk, she said she damn near froze to death in the wind. If it hadn't been so cold, she might have seen something of the city. As it was, she pulled her hat down, buttoned her coat up all the way and cursed herself for not having brought gloves.

Union Station, like the Chicago and Northwestern Terminal she'd just left, was a vast, echoing, marble building with a vaulted ceiling. She'd never seen such a place, and now she'd been in two of them. What else was out there?

She bought another sandwich for dinner and found the Pennsylvania Railroad waiting room. A few other single women were there. She sat on a bench next to a girl about her age who looked as unsure of herself as Connie felt. Connie asked if she minded her sitting beside her. The immediate grateful smile told her all she needed to know. It turned out that the girl didn't speak English, not that it mattered. Nobody bothered them as they watched the big board with words and numbers that clacked as they spun around and announced the trains that were there or late or departing.

The other girl's train came in at six and she left. The Juanita showed up a couple of hours later. Connie explained to the gate agent that Mr. Casta had told her to see Mr. Dane, the conductor. Instead of taking her out, the bored agent told her to sit down and wait with everybody else. She did, and when they finally boarded, she was part of the crowd.

Mr. Dane turned out to be a sharp looking blond who gave her the once-over when she told him about Mr. Casta. He took her ticket and her suitcase, and said, "I'm sure we can work something out for you. Newark, you're going to Newark. Not staying with us all the way to New York? That's a shame. You'll miss so much fun. But I'll tell you what I'm going to do. It looks like we've got one berth left in the new sleeper, and it's yours. Go to the third car there, and tell George I said to put you in number eleven."

She went to the third car and told this George what Mr. Dane said. He showed her to her seat and said they'd be leaving soon.

She ate her sandwich, and worried over the few coins left in her little purse, and the bills in her shoe. Then she told herself that this was the last leg of the trip. In less than twenty-four hours, she'd be at the Pennyweight mansion. She slept poorly again that night, alone in another upper berth.

She worried about how she looked, what she was going to find, what she would do when they hated her.

She woke up in Ohio where she lost another hour, and spent the day crossing Pennsylvania from Pittsburgh to Philadelphia. It was dark when the train stopped in Newark. As Mr. Dane gave her her suitcase, he tucked a card into her hand. Then he winked and said, "If you get into the city, call me. I know all the best places."

Chapter Twenty-three

1931
NEW YORK CITY

After my short set-to with the Abbé in Ruby's apartment, I took a cab back to the speak. It was about three in the morning. I was exhausted and my hip was screaming for another pain pill. Willie and Mrs. Opperman were at my table. They were pissed off. At me.

Willie said, "What the hell did you think you were doing?"

The detective said, "I told you about this. At this stage of an investigation, the last thing we need is an amateur sticking his nose in."

I held up three fingers. Marie Therese brought three brandies.

I was as pissed off as they were. "And what is it you're investigating? When Ruby Rose was here earlier, Willie told her that Miss White has recovered. No more stomach aches. Is that right or were you throwing her a curve ball?"

"She seems better but that simply means my strategy is working and Ruby is afraid of us. That's why she came here tonight. What did you hope to gain by seeing her home?"

"I hoped to get my ashes hauled. Didn't work out, but it was an interesting trip if you'd like the details."

I told them that I'd fed Ruby a phony story about A'Lelia Walker and a priest sacrificing a chicken and it scared the hell out of her. "She almost admitted that Willie's screwball business of sticking pins in the puppet worked on her, made her feel bad."

"Did you see her puppet?" Willie asked.

"No, I looked around a little after she passed out."

Willie drained his brandy and muttered, "She never could hold her liquor. Women." The detective cut her eyes at him.

"I was in her bedroom when I was interrupted by a third party—the Abbé. He had a key and claimed that he was taking care of the rent on her apartment."

Willie shrugged. "He probably is. As I told you, money has never seemed important to the man."

"It was important enough for him to lift some cash from her purse."

"That means nothing," Willie said. "What else?"

"He said that booze is killing you, and then he enjoyed a snootful of cocaine. Didn't care for it when I accused him of living off Ruby Rose."

Willie shook his head. Mrs. Opperman took out her notebook and wrote in it. She said, "Did you learn anything that would connect this Abbé character to the Instructor or to Tudor City? We still don't know enough about what's going on with these three women who are seeing him every week."

"That's what I was trying to say. Willie, all this got started because you said your friend Lily White thought that her friend Ruby Rose was using voodooism to make her sick. Then you let Ruby know that you were putting the whammy on her, right? So nobody has physically harmed anybody. In fact, nobody has even directly threatened anybody."

"The threats are real. So is the harm."

"You want to take that to a cop or a judge?"

He started to answer but Mrs. Opperman cut him off. "It's not that simple anymore."

She stopped. When Willie and I didn't answer, she went on, flipping pages in her notebook. "I can tell you more about the two other women who are visiting the Tudor City apartment. We're beginning to see what this man's game is. He's already milking one of them. He's set the hook with another, and he's ready to make his move on Helen Stiles."

Since Willie was picking up the tab, she and Hacken and Begg, the other two Continental detectives, had been investigating the women who were visiting the Instructor. She said that the plump woman in the shiny blonde wig was named Cassandra Hickey. She had gone to her bank and cashed a check for fifty dollars before her last visit. The widow was Mrs. Garner. She had given him almost four thousand dollars over the past two months.

Four thousand was more than most guys made in a year.

"How do you know that?" Willie asked.

"We're shadowing Cassandra Hickey. With Mrs. Garner, it's the doormen in her building. They take her checks to the bank and bring back the cash. We don't have the details yet but it's some kind of spiritualism game. With Helen Stiles, he has changed her 'treatments' to address her vocal difficulties. They're becoming more expensive."

Willie drummed his fingers on the table. "I'm not ready to accept that the Abbé is really involved in this. No matter what Jimmy says, he's not a charlatan. People are attracted to him. He is a forceful personality and if, as you suggest, the Instructor is purporting to be a spiritualist, he might well have attached himself to the Abbé. But the man I know is no phony. He has many profoundly wrong ideas. He believes himself to be a superior being and so he has nothing but contempt for society's rules and expectations, but he would never stoop to cheap theatrics."

I had to say, "This business with the puppets isn't cheap theatrics?"

Mrs. Opperman lit a Fatima. "Did you see how much that puppet maker charged? It may be theatrics but it ain't cheap."

Willie said, "Stop it, both of you. This isn't getting us anywhere."

"Then let me and Begg and Hacken do our jobs. We can discover what's really going on with Miss Stiles and the other two women. Then we'll know how to proceed."

Willie nodded and waved to Marie Therese for another Five Star. Mrs. Opperman left and I went up to my office for another pain pill. I slept on the divan.

The next night, Willie was back to staring at the puppet in the cellar. Mrs. Opperman came in after eleven. She had more to say.

They'd learned that Cassandra Hickey, the plump woman in the shiny blonde wig, spent most of her time alone. Her husband owned a sweatshop in the garment district. He was there for twelve hours a day when he was in the city, and he traveled out of town several days and nights every month. Those were business trips, and he treated himself right when he was on the road with the best hotels, good liquor, fancy restaurants and fancy women. His wife knew about those. She didn't know about his mistress in Brooklyn. The friends that she played bridge with every week had convinced her that she could stop his screwing around if she just lost a little weight. Then she'd get him back and then they'd have the children she wanted so desperately.

Mrs. Hickey's usual schedule with the Instructor was Monday and Wednesday nights. On the afternoon of her last visit, she stopped at the bank on the way and cashed another check for fifty bucks. She told her friends that the new vitamin supplements he was giving her were working wonders. She took the supplements through a special inhaler and she was finally able to get into clothes she hadn't worn in years. Even better, she was simply full of energy.

Mrs. Opperman said, "We haven't seen the 'inhaler' yet but I've got a pretty good guess as to what's in it."

"That could be the connection between the Abbé and the Instructor."

Willie shook his head. "The man I knew was no drug peddler. He—"

The detective interrupted him. "With Mrs. Garner, the widow, it's more serious and much sadder."

Before Mrs. Garner married, she was Victoria Vandergeld. Like the Garners, the Vandergelds were a prosperous old New York family. Her husband Bartholomew Garner was an executive with the National City Bank, an important guy who could have had a driver take him to work every morning but walked because he liked to. They lived in a huge apartment on the Upper East Side with room for four children, and they had a big house on the North Shore of Long Island. For nineteen years, the Garners had a fine life. The right schools for the kids, the right clubs for him, the right organizations for her. Then the middle daughter and a son were early victims of the Spanish flu, and not long after, their oldest son was killed in the Great War. Their third son was twelve when he tried to move a radio aerial. It touched a power line and he was electrocuted. Soon after that, on a Sunday while Mrs. Garner was at church, her husband drew a warm bath and opened an artery in his thigh. She moved to the smaller place on the East Side where she still lived.

"Her husband killed himself less than a year ago," Mrs. Opperman said. "Now this Instructor is telling her that he's a clairvoyant and a clairaudient." She saw that I didn't know what she was talking about. "He claims to see and hear her dead family."

Just listening to her read all that from her notebook, you couldn't tell how angry she was. It didn't show in her face either. But I figured Mrs. Opperman had been telling the truth to Helen Stiles when she said her own husband had liked her version of "Meet Me in the Shadows," and she knew what it was like to be a widow. Willie missed that part.

"But," she said, "None of this has much to do with Miss Stiles' situation and we've made progress with that. Her supplements—she drinks them, by the way, she doesn't inhale them—her supplements are becoming more exotic and expensive. She didn't say it in so many words but we've talked."

"That settles it." Willie had another slug of brandy and his face took on that cagy look that guys get when they've drunk enough to think they're smart. "I'm going to host another party."

Chapter Twenty-four

1931
NEW YORK CITY

Willie was as good as his word. The next day, he had invitations printed. It was a thick engraved card in a heavy envelope with gold foil. He must have shelled out a nice piece of change to get it so quickly. I've still got mine. It reads:

Please join Mr. William Buehler Seabrook
This Friday at 66 Fifth Avenue
Cocktails at 6:00
Refreshments and light supper at 8:00
Followed by an evening of
Fantastical experiments, occult esoterica
And a demonstration of Haitian voodooism.

"It's all nonsense, of course," Willie said as he sat on my divan and sipped his first Five Star of the night. The puppet was in a box on the coffee table. "But after I heard what Mrs. Opperman has learned, I felt I had to do something. Even if the business between Ruby and Lily is nothing more than a jealous spat, I fear that the women who have fallen under this Instructor's influence may be in danger. I've got to do something, and, as you pointed out, there's really nothing to take to the police, as if I trust them anyway."

"So, you're going to invite them all to your place?"

"Yes. Remember what I told you about Rhine and the experiments in telepathy he's conducting at Duke?"

"People guessing symbols and something that somebody else is thinking about?"

"Precisely. I said and I believe that those will never amount to anything because he's working in a cold, sterile laboratory. You need the heat of passion. If human beings do possess such powers, they need extreme circumstances of lust, fear or hatred to manifest them. I am inviting everyone who has any connection with this matter and then I'm going to apply that heat, that passion."

"What's going to happen?"

"We'll see."

Mrs. Opperman came in later. She and Willie used my office to talk. I listened.

She and the two other detectives had been shadowing Mrs. Hickey and Mrs. Garner. Mrs. Garner, the widow, didn't give them much to work with. She didn't leave her Upper East Side apartment very often. The doorman who'd told them about the checks he cashed for her said that she had most of her groceries and meals delivered. When she went out at night, she hired a car. Never used a taxi.

Mrs. Opperman said that at first the doorman wouldn't give her the time of day when she asked about Mrs. Garner. "I expected that," she said. "It's a good building. The people who can afford to live there pay extra for privacy, and it would take a lot to bribe the staff to talk about them. But the first time I saw them talking in the lobby, I could tell that he cares about her. I've seen pictures of her family and this doorman has a resemblance to her youngest son, the one who was electrocuted. He's older but he has boyish features. It looked to me like she was more than just another tenant to him. Then I gave him the details about what has happened to her family and explained to him what we were investigating. He came right around. He's helping us because he doesn't want to see her harmed."

"But he took money," Willie said.

"Of course, he's not stupid. With Cassandra Hickey we've got more to work with."

Even if she could fit into her old clothes because of the inhalants the Instructor was peddling, Mrs. Hickey was buying a new wardrobe. In the mornings, she went to Bonwit Teller, Madame Alsten, Gimbel's, and the rest. In the afternoons, her new duds were delivered to her place in

Murray Hill. The detectives who were following her said that they'd seen a difference in her manner. She was more energetic, even frantic. More than once, they'd caught her sneaking a quick toot from the inhaler she carried in her purse.

Her husband had been out of town for a week and wasn't due back for a couple of days. The detectives had no trouble getting the doormen and concierge in that building to talk about the Hickeys. They were demanding, never satisfied with anything or anyone, and they tipped lousy at Christmas.

Willie listened to all that and thought about it for a while. Then he said, "The reason I first became involved with this mess is my reputation as an expert in these extraordinary subjects that lie somewhere outside the understanding of conventional religion or science. I do not automatically disbelieve in 'miraculous' occurrences, but I'm skeptical and difficult to fool. That's why Lily White sought me out when she learned what Ruby was up to. I say that so you'll understand what to say when you deliver the invitation to Mrs. Garner. Whether she remembers any of my newspaper columns or reads my books, she knows who I am. My name carries some weight."

"What invitation?" the detective asked.

Willie paid no attention to the question. "I want you to tell her that the man she's seeing in Tudor City has come to my attention. I want to know more about him and that's why I have invited him and his coterie to this affair. Even though I have never met them, I sincerely hope that I will see them this Friday night. I'll take care of Mrs. Hickey's invitation myself."

I wrote the word *coteree* in my notebook.

"After I saw what has happened to Lily White, my initial idea was to frighten Ruby off. I hoped that, at best, she would make some sort of public or personal reconciliation. Failing that, I'd arrange a meeting and force Ruby to admit what she's done. But once Helen Stiles entered the picture, I had to reconsider. Now with two more women who appear the be targets of a confidence operation, I've got to come up with something else."

"And there's the Abbé," I said.

"Yes." That seemed to spark something in Willie and he smiled, but not like anything was funny. "The Abbé. We can't forget about him. He could be the key."

Mrs. Opperman looked like she wasn't buying any of this. "What are you talking about, Mr. Seabrook? Invitation to what? This investigation isn't finished."

"Possibly," he said, looking distant. He handed her one of the invitations from a short stack on the table.

She read it and said, "What the hell is this?"

"I was just telling Jimmy that to get the right reaction in some conflicts, you've got to turn up the heat, apply some pressure. I'm going to get everyone involved in this business together in one room and make them sweat. I will show them things that they won't be able to explain."

Mrs. Opperman looked at him like he was nuts and shook her head.

Willie said that messengers were going to deliver the invitations to Ruby Rose, Helen Stiles, Lily White, and their friends. He was going to invite "the Instructor," but he didn't expect that the man would show up. He'd arranged food with Klaus Cassell at Longchamps, and he was leaving the booze to me.

Then he picked up the puppet in the box, the bottle of Five Star and headed for the cellar.

Mrs. Opperman said, "What the hell is he up to?"

"I don't know, but you should've seen what he brought to the last party he threw."

As it turned out, the man outdid himself.

Chapter Twenty-five

1931
NEW YORK CITY

By Friday evening, the pain in my hip was better. It wasn't gone but I didn't feel like I had to stay close to the pain pills. I showered and dressed in an older English flannel three-piece. It wasn't as sharp as some of my suits but it was comfortable and I wouldn't mind so much if red wine and booze got spilled on it. You see, I'd thought about bringing Brenda with me to tend bar at Willie's soirée, but we couldn't be shorthanded at the speak on a nice cool spring weekend. So I arranged with Frenchy to bring his truck and drive me and the hooch down to Willie's digs on Fifth Avenue. Then it came to me that some of Willie's well-heeled acquaintances might be in attendance so I loaded my vest pockets with cards that would get them into Quinn's Place.

Frenchy helped me take the stuff up in the elevator. The guys from Longchamps must have been just ahead of us with the steam trays because the elevator smelled so good. Frenchy said he wished he could hang around for dinner.

Up on the top floor in the converted ballet studio, I saw that Willie had brought in palm fronds and six more of the plaster columns, like the one he had at my place. They were spread out here and there in the big room. I was pretty sure they hadn't been there the first night when I brought the booze for the party with A'Lelia Walker. These didn't have naked girls chained to them either, but it was early. A professor was noodling tunes on the Steinway. There were curtains on the big windows over Fifth Avenue. Most of the light came from a fireplace near the back.

Willie was dressed in denim pants, a striped jersey with a red bandana around his neck and a floppy beret that sagged down to his ears. He was talking to the dark-haired worried woman I'd seen there before. That night, she was more angry than worried. He waved me over. She stood with her arms crossed over her chest.

"Mink, this is the man I've been telling you about."

"Don't bother," she said. "I told you. I love you but I will have nothing to do with this. I'll be back Sunday. Have fun with your…" She glanced at me and frowned. "…friends."

She looked like a one-woman parade as she stomped to the elevator and stabbed the button. When it opened, three girls got off. One of them was Deborah Luris, who'd been on the job at my place. Under the girls' open coats, I saw dozens of chain necklaces and metal hoops around their necks.

Mink shouldered them out of the way. She shot Willie one more cold-eyed glare as the doors slid shut. He paid no attention.

Willie told Frenchy and me to set up the bar at a long table covered by a white cloth. He said he had to help the girls get ready and took them to an area separated from the rest of the room by Oriental screens at the back. On the way there, something he said made them yell and laugh like they were happily shocked.

It looked like Willie had enough glassware stacked on a side table. Frenchy and I unboxed the wooden cases of liquor, wine, and mixers, and set up as much as we could. We put the white wine and beer in a tub of ice, and stowed the rest under the table. Frenchy went back to the speak. I charged a siphon of seltzer, and put a dime and a dollar in a beer pitcher to prime the pump.

Jimmy's Rule Number One: Always Leave a Tip.

The steam trays from Longchamps were over by the opposite wall. I took a look. Sliced ham, chicken, roast beef and French bread. Lots of cheeses, some sort of peas or lentils that smelled great. Stuffed grape leaves. There was more but Willie came back with the Ruby Rose doll in its coffin. He stashed it with the booze under the table.

I reached for the Five Star but Willie said Scotch. I cracked the seal on a fifth of Black & White and poured a double. He invited me to join him. I said no and gave myself a splash of seltzer.

"What's the matter?" he asked.

"I'm working. I don't drink when I work."

"You drink at your place."

"At my place, I'm the host. Frenchy and Marie Therese are taking care of that tonight. What's going on here?"

After a sip, he said, "It depends on who shows up. I expect everyone. I'll know more after I see Mrs. Garner and Mrs. Hickey. When I give you the high sign, hand me the doll in the coffin. After that, things could go in several different directions."

Mrs. Opperman was the first to show up. She wore a black coat and a long black skirt over a dark gray blouse. As she walked over to the bar, I noticed that she touched her right pocket, and I guessed she was carrying a pistol.

She asked for seltzer over ice. I made one for her and another for myself. As I hit the siphon, Deborah Luris and the other two girls came out from the back and went to the steam trays. Willie had them decked out in more chains. They wore necklaces and sequined brassieres and headdresses like they'd come out of a movie about ancient Egypt. The detective cocked an eyebrow and chuckled when she saw them.

The elevator doors opened, and an older woman in a black dress, black hat and full veil stepped out. When she got a load of the big room with the palm fronds and the girls in their get-ups, she looked like she was about to turn around and get back on the elevator. But before she could do anything, Mrs. Opperman hurried over and started talking to her. The next time I saw them, they were sitting in two chairs close together and yacking away like they'd known each other forever. She had to be Mrs. Garner, the widow.

By then, the place was filling up. As it got busy at the bar, I hung my suit coat over a chair and rolled up my sleeves. The biggest sellers were Manhattans, Martinis and Cuba Libres. As people caught on that the liquor wasn't the panther piss they were used to drinking at other speaks, business picked up, and I handed out about a dozen cards.

A middle-aged couple got off the elevator. He was a big guy with thinning hair and a tailormade suit with a wide pinstripe. She was about half his size and wore a loose shimmery dress meant for a younger woman. Her eyes were wide open with excitement. He looked like he'd rather be at the dentist. Then he spotted the bar and dragged her with him. He shoved to the front of the crowd and yelled, "Hey, boy, gimme a Scotch." They had to be the Hickeys, the other woman who was trying to lose weight and her philandering husband.

I ignored him and poured a glass of wine for the guy who'd been in front. Then a beer for the next guy, and two Martinis for the one after him. Like any bartender worth a damn, I knew how to focus. When Hickey's turn came, I said, "What'll it be, sir?"

"I've been asking for a Scotch for twenty minutes, goddammit."

I poured a King's Ransom, the nastiest stuff I had, and asked what the little lady would have. He said she didn't want nothing. She said ginger and rye. I mixed ginger and rye.

By then, Willie's place was filling up. They kept me moving, and as the hooch loosened tongues, the room got louder with more laughter. Since Willie had already paid for the juice, I was generous. But not with Hickey. He made his way back several times and always had to wait.

Deborah Luris and the other two in the slave girl outfits served food. After an hour or so, Deborah brought me a plate of stuff to nibble on and I saw that Willie had worked something out with the bracelets and chains to turn them into handcuffs.

They jangled when I shook them, and I asked her what it was.

"Just another of Willie's chains. Whatever you do with him, there's always chains. These ain't so bad as some. A little difficult to scratch your butt though."

I said, "If you need a hand with that, I'm available."

She winked and went off to get more food. I mixed drinks.

Lily White and Helen Stiles came in together, and, to my eye, they'd changed in the weeks since I met them. Lily, who had been wasting away on account of the voodoo hex doll, didn't look bad to me. Like most actresses, she could've used a few more pounds here and there. But if she'd shown up at my place, I'd want to talk to her. The same went for Helen Stiles. Remember, she started out with the opposite problem. The guys out in Hollywood convinced her that she needed to be more svelte to make it singing in moving pictures. Now, you may be thinking that I was just another salty young guy ready to make a move on any doll in skirts but there was more to it. The first time I saw those women, they were scared and something was causing them pain. Maybe they were still frightened but that night in Willie's big apartment, they looked confident and proud. Just like Miss A'Lelia Walker, come to think of it.

Their hair was done up under smart little hats, and Miss White was wearing that dress that Willie had described—the pink and gray Chanel gown. Helen Stiles was in a green dress that looked like silk. Willie hurried over to them. He had Cassandra Hickey in tow, and you could tell how star struck she was to be introduced to an actress and a famous singer.

Theodora Opperman was still huddled with the widow, and I was too busy to talk to anybody. Hickey was my most frequent customer. By his fourth drink, he'd forgot he was mad at me. He leaned on the bar and went into what must have been a well-practiced spiel about how terrific King's Ransom Scotch was, much better than any of those fancy-pants labels. I didn't tell him what they did to the stuff. It was the only rotgut we sold, but enough guys had developed a taste for it that I had to stock it.

I was keeping an eye on the elevator and so I saw Ruby Rose when she got off. She was with a group of people who headed straight to the bar. She hung back. Like Lily White, she was wearing the black and white striped dress that matched the one on the puppet. She stayed near the elevator and scanned the room. When she saw me, I gave her a quick wave. She paid no attention. Didn't remember me. A few seconds later, she stopped searching and stared at Lily White and Helen Stiles. They were surrounded by guys and didn't see the third member of their trio, the Gay Greek Chorus Girls.

By then, everybody had enough to drink and Willie's apartment was sounding and feeling like my place on a Friday night, people telling stories and talking and flirting and arguing and getting mad at each other until their friends broke it up. As often as not when the evening has reached that point, one conversation will somehow take over and everybody else stops talking and listens in. That night, it was Willie. Who else?

He'd been standing between two sofas where the Hickeys sat. As he spoke, he moved closer to the open area in front of the bar. Everybody found seats or shifted to where they could see and hear him.

"I was just saying that the mind is a curious thing. Can it truly comprehend itself?" He paused and looked at different people like he was expecting an answer.

"I can't say with any certainty and I have made a study of the subject for all of my adult life. Think about it. We use our brain to translate what we comprehend through our senses, to judge heat and motion, to understand the written and spoken word, to appreciate music. And thanks to Professor Einstein, we know that the brain can perform the most beautiful computations that were inconceivable a generation ago. But can the mind examine itself?"

He was walking around, working the room. You could tell that he was serious but he was playing at the same time.

"Can one mind actually connect or communicate directly with another?" Ruby Rose was still near the elevator, staring at Willie. He hadn't seen her yet, or he was acting like he hadn't seen her.

"Many say it is impossible, it's the stuff of fantasy and mystics. Once I was one of them, but I have found that under the most extreme circumstances of fear, hatred, lust, and… of course, drunkenness," That got a laugh. "In those conditions, something approaching that direct communication is possible, one mind 'reading' another."

He strode around some more and moved over by the fireplace where the lighting was better. "I bring this up because for the past several weeks, I have undertaken an experiment, an attempt to make that connection, to achieve one specific goal." He let that sink in. Ruby Rose looked grim.

"I have succeeded. To a degree."

That made one guy in the back give him a big raspberry. Willie had been waiting for it and shot back, "Pipe down, you freeloaders, you want proof? I'll give you proof. But first I need another drink." He handed me his glass. I filled it.

"Now, I'll need a volunteer." He looked around the room and then hustled back to the sofas where he'd started. "Mrs. Hickey, would you be so kind…"

She protested, but not too much as he helped her stand. They came back to the bar and he took his drink.

"Mrs. Hickey and I have not met before this evening, isn't that right?" She was close enough that I could see the flush on her face and neck as she stood there, embarrassed to be up in front of a group of strangers, but pleased as punch that Willie chose her.

"Yes, that's right." she said.

"That gentleman over there is your husband, is he not? Sir, have I ever met you or your wife? No? Good."

Hickey blurted out, "I still don't know who the hell you are or why we're here." That got another big laugh.

"I have chosen Mrs. Hickey because we are strangers. I have known most of the rest of you for a number of years and so, quite rightly, you wouldn't trust me not to cook up some parlor trick with one of you. Right?

I could hardly have done that with Mrs. Hickey in the few minutes we have known each other."

She shook her head, said, "Oh, no," and stood there like she didn't know what to do as Willie moved around.

"Now, as I said, for the past few weeks I have been engaged in what you could call a mental weightlifting exercise. I have continuously and repeatedly focused all of my mental, emotional and even spiritual energies on one object. Blocking out all other external sights and sounds, I have finally been able to accomplish what I started out to do."

He stopped and smiled. Nobody said anything. Ruby Rose hadn't moved from the elevator and her expression hadn't changed.

"Under the right circumstances, which I believe I will recreate here, I can receive a thought, an image from another human being. Jimmy Quinn, who's handling the refreshments tonight has seen me do it. Isn't that right, Jimmy?"

I said yes, not knowing what the hell he was up to.

"Now, I'm going to ask for another volunteer. You, miss." He offered his hand to a girl in a sequined dress. She had bobbed hair and a glass of champagne, only her second of the evening.

"I want you to pick an object in this room. Don't do it yet. Wait until I tell you, then whisper it to Mrs. Hickey. Mrs. Hickey will select a series of objects and when she reaches the object you have chosen, I will know it." That's when people started talking and whispering to each other.

Willie said, "I understand what you are thinking. I will be able to observe some change in her voice or her posture, so I will be blindfolded. Deborah, if you would be so kind."

She came over with a bright red silk scarf.

"And I'm going to ask for another volunteer who also won't know the object to state the names of the other objects that Mrs. Hickey points to."

A young fellow in a tan suit hopped up. More hubbub from the crowd as Deborah Luris wrapped the scarf around Willie's eyes. None of the people in the room knew what to expect but those of us who knew Willie figured it would be good.

Willie said, "Now, pick the first object."

The girl in the sequined dress looked around the room and whispered something to Mrs. Hickey, who nodded. The girl giggled and said they were ready.

More laughter and chatter as Mrs. Hickey looked around. She pointed at a table, and the guy in the tan suit said, "End table."

Willie said no.

"Palm leaf." No.

"Cocktail shaker." No.

"Silk top hat." No.

"Wine bottle."

Willie said, "Yes." Mrs. Hickey gasped. The girl in the sequined dress yelped. The guy in the tan suit said, "I'll be damned," and the hubbub took on a different tone. Willie smiled.

He said, "I know some of you think that this young woman is in on the act. I assure you she's not. But let's have another volunteer choose the next object."

Several people started talking but one woman stood next to Mrs. Hickey and whispered to her. Mrs. Hickey raised a hand. She and the girl in the sequined dress started around the room again.

"Arm chair." No.

"Cigarette case." No.

"Yesterday's *Gotham Gazette*." No.

"Neck tie." No.

"Fireplace poker." No.

"Silver bracelet."

"Yes."

That set all of them talking and buzzing and trying to get Mrs. Hickey's attention. She looked confused and uncertain until Willie pulled the blindfold off and spoke up, loud and serious.

"Listen to me. Be quiet, please. All of this will be explained. In Haiti, I met a very wise woman, Maman Célie who showed me rituals and concepts that I had never encountered before. *The Magic Island* is dedicated to her. It was her teachings that have brought me to this place. True black magic. But I see that some of you still doubt what you're seeing. Would you like another demonstration?"

As everyone nodded and yelled yes, Willie turned and stared directly at Ruby Rose. His face showed nothing. She stared right back at him. I saw that Lily White and Helen Stiles had spotted her. They moved away from the guys they'd been talking to. Willie put the blindfold back on. A guy in a tux said something to Mrs. Hickey. She nodded and began pointing to things that the girl in the sequined dress named.

"Rum bottle." No.

"Napkin." No.

"Tie clip." No.

"*Town and Country* magazine." No.

"Feathered boa." No.

"Ashtray." No.

"Steinway." No.

"Serving girl's headdress."

"Yes." Willie pulled off the blindfold and walked toward Ruby Rose. He stopped at the bar. "You see, it's possible. If you can absorb the essence of a thing or a person, and if you can then focus your mind as a magnifying glass focuses the sun's rays into a single burning point, then anything is possible."

He held out a hand. I gave him the doll in the coffin.

Ruby's face went pale beneath her makeup. By then, everybody was watching her and Willie. When Lily White and Helen Stiles made their way through the crowd to her, the room went dead quiet. Again, nobody knew what was going on but everybody thought something interesting was about to happen.

Willie spoke to Ruby like they were the only two people in the room. "We have a mutual friend, though 'friend' isn't the right word, really, who knows almost as much about these matters as I do. When you confided to him the betrayal you felt, he said he could show you how to get even."

She nodded, still looking frightened.

"He bought you the puppet, and when it was right there in front of you and you could direct all of your anger and pain and humiliation at that doll, it felt good. After you showed your friends what you could do to her, you felt even better."

Ruby didn't do or say anything.

"Then you learned that someone was doing the same thing to you. At first, you tried to deny that it had any power over you. But if you had seen that it worked once, you feared that it was working again. And it did work, didn't it?"

She caught her breath like she was stifling a sob and nodded. "I didn't mean to hurt anyone. He said it was…"

"It's all right, Ruby." Lily White was blubbering, too. When Ruby saw her, both women raised their arms and hugged each other. Willie looked like he was getting a little misty-eyed himself. I looked for Helen Stiles in the crowd that was gathering around the two women. She was not as emotional. Judging by her cool expression, she thought her old partners were putting on quite a show.

People were packed in around Willie and the women as they went back over the business with the dolls and the hatpins. The guy in the tan suit who'd picked the first object in Willie's "demonstration" piped up, asking how he'd done it.

Willie smiled again. He was doing a lot of that. "It's exactly what I said it was, black magic. Now, where's my drink?"

Damn, these people were easily fooled.

I poured a Scotch and muttered to him, "Yeah, that was real *black* magic all right."

Willie took his drink and stepped up on the stage by the Steinway. "Let me explain," he said and waited for everybody to settle down before he went on. "What you just saw was a simple little parlor game dressed up with the usual trappings. But before I explain anything, I want each of you to take a moment and remember what you were thinking while Mrs. Hickey and I were at work. You don't have to admit it to me or anyone else, but be honest with yourself. No matter how skeptical or clear-headed you think you are, wasn't there a moment when you believed you were witnessing something extraordinary? When I was blindfolded and she was silently pointing out objects and I was identifying the right ones, didn't you suspect that Seabrook had parted the veil a fraction of an inch? You believed that perhaps there is something greater, something beyond our understanding and you had been given a glimpse of it. I know I've had that feeling many times and even though it has been proven false time and again, it is impossibly wonderful while it exists. I hope to feel it again. But tonight was simply a trick, not a trick because I wanted to fool you but because I want you to understand how powerful that search can be."

A guy in the back said, "Cut the horsefeathers, Willie, and tell us how you did it."

I was looking straight at Willie when the guy said that, and I saw some of the brightness go out of his face. When Willie talked about wanting to believe, he was as serious as he could be, and that guy didn't understand it. That guy thought he just was a clown.

"The point I'm trying to make is that the search for something beyond the everyday world is natural and it is important. Perhaps it is the most important thing we can do. But sometimes that desire to know more can be manipulated, as I just showed you. That doesn't make the search any less valid or important. It just means that we must be careful about trusting people. Mrs. Hickey, come up here."

She made her way quickly to the stage and stood, blushing, beside him.

"The one white lie I told you was that Mrs. Hickey and I had not had time to arrange trickery. We did. It was so simple that it took us only a few moments, really. The secret to black magic is the color black. Whenever she chose something that was black, like the fireplace poker or this piano, I knew that the next one she named was the right one."

When he said that, most of the guys in the room grumbled and hooted. I looked through the crowd to see how the women were taking it, the women Willie had been working on. Ruby and Lily were sitting together on a sofa and pouring their hearts out to each other. Theodora Opperman and Mrs. Garner were on the other side of the room. I couldn't tell what they were doing. Helen Stiles showed up right in front of me and asked for a glass of wine. It was the first thing she'd had to drink that night. I poured and asked what she thought of Willie's show.

She whispered, "It made more sense than I thought it would. It's easy to fool someone when they want to be fooled."

"That's the best time."

The professor started noodling more tunes on the piano, and things were slowing down when Marie Therese came dashing out of the elevator.

Blood was smeared around her hairline and one side of her face was swollen.

"You gotta come back right away, Jimmy. We've been robbed."

Chapter Twenty-six

1931
NEW YORK CITY

Fat Joe looked like he'd been beat worse than he ever was in the ring. His cauliflower ear was bloody. Both his eyes were swollen shut. His nose was a mess and he'd lost some more teeth. He held a bloody bar towel to his mouth. Frenchy wasn't as bad. He had a split lip and a red welt across his face. He'd put his hogleg on the bar in case they came back. Brenda and Dorothy, the barmaids, were crying at one of the two-tops.

Marie Therese and I had scrammed out of Willie's place without saying anything to anybody. I drove Frenchy's truck back to the speak with my foot on the floor. I gimped inside as fast as I could, and, at first, I thought it wasn't so bad. No customers, but the furniture wasn't broken. Then I saw how they'd been hurt. Fat Joe tried to explain but his mouth wasn't working so good. Frenchy did most of the talking.

There were three of them. Fat Joe didn't know that when the first guy knocked. Fat Joe just opened the little spy door like he always did. The guy held up a Quinn's Place card and said he got it from me. Fat Joe let him in. Didn't pay much attention to what the guy looked like. Medium height, coat and tie, no glasses, no hat. He just went straight to the bar, ordered a beer, took a few sips, and got up to leave, like the place wasn't to his liking.

Fat Joe didn't get up to let him out and didn't notice when the guy opened the front door and two other guys rushed in. Those two wore nylon stockings over their faces. They jumped Fat Joe before he could get up from his seat and laid him out. The first guy turned and punched Brenda right in the face. She was working the coat room. He reached in and grabbed the change in the tip drawer, leaving half of it spilled on the floor. Then he saw the little packs of cigarettes we sold and took all that he could cram into his pockets.

Before anybody really knew what was going on, the three of them rushed into the bar. One pulled a pistol and yelled at the customers to stay put. The other went behind the bar and clubbed Frenchy with a short billy stick. When Marie Therese tried to help, he smacked her, too. They emptied the till and beat it out of there.

Marie Therese said there were less than a dozen customers in the place then, most of them regulars. One guy started to run after them but thought better of it. Somebody else said they should call the cops. Sure. The rest of them either tried to help or decided to call it a night.

I asked Fat Joe if he'd taken a close look at the card the guy showed him. He shook his head. Hell, he probably couldn't have told me his own name. Frenchy couldn't add much. I asked him how big they were. He said one guy in the stocking mask was about as tall as Fat Joe, maybe. The other guy was smaller but he was quick with the billy stick and knew how to use it.

Dorothy piped up, "The guy with the gun. He was wearing two-tone shoes."

That set me back. I guess it made sense that Xeno Pool was pissed off at Lansky and me, but I was surprised that he was still around. After the business at the garage, you'd think he'd cut his losses. First thing to figure was the card. A few years earlier, when I bought out Carl Spinoza, I had the cards printed up. I had to because I changed the business. Carl ran your basic neighborhood speak. He served some rotten booze that had been doctored and poured into phony bottles. It was the same stuff you could get in a hundred joints in Midtown. Hell, a thousand joints, probably. I decided to buy the real stuff straight from Lansky, and I sold it at top dollar prices. When you make a change like that, you've got to let people know. I handed out a lot of cards in the first year or so we were open. But until Willie's party, I couldn't remember the last time I'd touched one. So maybe somebody left Willie's apartment and knocked over my place.

Marie Therese pulled out the medicine kit we kept behind the bar. She said she thought she could take care of everybody except Fat Joe. He needed to see a doctor. Fat Joe said he didn't need to see any fucking doctor.

They were trying to get him to go to the emergency room at Bellevue when Willie and Theodora Opperman came in. He was full of questions.

I held up my hand to stop him, and said, "Do you have a cab?"

He said yes. I said, "Let's go."

In the taxi, I told the driver to take us to Tudor City, and I explained the cards to Willie and the detective. "It seemed to me that not everybody you invited showed up. At least, I think they didn't."

Mrs. Opperman said, "The Instructor and his Assistant."

"Right. Willie, did you know everyone who was there? Were there any strange faces?"

"I want to say yes but I'm not sure. Once the place filled up and I got warmed up for my act, I wasn't paying attention to everyone. And then I was blindfolded."

"Remember, I told you the Instructor doesn't need those two sticks or the wheelchair. And nobody's got a good look at him in street clothes."

"But why would he want to rob your speakeasy?" Mrs. Opperman asked.

I didn't know how to answer that without bringing in Xeno Pool and I didn't see how he and the Instructor had anything to do with each other, so I said, "Call it a hunch, but it's all I've got."

It was sometime after one o'clock when we stopped in front of the Instructor's apartment building. While Willie paid the taxi, I asked the detective if she'd had any dealings with the doormen. She said yes, she'd been there with Hacken and Begg, the other two operatives when they first approached the doormen.

"Good. Say whatever you have to say, pay whatever it takes to get me past them."

She said, "I don't need to do that."

We went through two heavy wooden doors with glass panels to get to a big desk and a couple of doormen.

Mrs. Opperman spoke to one of them by name. "Dennis, I know it's late but I need to speak with Florence Pruskaya."

Willie looked confused. I murmured to him, "Florence Pruskaya, the woman who knows everything about everybody. Lives down the hall from the Instructor."

Dennis the doorman got on the house phone. A minute later he nodded for us to go up to the fourth floor. That late, the elevator was self-service. On the ride up, Mrs. Opperman said, "I don't know what you've got in mind but don't do anything stupid. You can't be sure this man had anything to do with the robbery."

I nodded, adjusted the knucks, and said, "It's 431, right?"

The doors opened on the fourth floor. Mrs. Opperman led us down the hall. A door at the end cracked open and a short woman peered out. When she saw Mrs. Opperman, she opened it wider. The detective hurried toward her. I stopped in front of 431 and rapped on the door with my stick. That was the moment when I realized it would have been smart to have picked up a pistol at the speak. The knucks would have to do.

I heard shuffling footsteps from inside and the door opened. A guy in his undershirt said, "What did you forget?"

Making as little racket as I could, I shoved through the door, grabbed a fistful of the guy's shirt and clipped him on the chin. He went bug-eyed as I pushed him back into the apartment. He was in stocking feet and they slipped on the floor. He was a head taller than me but I had leverage and hustled him down a short dark hall into a larger room. We stopped when he backed into an upholstered chair and sat down hard. I let go of him but stayed in his face.

He was a round-faced guy with wispy hair and a thin mustache. He was wearing an undershirt and suit pants with his suspenders unfastened. Sweat beaded on his face and darkened the armpits of the yellowed undershirt.

"Take whatever you want, please, just leave me alone. This is some kind of mistake."

"You shouldn't've robbed my place."

The guy's eyes opened even wider. "Robbed? What robbed? This is crazy. I didn't rob anybody. I don't know what you're talking about." His voice started to sound panicked, hysterical. "This is insane. I've been here all night. How did you get up here anyway? I don't know what you're talking about."

He was crazy with fear. I nodded to the bedroom door and stabbed him with the tip of my stick. "Let's take a look at the rest of the place."

He stood, still shaken and scared, and edged toward the door. I followed.

It smelled of incense. The stuff Theodora Opperman had noticed was still there—the wheelchair, canes, the robes and crystal ball. A curtain that separated the bathroom and closet from the rest of the room was pulled back. A black suitcoat was draped across the steamer trunk. It looked like he was throwing stuff into it for a fast getaway.

The guy backed away from me. He stammered, "I don't know what's going on here but you've made a mistake, mister. I don't know anything about any robbery. Like I said, I haven't gone out this evening."

He sounded so sincere I was about to believe him. Then I picked up the suitcoat and a dozen of the little ten-cigarette packs of Camels fell onto the floor. We sold them for a dollar each.

I don't know where he got the straight razor. It flipped open, and he held it waist-high like he knew what he was doing. He came at me with a pigeon-toed lunge and slashed at my stomach, back and forth in a narrow arc, the shiny blade never moving away from me. The stick kept him away and even though he was taller than me, the stick gave me an edge in reach. When I jabbed him in the gut, he turned and ran toward the door, straight into Theodora Opperman. She cracked him on the crown of his head with the butt of her pistol. He went down and didn't get up.

When he came to, he was back in the chair. I'd found a roll of friction tape in his steamer trunk, among other interesting items, and used it to tape his hands behind his back and his ankles together. While I was taking care of him, there was some conversation going on out in the hall. Mrs. Opperman and Florence Pruskaya told the neighbors not to worry about the noise we'd made. It was nothing. I guess the neighbors bought it.

The guy opened his eyes but couldn't focus or pretended he couldn't until I gave him a couple of taps with the knucks. Then he noticed the three of us facing him. Willie and Mrs. Opperman fired up smokes. The detective gave him a hard look, the same hard look she'd given me, and said, "I know this man. I don't forget a face I see on a wanted poster. His name is…"

He looked at her and squirmed. "…Emmanuel Hoyt, alias Manfred Hoyer, also known as Manny the Dip. Height, five foot seven. Weight, one forty-one. Hair, brown. Eyes, brown. Complexion, light. No known relatives or associates. We collared him working Herald Square with four other pickpockets. We pinched him again a year and a half later when he was writing bad checks."

Manny tried to sit up straighter. "Bastards broke my fingers but they couldn't make the charges stick. Not for the checks, either. That was a misunderstanding."

She ignored what he said. "We know that you rented this apartment under the name Robert Haldorn. We know that you've been calling yourself 'The Instructor' and duping three women with different schemes."

"Listen, lady, I don't know where you're getting your information but you've got it wrong. There's no paper on me." He looked at Willie and me like we were going to help him. "This lady's crazy."

She said, "I'm an operative of the Continental Detective Agency. This gentleman hired me and my associates to investigate your activities."

"I don't know what you're talking," he said. "I ain't broken no laws. Those dames came to me and they got what they were looking for."

I said, "That might have been true until tonight. You stole from me. You beat my people."

Then he started squirming, trying to loosen the friction tape. "They made me throw in with them on that, and I didn't beat up nobody. It was those other guys. I was just with them, that's all. I didn't do anything, you gotta believe me."

"Who are they?" she asked. "How did they force you to join them?"

He started out, "Lady, you gotta understand that they..." and I could tell he was cooking up a story, so I slipped the knucks back on and gave him a solid pop that snapped his head back. I wiped the blood off my knucks on his grimy undershirt. Made me feel kind of sick to hit him when he was helpless like that, but it was getting late.

"Don't even try to lie," I said. "Right now, you've got one chance to walk away from this. One chance. Don't screw it up. Talk straight."

He sighed and looked at the three of us. Most of what he said next was true. Probably.

Manny had been working variations on the table-rapping spiritualism game in Florida. In winter, he could count on finding rich New Yorkers in resort hotels. He paid the staff to clue him to the ones who had recently deceased family members, and he had a girl in the city, a girl he called Sally, who dug up the information he used to prove that he could reach across the ether to contact the lost loved ones.

In Miami he met a guy who was working the same racket and they decided to team up and move back to New York when the weather got too hot in Florida. It was this guy, Sidney Abbey by name, that came up with the weight-loss angle. It only worked with well-heeled dames because most people were struggling to put any food on the table. Sidney had a supply of exotic drugs and powders that had a mild kick and "enhanced the metabolism." It was Sidney who came up with the mumbo-jumbo about refocusing the seven energies that formed a fan-shaped pattern.

When he said that, Willie frowned, like he did when Lily White used the same words.

Sidney Abbey, aka the Abbé, set Manny and Sally up in the Tudor City apartments. They had a one-bedroom in Tudor Tower and they worked out of The Cloister. I asked him where Sally was. He went antsy again and said she got scared and left.

When they got the invitation to Willie's party, she said that was the last straw for her. First there was the guy who'd made them on the sidewalk. That worried her but Manny convinced her it was nothing until they got the invitation. She said Willie was a famous writer who knew all about real magic and spiritualism. If he knew about their racket, the game was up and she was getting out. She packed up and left. He didn't know where. He was thinking about doing the same when Abbey showed up with another guy. He didn't tell Manny the guy's name and Manny didn't ask because the guy scared him. Abbey said they didn't need to worry about Seabrook. Willie was a weak sister who thought he understood things.

Anyhow, Abbey said that Willie was trying to trap them with this invitation, but they didn't have to bite. And it was an opportunity for them to beef up their cash supply which was running thin because it was taking longer than they thought to close the deal with their three marks. He knew a speakeasy that was going to be flush with cash and poorly guarded that night.

"Wait a minute," Mrs. Opperman said. "All this time you're stringing along Helen Stiles and Victoria Garner and Cassandra Hickey, what is this Sidney Abbey doing?"

"Coming around every other day and taking most of the money we made." He whined. "That's all I know. He had his own racket on the West Side and didn't cut us in on it."

"Where are they, Sidney Abbey and the other guy?"

He got that panicked look again. "They're gone. They left an hour ago, I swear."

"But first you came back here and divided the money," I said.

He nodded quickly.

"I took $36.50 out of your suitcoat, most of it in change. Since it was a busy Friday at my place, you didn't get a full third."

"You don't argue with those guys." He seemed to shrink in the chair when he said that, and he looked like what he was, a smalltime grifter who preyed on women and then got in over his head with the likes of Xeno Pool and the Abbé, aka Sidney Abbey.

Mrs. Opperman said, "I've got his key to the apartment in Tudor Tower. I'll have a look around, see if he's telling the truth, and then we can decide what to do with him."

"Good idea. I found another roll of bills in the steamer trunk but there could be more."

Manny got even smaller then and started crying at the loss of his cash. That embarrassed Willie. He said he'd help Mrs. Opperman and went with her. It didn't take them long to find the empty one-bedroom. When they got back, she said, "A woman was living there. I could tell that from the trash she left, but the place had been cleaned out. I think he's telling the truth that Mr. Seabrook's invitation scared them off. You should've gone with her."

"Don't I know it," he said. "That's the story of my life, leave too early or stay too long. Just go ahead and shoot me, why don't you. I'm no good to anybody."

I stuffed a dirty undershirt in his mouth to shut him up. "So, what do we do with him?"

Mrs. Opperman shook her head and said, "We know Mrs. Garner has given him four thousand, and after talking to her tonight, I know that she still thinks he's the genuine article."

He spat out the undershirt. "I AM the genuine article I can—" I stuck it back in his mouth.

She said, "It's late but I may be able to get some information from the office. I'll be right back."

She went downstairs to the lobby. Dennis the doorman let her use the telephone. When she came back into the apartment, she said, "It looks like Manny wasn't lying about there being no outstanding warrants on him, so that really just leaves what he did tonight at your place. What'll it be, Quinn?"

I said, "While you were out, I examined his bankroll. It adds up to a shade under four hundred dollars." I held up the money. Nothing larger than a ten spot so it looked like a lot. He spat the undershirt out but didn't say anything. He was remembering that I'd said he had a chance to walk away from this, and he didn't want to screw it up.

"Normally, on a Friday night, we'd take in two-fifty, three hundred dollars. Now, I'm going to be generous and say it wasn't that busy, so I'll take two seventy-five."

I counted the bills. Manny didn't take his eyes off them. He looked sad when I folded them into my pocket. "That leaves, let's see…" I counted again. "One hundred and sixteen dollars." I held the money up to focus his attention.

"I got involved with this business because Mr. Seabrook hired Mrs. Opperman and her associates to look after some friends of his. As you can see, money doesn't mean a damn thing to him. He's a wealthy, famous guy, and he is going to continue to pay the Continental agency to keep an eye on Mrs. Garner. Isn't that right?"

Willie and Mrs. Opperman nodded.

"And you are not going to have anything else to do with her," I said to Manny. "You're going to pack up that trunk and you're going to get the hell out of the city. Right?"

I knew he was going to say yes, and I knew he was lying. What else was he going to do?

I opened his razor and sliced through the tape at his ankles and wrists.

Chapter Twenty-seven

1931
NEWARK, NEW JERSEY

Connie got off the train in Newark, and collected her suitcase at dusk on a foggy, chilly Friday. She turned toward the station and saw a ginger-haired young guy in a black chauffeur's uniform. He stepped up to her and said, "You must be Miss Constance Nix. Oh boy, I been waiting all afternoon. The car's over this way. I'm Oliver, by the way." He touched his cap. "Here, let me take your bag. Oh boy, this is heavy, whatcha got in here? Anyway, they didn't tell us the train was gonna be late when we called, so it's been..."

From the time we were kids together, whenever Oh Boy Oliver got nervous, he'd talk nonstop like that. Girls made him nervous, and pretty girls made him really nervous. Connie didn't try to get a word in. She just let him go on as they walked. When she saw the car, she did a doubletake. The Duesenberg J was about half a block long. Even dotted with rain, it gleamed under a streetlight.

Oh Boy put her bag in the trunk and opened the rear door. Connie said, "No, I'm staff, just like you," and got in the front seat. That rattled Oh Boy even more.

As they started off, she asked him if they were going to Valley Green.

Oh Boy said, "It's less than an hour from here, paved roads all the way."

She couldn't tell much about Newark except that the streets and sidewalks were crowded and wet. It didn't smell like San Francisco. Outside the city, they drove through dark fields and small towns. Oh Boy talked all the way.

"It's really good that you finally got here what with Miss Flora expecting the way she is, and none of the girls from town want to work for Mrs. Pennyweight. It means a lot more work for the rest of us, I can tell you that.

Mrs. Conway said she didn't know what we'd do if you didn't work out. Oh boy, some of the girls that the other agency sent over, they didn't even get in the front door."

"Who's Mrs. Conway?"

"She's the cook. Her and Mr. Mears, they run things."

"How many others are on staff?"

"There's Dietz, the groundskeeper. And me."

"That's all? Four people?"

"Well, there's only Mrs. Pennyweight, her daughter Flora, and Walter Spencer. Spence is Flora's husband. He's the one who hired me on account of we kind of worked together before he married Flora. He's a swell guy, and Valley Green is a great place. You'll see."

Oh Boy turned at a white metal sign, VALLEY GREEN BOROUGH 2 MILES, and they drove through woods and dark pastures with white rail fences on both sides of the road. He turned again at a stone gate and went up a long gravel drive that curved in front of a Tudor house. He stopped at the front doors and said, "I dunno. Staff uses the back door but this is quicker, and Mrs. Conway wants to see you right away, and we're late already. Follow me. I'll put your bag in your room."

Connie was whipped from four days on trains, and an hour of Oh Boy. She wanted a shower, a change of clothes, a cup of coffee, and a slice of pie with ice cream. But, not yet.

She and Oh Boy went into the big hall with the fireplace at the end, and down the narrow servant's stairs to the kitchen. The kitchen was a warm bright room that smelled of cooked onions and meat. A wooden table with six chairs was in the middle. An older gent with a walrus mustache sat at one end. A jug of red wine was at his elbow. He drank from a half-full glass. She figured him to be Mears. Mrs. Conway was at the stove stirring a pot. She had gray hair and sharp features.

Mrs. Conway glanced at Oh Boy and said, "Well, it's about time. And this will be Miss Nix." She gave Connie a long once-over and looked to be a little unhappy at what she was seeing. Connie didn't know then that Mrs. Conway looked that way at just about everything and everybody.

"I'll let Mrs. Pennyweight know you're here. I'm sure she'll want to speak with you right away."

She made to leave but Connie said, "Excuse me, ma'am, may I have a glass of water. The trip was—"

"You'll not call me 'ma'am.' I'm staff. 'Ma'am' is for Mrs. Pennyweight and Miss Flora and any of their friends." Then her tone changed and her voice softened. "But of course, you'll have a glass of water. What was I thinking? How about a cup of tea? You've come from Chicago, haven't you?"

"Actually, California."

"Goodness, such a long trip. Mr. Mears, tell Mrs. Pennyweight that Miss Nix is here."

The old guy mumbled something and wandered off. Mrs. Conway poured two cups of tea from a pot on the stove, and gave Connie a plate of gingersnaps. She slapped Oh Boy's hand when he tried to take one. Connie had taken her first sip of tea when a loud electric bell sounded. She looked up and saw a grid of numbered squares on the wall. The light on number one was glowing.

Mrs. Conway got up and muttered, "When you want him to take his time, he steps right to it. Follow me." She led Connie back to the servant's stairs, up two flights to the second floor and down a hall to a suite of rooms. Before they got there, she stopped and lowered her voice. "Mrs. Pennyweight can be… abrupt. It appears to me that you have the qualities we've been looking for. Let her say what she wants—she will anyway—and nod agreeably. You'll be fine."

Connie nodded agreeably and went into the suite.

Catherine Pennyweight stood warming her rump at a fireplace. There was a glass of sherry on the mantle. A gleaming black cane leaned against the wall beside her. She had a way of standing that made her seem taller, and she liked to tilt her head back when she looked at you with those pale blue eyes. She was a striking woman with brown hair going to gray.

"You're late," she said. "You were supposed to be here hours ago. Explain yourself."

"The train from Chicago was—"

"I know, I know. You can't control the trains, but you must understand that you have created a very unfortunate first impression and I'm not sure you'll be able to overcome it."

It looked to Connie like the woman was daring her to answer. Just nod agreeably, Mrs. Conway had said, and Connie might have done that if she'd had time to drink her tea and eat a gingersnap, and if Oh Boy hadn't blabbed so much.

Instead, she stood as straight as Mrs. Pennyweight and said, "You're probably right. I won't be able to overcome this. It was my fault the trains were late, so I'll just ask your driver to take me back to Newark and you can find someone more suitable."

She heard Mrs. Conway's quick intake of breath through her teeth.

Connie and Catherine Pennyweight stared at each other. In time, her highness said, "Don't be ridiculous. Mrs. Conway will instruct you on your duties. That will be all."

As Connie and Mrs. Conway went back down the hall, they heard a young woman's voice yelling from another room, "Goddammit, Walter, I will not do this!"

Chapter Twenty-eight

1931
NEW YORK CITY

While Manny threw on clothes and stuffed his steamer trunk, the detective went downstairs and had Dennis the doorman call two cabs. Dennis helped Manny with his trunk and we put him into a taxi to Penn Station. The three of us got in the second cab. Willie told the driver to take us back to his place down on Fifth.

Willie said, "I'm not sure we did the right thing but I can't see another course of action." I didn't say anything but I was having the same doubts. Mostly I was mad that I couldn't get to the Abbé and Xeno Pool. They were the ones who came after me. They were the ones who beat my friends and stole from me. Taking it out on a mug like Manny didn't make things right, money be damned.

Mrs. Opperman said, "Are you talking about tonight with Quinn, or your party and all that led up to it, including the puppet?"

"I'm not sure. At first, I was thinking only of that frightened, ugly little man. I haven't really had time to consider the business between Lily and Rose, but I have to say that it seems to have been resolved more successfully and peaceably than I dared hope. To see that tearful embrace of women who'd been so spiteful to each other, all I can say is that I'm glad it ended that way."

Mrs. Opperman had more on her mind. "What Quinn said about your having the agency keep an eye on Mrs. Garner for another month, is that agreeable to you?"

Willie said, "Of course, though I'm sure we've seen the last of him."

"Perhaps." She didn't say anything else until Willie looked at her and she knew he was listening to her. "That woman genuinely needs help. I know what it's like to lose a husband and a child, and I can't imagine how she has managed to go on after everything else that's happened to her family. That's why Manny was able to convince her that she had not failed her family and he could contact them. She and I had a long talk tonight, and she still believes that this 'Instructor' can 'pierce the veil,' as she put it. I'm going to try to make her see the truth. I don't know that I'll be able to do it, but if nothing else, I'll make sure he doesn't get his hooks into her again."

Willie nodded. "Of course. Is there anything else?"

"Yes. I'd like a better explanation of who was involved with tonight's robbery. You've certainly made it sound like this Abbé character was the connection between Miss Rose and Manny's spiritualism and weight-loss confidence games, but who was the third man?"

She looked at me.

I said, "He's a guy I thought I'd taken care of. It has to do with a business I'm involved in with some other parties. I didn't think he had anything to do with this, but this individual did tell me that he knew who Willie was and that another guy, who was probably the Abbé, had been following Willie and watching my place when Willie came by. So I guess it's possible they got together."

"Does this individual have a name?"

"Yeah. Xeno Pool."

She whistled low between her teeth. "You play with some rough customers, Quinn. Xeno Pool. Height, five foot ten. Weight, one sixty-five. Hair, black. Eyes, brown. Complexion, dark. Known associates, Frank Muldoon and Harry Shaw, both deceased. Last known address, Kansas City, but he's not from there. Sharp dresser. I remember his face from the picture in his file. Fine looking man."

She was misinformed about the sharp dresser part.

"In Kansas City, he was with the DiGiovanni gang. Part of the Pendergast machine, but he had a disagreement with Sugarhouse Pete DiGiovanni and vamoosed. That was a year ago. Pool was rumored to be in New York but the agency doesn't have anything definite."

I guess I could have said a lot of things then, but you didn't talk about business with a detective, even a private operator. So I asked both of them if they thought the Abbé and Xeno Pool had taken a powder.

She shrugged. Willie said, "I still have trouble reconciling the Abbé I knew, a man who believed in the possibility and power of real magic, with this cheap fraud. And the man I knew was from a wealthy family."

"A lot of families were wealthy before the Crash," I said.

Willie shook his head, still not understanding. "Admittedly, it's possible, much as I doubt it. You think he tricked me on the sidewalk but I simply didn't explain it properly. That wasn't possible."

"Doesn't matter. Whatever this joker believes or doesn't believe, he knocks over upstanding speaks when his money runs thin. That's all I need to know. I see him again, I'm going to shoot him."

It also figured that the Abbé was outside of the garage the night Pool tried to persuade Lansky to hire him. The same night he saw me at Ruby's apartment. But I wasn't going to bring that up either. I wasn't going to mention Meyer in front of the detective, and I could tell she knew more than she was saying, too.

When we got to Willie's place, he paid the hack, and we took the elevator up to his apartment. It was a little after three. The place smelled of spilled booze and overflowing ashtrays. Lights were on in the back behind the Oriental screens, and we heard drawers being opened.

Somebody was going through Willie's things. He yelled out, "Who's there? What are you doing?" and ran across the room. He stopped when he saw the Abbé.

I cursed myself again for not bringing a pistol, slipped my fingers into the knucks and choked up on the stick. It figured Pool was there somewhere.

The Abbé's big voice boomed, "You disappoint me, Seabrook. Cheap theatrics to fool little Ruby? I thought you were above that."

The only light in the front of the room came from the windows over Fifth Avenue. I could make out the shapes of the big plaster columns and furniture. Nothing else until a shadow moved away from one of the columns and I saw an extended arm and a bandaged hand holding a pistol.

I reversed the stick and shuffled forward two quick steps. Pool heard me and turned. I smashed the stick down on his gun hand. The pistol clattered to the floor. Pool screamed in pain and grabbed his hand. I moved closer, took a baseball grip on the stick and swung for his body. It connected. He howled, almost fell to his knees and staggered away, toward Willie, Mrs. Opperman and the Abbé.

I tried to follow but he got his balance and hurried away fast as a rat.

As I got used to the dim light, I saw more of the low furniture and stepped around it, always looking for Pool. The truth is I remembered how he handled the three sluggers in Meyer's garage, and I was scared of him. He was bigger and faster and stronger than I was, and he hated me as much as I hated him.

I thought about trying to find his pistol but, no, I had to keep him in front of me.

I heard him as he came around one of the columns and picked up something. Turned out to be a big chair that was heavier than he thought. He grunted and heaved it at me with both hands. It hit the floor with a loud bang right at my feet and toppled onto my bad knee. The brace took the worst of it but pain shot through my knee and hip, and Pool got away again, ducking behind the Steinway. I gimped after him.

While I was occupied with Pool, the Abbé had grabbed Willie in a headlock and Mrs. Opperman was hammering the back of the Abbé's head with the butt of her pistol. I kept moving forward, step and slide, trying to figure where Pool would come at me from. He was up on the stage near the Steinway. He shoved the piano bench onto me, and put me on my back. The pain was sharp and sudden, and knocked the wind out. I made it to my feet before he got to me, and jabbed at his chest with the stick.

It hardly slowed him. He came in fast and hit the crown of my head with his fist. I saw a spray of stars. He howled and grabbed his right hand with his left. That was the hand that had been sliced open by the high-pressure hose, the hand I'd just cracked with the stick. Hell, I shot the bastard that night in the garage, too, but I didn't shoot him good enough.

Pool staggered backward. I attacked, jabbing at his gut, harder this time. He bellowed, cuffed me with a left that stung, and tried to wrap me up. I ducked inside and hammered his ribs with the knucks. Something crunched. He grunted, grabbed at my head and tried to knee me in the crotch. I twisted away and cracked him across the mouth with the cane.

He went to one knee. I was too scared of him to stop until he was out of commission, so I stepped to one side, smacked him across the kidneys with the stick and rabbit punched him with the knucks repeatedly until he collapsed face down, and I was sure he wasn't going to get up.

I staggered and almost fell myself. Fear, excitement and exhaustion left me shaky, and I had to lean on one of the columns before I trusted my legs to keep me standing. I saw that I'd ripped the shoulder seams out of my coat and torn the knee of the slacks. It wasn't a new suit or a particularly nice one, but still. When my breathing came back to normal, I gimped back the way we'd come and found his pistol on the floor by the fireplace. It was a little German automatic. I took off the knucks and picked it up. Nice piece. I walked over to the others. Willie and the Abbé looked scared. The detective was frowning.

Willie said, "I haven't seen one man beat another man that savagely since the war."

Pounding Pool hadn't settled anything. I was still steamed, wound tight. "He tore up my place, beat my people and stole from me. So did this son of a bitch." I pointed the pistol at the Abbé. "Turn out your pockets."

He pulled out a wad of crumpled bills and put them on a table.

I flicked the pistol at Pool. "Now, empty his pockets."

The Abbé came up with another wad of nasty bills about the same size. I told him to count the money. Ninety-three dollars.

I said, "You got more than this from my place. Where's the rest of it?"

The Abbé said, "I have no idea what you're talking about, little man."

I raised the pistol.

He grinned and said, "You won't shoot."

The first shot was less than an inch from his ear. It went through one of Willie's Oriental screens. The report shocked all three of them. The Abbé yelled that I was insane. I pointed the muzzle at his head.

"Don't lie to me. Where's the rest?"

"That's all of it. What's the matter with you?"

Mrs. Opperman said, "Put it down, Quinn." I glanced at her. Her gun was pointed at me.

Years before then, when I was a kid, I stole cars with Spence. One of the first really nice ones we boosted was a Packard Twin Six. The previous owner took exception, and managed to stay on the running board as we were trying to get away. I can still remember his expression when I stuck a pistol in his face. In my memory, I was ready to shoot him when he let go and we drove off. But ever since, I've wondered about myself. Was I going to kill that man to get his car? I like to think that I wouldn't have.

Now, what I'm getting at is that I had less reason to hurt the guy with the Twin Six than I had with the Abbé, and when I heard the detective's voice, I realized what I was about to do. I put the pistol in my pocket. You don't kill a guy just because he's an arrogant asshole. There are better reasons.

Then the son of a bitch smirked at me. I put on the knucks on my right hand. He was dressed like he'd been when I met him at Ruby's apartment. Cheap suit, dirty white shirt, no tie. I counted the buttons, figured his solar plexus was between the third and fourth, and knucked him right there three times as hard and fast as I could. His knees went and I had to hold him up for two more shots, until he collapsed facedown and threw up all over Willie's floor.

Mrs. Opperman stepped between us. She put her pistol in her bag and pulled out a pair of handcuffs. "Are you going to let them go like you did with Manny?"

"I don't deal with cops, you know that."

"This one," She gave the Abbé a kick. "I don't know or care about, but somebody's bound to have something on Pool."

"He's yours," I said. She pulled his hands around behind his back and snapped the cuffs on.

When Pool and the Abbé were able to stand, Mrs. Opperman and I frog marched them into the elevator and went downstairs. I stood with the detective on the sidewalk while she hailed a cab. The Abbé, still doubled over and holding his stomach, hobbled away down Park Avenue.

The detective said, "Tell Mr. Seabrook I have a few loose ends to check. I should have a preliminary report and a bill ready for him tomorrow." She checked her watch. "Actually, that will be later today."

A cab pulled to the curb. She shoved Pool into the back and said, "I'm still not sure what to make of you. Something doesn't add up."

I didn't know what to say so I said nothing. She was right.

Upstairs, I found Willie pouring warm gin over mushy ice. He offered me a drink, and I was about to say yes when it hit me how long it had had been since I'd had anything to eat.

"Willie," I said, "I'm starving. There's an all-night hash house around the corner. Let's get some breakfast."

The place smelled of fry grease, and it was too bright but there was an open booth. They fixed up a couple of eggs over easy and a side of salami for me. Willie stuck with the gin. By the time I had finished eating and downed a couple of cups of coffee, I was back among the living.

Willie had a curious look on his face. He drank and smoked and said, "You know, this isn't at all how I expected this to end."

"You mean the women, or dealing with these common cocksuckers who tapped my speak?"

"Ruby and Lily."

"That was crazy, wasn't it? I gotta admit that when you explained what you were trying to do with the dolls and puppets, I thought you were nuts, and I guess I was wrong. Still seems crazy to me, but your going down and staring at the thing, it did what you said it would do, and then tonight, you tossed in your 'black' magic."

"That's right." Willie said, giving me a level look.

"And to think, you threw it together in a few seconds with Mrs. Hickey."

"What are you getting at?"

"Nothing. When you were explaining things at your party, you said that you were able to cook up that routine right there on the spot. I'm impressed, that's all, that Mrs. Hickey was so comfortable with you and so convincing. With no rehearsal."

He smiled a little and stared into his gin. "We might have met yesterday and had a little tête-á-tête in her apartment. She's an attractive woman."

I didn't know exactly what tête-á-tête was but I had a pretty good idea what Willie had done, and I was right.

"Something else. Every time anybody mentioned the Instructor's fan-shaped powers razzamatazz, you got pissed off. What gives?"

He forgot his tête-á-tête and looked serious. "It goes back to what I was saying before, when Crowley and the Abbé and I were talking about the possible ways to reach heightened states of consciousness. I was intrigued by the idea of destiny or fate. Some philosophers and theologians believe in predestination, that God knows exactly what is going to happen to every person and there's nothing that any of us can do about it. Are you familiar with the concept?"

"Maybe I read something about it in the papers. Can't say I've ever given it any thought."

"Actually, it's connected to what I was attempting with the puppet. What if there is not one destiny for each of us, but several destinies? Or even an infinite number of destinies, and whenever we make a choice, we move toward one destiny and away from others."

He could see I didn't understand. "Imagine you're walking on a path in the forest… No, not a path in the forest, you're walking on a street in the city. At every intersection, you can go straight or turn right or turn left. At some intersections, there may be even more choices, an alleyway, perhaps, or two streets fanning out in different directions. Some of them may lead to the same place but not all of them. The ones you choose to take determine your destination. Got that?"

"Got it."

"Now, imagine an infinite number of streets and alleyways and an infinite number of Jimmy Quinns making their choices, each taking a different route to a different destination, a different destiny. Who's to say that's impossible? In Africa, I came to know a very wise Negro woman named Wamba who had studied these matters even more deeply than I have and she believed, as I do, that we can actually shape our destinies. By creating and consulting fetishes, charms, figures and the like, we can use those objects to focus our mental energies and enhance the results we desire to achieve. I have seen it work. The puppet worked with Ruby Rose. You heard her admit it. Was it religion, magic, or a science we do not understand that brought her to forgive Lily White? I don't know but I know it's real and I hate to see charlatans using it to turn a fast buck. Can you understand that?"

"I was with you up until the infinite number of Jimmy Quinns. After that, I dunno."

I finished my toast. "Now, let me tell you a story. This isn't a made-up, what if there are a million Willie Seabrooks story, this is a real story. It happened to me when I was a kid working as a messenger. I delivered this and that, and picked up this and that for some individuals who needed a kid who knew his way around the city and could be trusted not to steal this and that. I stayed pretty busy. One morning, it must have been a Sunday because there wasn't much traffic, I was at an intersection downtown, crossing Broadway. I'm on the sidewalk, waiting for the light to change because when traffic is thin, the cars move fast. You gotta be more careful.

"So I'm checking both ways and on my left, I see a sedan slowing down. The driver and I make eye contact. I know he sees me and he's slowing down, coming to a stop. The traffic light changes to red for him, green for me. Other cars stop. I go to step off the curb and a woman beside me sticks her arm in front of me and stops me. At the same moment the guy in the sedan who'd been slowing down, he hits the gas pedal and screams through the intersection. In a fraction of a second"—I snapped my fingers—"he's right in front of me, real close, and he's looking at me again, and his mouth is wide open because he's surprised that he's plowing through the intersection, and he knows that I ought to be dead. I should be smeared across his grill and windshield. I know that, too. I should've died right there. Then the sedan flits through the intersection, and it's gone.

"Funny thing, I never did get a good look at the woman who stopped me. She just grabbed my shoulders and asked if I was o.k. I don't even know if I answered. Probably not. I had two good knees in those days, but just then, both of them were jelly."

I stopped talking and remembered that Sunday much too clearly. It chilled me that morning in the hash house with Willie and it still does today.

"What did I learn? I was careful on the street before then. I was more careful after it. Since then, I've crossed a lot of intersections and I'm still alive. Now, I don't think that's what you and the infinite number of Jimmy Quinns were getting at, but you take my point. Whenever you start thinking you know how things work, you forget it's a crazy world where things happen for no reason at all. Yeah, you've got to be careful, but sometimes somebody's got to stick her arm in front of you."

Chapter Twenty-nine

1931
VALLEY GREEN, NEW JERSEY

Connie came to believe that something strange was going on in the Pennyweight house. It wasn't anything she could point a finger at or even describe, but it was there all the same.

Her room on the third floor was small, and she shared the bathroom with Mrs. Conway, but it was warm enough for the rest of the winter and the bed was fine. Her uniform was a shapeless black woolen dress, starched white apron and hat. She hated it. She got Sunday morning off and all day every other Tuesday. She was paid monthly and part of her money would go directly to the agency for the first year. Connie sent two dollars to her mother from her first pay envelope just to show her that she could. She didn't get anything back. Didn't expect to.

Most of her work was cleaning—washing dishes and clothes and bedding, dusting, using the Hoover on floors and rugs. She also helped Mrs. Conway with food preparation. The family never took meals together anymore, Mrs. Conway said, so Connie and Mr. Mears were responsible for preparing trays three times a day, and sending them up to the second floor on the dumb waiter at any time day or night. Staff ate together when their schedules allowed.

She met Dietz, the groundskeeper, at dinner the first night she was there, right after her talk with Mrs. Pennyweight. He was a bright-eyed little gnome with a forked beard and a briar clenched between his teeth. He and Oh Boy had rooms in the garage. Dietz smelled of moss, leaves and gasoline, and kept a bottle of disgusting yellow bootleg liquor in the kitchen. Mr. Mears' wine was dago red that he bought from the Italians in Morristown. He also got aquavit from them.

It didn't take Connie long to figure that Mrs. Conway was the boss. It seemed like Mrs. Pennyweight didn't give many orders. Mrs. Conway knew what needed to done, and ruled the house from the kitchen. Most days, she didn't leave it. She and Connie were the first ones up. They got breakfast started around dawn. Mr. Mears appeared when the coffee was ready. Oh Boy brought the New York newspapers from Morristown. When Mrs. Pennyweight's light flashed around eight o'clock, Connie would load a tray. Fresh fruit, dry toast, a carafe of coffee and a pitcher of water, a rose in a bud vase, the *Times* and the *Daily Mirror*. The tray went on a cart, and the cart went on the dumbwaiter.

Dietz would show up when he was hungry and disappear after he ate. Oh Boy spent most of his time in the kitchen. After bringing the papers, he'd stay at the table and wait for one of the squares to light up. Then he'd bring the Duesenberg around and wait for another call from the second floor.

The household was not what she'd expected. Everybody knew Pennyweight Petroleum. It was usually mentioned with companies like Standard Oil and Dow Chemical. Given that, Connie figured she'd be working in a large house with a lot of other girls and a few men. She'd be at the bottom and so she'd do what she'd always done—keep her head down, listen, remember what she was told, and learn the work. If she handled it well enough, she'd be able to save some money, and in a couple of years, she'd know more about how the world worked outside of Napa. Then she'd go on to something else that paid better. But after the Crash, there were no more parties or dances in the big ballroom, and staff was cut back.

The night she told me that part of her story, I realized again how much smarter she was at seventeen than I had been. Me, I was just reacting to whatever happened in front of me and trying to get through the day. She understood that there was a lot she didn't know, and she was careful not to jump too soon when something new popped up.

Flora and Mr. Spencer weren't as predictable as Mrs. Pennyweight. Their breakfast was different every day. His might be half a dozen eggs and a rasher of bacon, or nothing, at nine o'clock, one o'clock, or five. On hangover days, Flora's breakfast was tomato juice and black coffee.

As best Connie could tell, Miss Flora and Spence really didn't know she was there. She was simply the girl who brought things and took them away later. They didn't know or care that she cleaned their rooms. And that was the way it was supposed to be. She was staff.

On her third day, Mrs. Conway came with her when she brought the breakfast trays to Spence and Flora's bedroom, and introduced her as the new maid. Flora smiled through cigarette smoke, and went back to the telephone conversation she was having, apparently with another woman her age. Spence glanced up from his newspaper. Connie thought they were the most handsome couple she'd ever seen, including the ones in moving pictures, and their bedroom looked like something you'd see in a moving picture. One wall was completely mirrored, floor to ceiling, and there must have been a dozen big mirrors on the other walls. They made Connie a little dizzy.

Spence looked like Gary Cooper and did everything he could to make sure you noticed it. He wore his hair a little long, and always kept himself looking sharp. Flora was one of those angelic blondes who always had guys swarming around. That first morning Connie met her, she was about a month away from having her first baby. Carpenters and painter were working on the nursery beside their rooms.

On her first Sunday morning off, Connie said no thanks when Mrs. Conway invited her to church. After Oh Boy drove Mrs. Conway and Mr. Mears away, Connie took off her ugly black uniform, put on her warm clothes, and went outside. She'd seen trees and water through the windows. Outside, she found that the woods were thick along the driveway and in front of the house. The land behind sloped down to a lake and boathouse. Farther on was a garage that had once been a stable. On the other side of the lake was a large gray stone building with a stone tower and wall that went all the way down to the water. It was Dr. Cloninger's Sanatorium. Oh Boy had told her about it. He said it was creepy but it reminded Connie of the Napa Asylum and she still liked that place. It was the memory of the nurses in the car that made her feel that way, and the nurse who treated her after the cop bashed her head, if she hadn't dreamed that. She still wasn't sure it really happened.

She spent the rest of the morning walking through the woods around the house. It wasn't like Napa or Browns Valley. She didn't see any other buildings or people. The Pennyweight house was about as remote as any place she'd ever been, and that was creepy.

Connie fell in step with the routine of the house. Monday was laundry, washing and hanging clothes and bed linen to dry in the hallways downstairs. Who would've believed that three adults could use so many towels and sheets? Ironing on Tuesday. Cleaning and dusting the rooms on the first floor on Tuesday afternoon and Wednesday morning. She was responsible for the big open hallway, living room, conservatory, ballroom, and library. Those were easy because nobody used them. After she finished, she went back to the kitchen. By midafternoon, Mrs. Conway would need help with cooking and dishes.

Mrs. Conway had a radio on a shelf near the sink and she kept it turned on all day. She told Connie she liked Sister Aimee MacPherson just fine, but she was more partial to Father Coughlin. As she got to know Mrs. Conway, Connie learned that the woman didn't care for Jews, Communists, gangsters, Italians, foreigners, girls with loose morals, boys who acted like "sheiks," women lawyers, drunkards, and dope fiends.

Oh Boy stayed busy driving Flora to the sanatorium where Dr. Cloninger was keeping track of her progress. Flora also had a steady stream of friends who visited and went out with her. Mr. Spencer spent his time on the telephone or in the city on business. When Connie wondered to Mrs. Conway if Mr. Spencer and Miss Flora ever went out together, Mrs. Conway got serious. She said that the Crash had hit Pennyweight Petroleum hard. If it hadn't been for Mr. Spencer's money, the company might have gone under. She'd heard rumors that he might have been involved in bootlegging in the city before they were married, but she couldn't believe that about a man as upstanding and handsome as he was. Besides, she'd once heard him telling someone that his money was in Coca-Cola. What kind of gangster would do that?

Still, there was something about Flora and Spence that bothered Connie and added to her sense that something was wrong.

Then there was the cat.

Connie met it the first time she cleaned the library. She'd opened the curtains to let in more light while she dusted. As she worked her way around the shelves to a corner near the fireplace, she noticed a wide curved mark on the dark carpet near a corner of the room. It looked like something had been dragged across the thick pile. But there wasn't any furniture in that part of the room, just tall bookshelves. Then she saw that two sections of the shelves didn't quite meet. The one closest to the corner stuck out about half an inch.

She knew Flora and Spence were away from the house and Mrs. Pennyweight was taking her afternoon nap. Telling herself she wasn't really snooping, she dusted that section more carefully. When she pushed the corner section, it clicked shut. She reached around one book and felt something on the upright between shelves. It was a flush mounted piece of metal. She pushed it, and with another click, the section popped open and she was able to swing it the rest of the way. Beyond it, she saw a narrow doorway.

She turned her shoulders and went through it. At first, she couldn't see anything but she smelled dry, stale air and paper. She felt for a switch, and turned on a light. She knew enough about the layout of the house to see that the little room was tucked beside the chimney. One section of the wall was metal. That was the dumbwaiter shaft. A colored glass lampshade hung over an old armchair. It was flanked by tables that held a decanter of brandy, a humidor and a stack of magazines. Rough shelves, nothing like the ones in the library, were stacked with more magazines, books and a stack of French postcards.

Those made her giggle and she was about to take a better look at things when the cat rubbed up against her leg. That made her jump but she didn't scare the cat. It was a thick, plump brindle that wove its way around her ankles and made a purring noise in its throat. It strolled out the door she'd opened, yowled and waited for her to follow. After she closed the shelves, it led her down the servant's stairs to the kitchen.

The cat then announced itself to Mrs. Conway who said, "There you are. Ready for dinner?" She put a bowl of scraps on the floor by the stove.

As the cat chowed down, Connie asked about the little room. Mrs. Conway poured two cups of tea and sat with her at the table.

"That was Mr. Ethan Pennyweight's reading room," she said. "Until the day he died, he thought it was his secret, but, of course, all of the staff knew about it. Probably best not to open that door again, dearie."

"Why should I? It's not on my cleaning list."

The cat wandered over and pressed against Connie's leg, waiting for an ear scratch.

"She's taken to you," said Mrs. Conway.

"What's her name?"

"I don't know that she's ever had one. She was always Miss Mandelina's cat."

"Who's Miss Mandelina?"

Mrs. Conway frowned and fussed with her teacup. "She's Miss Flora's older sister. It's a tragic story, it is, but the long and the short of it is that Miss Mandelina fell from a galloping horse some years ago. Near here, in the woods. She injured her head so severely that we thought it was the end for her, and maybe that would have been a blessing. But Dr. Cloninger worked another of his miracles and saved her. The damage was done, though, and she was afflicted with dementia praecox, poor dear. She stays at the doctor's clinic now. As far as he's able to treat her, she's fine but she can't deal with the world. And now there's Miss Flora's condition to think about."

"The baby?"

Mrs. Conway nodded. "It's been a difficult pregnancy and the poor girl has always been so emotional and guilty about her sister—she was riding with her when it happened, you know—and she's likely to burst into tears at the mention of her name. That's why Mrs. Pennyweight decided to tell her that Miss Mandelina passed away."

Mrs. Conway said that last part like it was the most normal thing in the world. Connie couldn't believe it. "You mean, Miss Mandelina is living at that place across the lake, but Flora thinks she's dead?"

"We had a lovely headstone carved for her. It's for the best. We can't let Miss Flora become too excited, you see. Now, it's time for you to prepare the bouillon for the fish. Do you remember how it's done? Of course you do."

Things at the Pennyweight estate got even stranger after little Ethan arrived.

It was about a month after Connie got there. Flora was out one night with friends when the telephone rang. Mrs. Pennyweight answered. Flora was hysterical. It was happening. Mrs. Pennyweight called Dr. Cloninger. Connie learned later that he sent an ambulance racing to get Flora at a nightclub in Newark. Oh Boy drove Mrs. Pennyweight and Spence to Cloninger's place, and the staff didn't hear anything until the next day. That was the last quiet time they had.

From the day they brought him home, little Ethan had problems. The biggest was food. He couldn't keep anything down. Cloninger sent wet nurses and called in other doctors. A stream of them paraded up to the nursery on the second floor for weeks. Flora always needed something.

Most often she called Mr. Mears to bring her a bottle of wine from the Butler's Pantry.

At the same time, Spence was going to the city more often. Oh Boy said he was meeting with lawyers and bankers and other men in the oil business. Something big was in the works.

Chapter Thirty

1931
NEW YORK CITY

By the time the speak opened on Saturday, we'd cleaned it up. Everybody who'd been working the night before showed up. You could hardly tell that Marie Therese and Dorothy had been hit in the face. Frenchy looked better. Brenda and Dorothy were dolled up even more than usual for a weekend. Fat Joe had been stitched and bandaged. I told him to take the night off. He ignored me. He knew there were women who went for wounded fighters.

Of course, word of the hold-up got about and everybody who came in wanted to know what had happened. Some terrific stories were told. In the first ones, Frenchy, Marie Therese, Fat Joe, Dorothy and Brenda had almost been killed trying to fight off an armed gang. Then, according to the grateful survivors, Willie and I cornered the guys, beat the hell out of them and got back all the money they took. In another version we had a shoot-out in the street.

Willie showed up around ten. As he told it, I was the deadliest fighter with a stick that he had ever seen, even deadlier than the savate fighters in Marseille. I guess I could have stopped it, but it was flattering and I knew it wouldn't hurt my overblown reputation as a tough guy.

Ruby Rose showed up late. I was at my table, and saw her after she'd checked her coat and scanned the crowd for Willie. She had on a tightly buttoned number that attracted a lot of attention, and she held a bundle wrapped in newspaper and tied with string. I motioned for Marie Therese to send her over and bring her a drink. When the actress got to my table, I saw that, like the last time, she'd already had a few. She sat heavily, breathing hard, and had trouble focusing her eyes. O.K., more than a few. She was boiled.

She stared at me hard and said, "I know you."

"You were here a few nights ago. To talk to Willie."

"No. Last night. At Willie's party. You were there. You saw what he can do. He helped me and Lily. I did something I shouldn't do."

"I know."

"And Willie sent me pictures—these horrible pictures, that were like me but not me. They were terrible."

Marie Therese showed up with a martini. I waved her away before Ruby saw her.

She held up the bundle. "It was just a joke, something for us to laugh at. Sidney came up with it on account of all the other things but now I can't find him. Do you know where Sidney is?"

"I think he's left town."

"Well, shit," she said and started crying

I caught Willie's attention. He came over and hugged her. As soon as he sat, she really turned on the waterworks. The bundle fell to the floor with a solid thunk. I picked it up.

She was blubbering and trying to talk but hiccupping. "You got it all wrong, Willie. It wasn't me, it was Sidney. He really had it bad for Lily and she wouldn't give him the time of day. Sidney's not very nice when he doesn't get what he wants. That's why he bought the doll. He said we'd use it to fix her wagon, now it looks like the lousy son of a bitch took off with all of our money." She threw her arms around Willie's neck and wailed, "What am I going to do?"

By then, she was crying so loud everybody was looking at us. I said to Willie, "Let me take care of this. Help me get her outside."

Marie Therese was already calling a taxi.

When we got to her apartment building, I was planning to tell the cabbie to wait, but she'd passed out and I knew that I couldn't get her up the front steps by myself. For an extra buck, he helped me pull and push her out of the back seat. Each of us got one arm over a shoulder and we walked her up to the front door.

That woke her up a little. As the cabbie worked the key, she swung around and plastered herself against me and laid a big kiss on me. He saw what she was doing and cocked one eyebrow.

"Keep the meter running," I said, walking her into the lobby.

He gave her a long look and said, "You sure?"

In the little elevator, she shoved me against the wall and reached for my fly. "Come on, doll," she slurred. "Little Ruby wants to be sweet. Don't you want to be sweet?"

"I'm sweet as hell. So are you." When we got to her floor, I maneuvered her out of the elevator, into her apartment and straight through to the bedroom.

She chuckled and pulled at my tie. "Oh, doll, you're in a hurry just like me. Come on."

Her fingers worked at the buttons of her dress. She shrugged it off her shoulders as I moved her to the bed and laid her down. She pulled me with her, closed her eyes and kissed me some more, and I was thinking I should've told the cabbie to go.

A few seconds later, her arms loosened and her face went slack. She snored. I rolled her over onto her stomach again and put a trash can beside the bed. I gave the place a quick once-over. Didn't see anything I hadn't seen before. I went back downstairs to the cab.

What a sap.

Things were still lively when I got back to the speak. I asked Marie Therese what the special was at the Cruzon Grill. She said it was brisket and it was good. I told her to have the guys send a sandwich to my office. She said that Willie and the detective were already there. I said make it three sandwiches, and put two of them on Willie's tab. Willie and Mrs. Opperman had Five-Stars. I poured one for myself. They'd cut the string and newspaper away from Ruby Rose's bundle. The puppet of Lily White looked like it had been pretty well knocked around. The hair was ratty and tangled. The face was chipped and the middle was shredded. The detective shook her head at it. "What foolishness."

Willie was more thoughtful. "Given everything that's happened, I'm not so sure."

"That's not the agency's concern. Here's my preliminary. You'll receive a bill and a more complete report, if there's anything more to add, within a week. I'll include our continuing observation of Mrs. Garner in that accounting."

Willie nodded, not really caring. "Tell me what you have."

The detective opened her notebook. "We can't fill in every detail but this explanation covers the facts that we have. Sidney Abbey recruited Emmanuel Hoyt, aka Manny the Dip, in Florida. They returned to New York several months ago. Manny and a woman we know only as 'Sally' rented two apartments in Tudor City. Sidney Abbey made contact with Miss Rose, and used her connections with people in the entertainment business to steer vulnerable women to Manny. By then, The Cloister apartment was decked out so Manny could impersonate a Hindoo healer, a weight-loss expert or a clairvoyant spiritualist medium."

Willie said, "Ruby Rose and the Abbé had several mutual friends, and we learned earlier this evening that he may have had designs on Lily White. She spurned his advances, and that was at least part of his motivation for purchasing the doll and using it to threaten her. When it comes to sexual conquests, his appetite is voracious. Some women are attracted to his sheer animal magnetism, and he believes any woman he meets is his for the taking. He has a particular taste for winsome blossoms like Lily."

Winsome blossoms? What the hell were winsome blossoms?

The detective said "We can find out easily enough."

"Please do."

"Whatever their motives, there's nothing for law enforcement to do about it. The man purchased a doll. The woman mangled it. Those are not crimes."

Willie looked like he wanted to disagree but all he said was, "Of course. What else do you have?"

"Now it gets more interesting." She looked at me. "Xeno Pool. We know that he was involved in hijacking two truckloads of illegal liquor. The first truck, on May fifth, belonged to Arthur Flegenheimer, aka Dutch Schultz. The second to Meyer Lansky and Charlie Luciano. Pool carried out both jobs with the help of Irving and Shmuel Rosen. They fingered their friend and associate Izzy Stern who was driving the shipment belonging to Flegenheimer. Stern was beaten and shot in the head. They went to the funeral. In the second job, they turned Lansky's merchandize over to Pool after beating each other up. Pool sold the liquor to an unknown party or parties. I'm sure Quinn could give us more details."

I didn't say anything. She went on, "Three weeks ago, the Rosens were murdered. Someone—possibly Pool, possibly Gordon, possibly Luciano or Lansky—shot them in their car."

I said, "Yeah. I read about it in the papers."

"And last night we learned that Pool and Sidney Abbey have been working together. What can you tell us about that, Quinn?"

I could've said that Pool came to the city wanting to sign on with Meyer Lansky but that didn't work out. Then he met Sidney Abbey and decided to throw in with him. But I didn't bring that up. I said, "Ask Pool the next time you see him."

Willie gave me a curious look. He didn't understand.

The detective closed her notebook and said, "I took Pool to the First Precinct where I have some friends. They're questioning him about the Rosens, and, for now, they can't find anything else they can charge him with. They'll hold him until he talks."

I didn't say anything, but I knew that wouldn't work with Pool, and it didn't. I asked around later and learned he walked out of the First Precinct when they couldn't find anything to charge him with.

After Mrs. Opperman was gone, Willie poured two more brandies and asked me what was going on. "Why wouldn't you tell us about this man Pool?"

"It's business," I said, finally able to relax without the detective listening in and noting down every detail. "Somebody asked me about your private business, I wouldn't tell them anything either."

One of the guys from the Grill tapped on the door, and brought in a tray of sandwiches. Willie asked what it was. I told him it was brisket and it was all part of the service. "Dig in," I said. "Rule number four."

"What's rule number four?" he asked between bites, and I realized he didn't know what I was talking about.

"Jimmy's Rules for Life," I said. "I've got five so far. Number one is leave a tip. It started as 'always tip your bartender,' but it applies to most situations where somebody's waiting on you or doing something for you. If you can afford it, you leave them a little something. If they do more than they have to, you bump it up."

"Makes sense."

"Rule number two. Wear comfortable shoes. I told you I used to be a runner, so I was particular about shoes that could help me get away from guys who wanted to take what I was carrying. But it's just as important now that I'm a gimp. You're not going to get anything accomplished when your feet hurt. Ruins your whole day. So, wear comfortable shoes."

"Never thought of it."

"Number three. Take an extra five minutes. If you've got a job to do, before you tell everybody that it's finished, take five minutes to look it over again. If you've got to be someplace at a certain time, give yourself an extra five minutes to get there. It's not always going to be possible, but if it is…"

"And number four is 'eat a brisket sandwich?' An excellent brisket sandwich, I must say."

"Ain't that the truth. The guys in the kitchen know what they're doing."

"But why 'eat a sandwich?'"

"Because you never know what's going to happen. Say somebody offers you a sandwich and you say no because you think you're going to have lunch in an hour. But then there's a huge thunderstorm and the sewers back up and the subway is flooded and the El shuts down and you can't get to a grocery store or a restaurant you trust, then aren't you going to be sorry you said no to that sandwich?"

"How true. One must be prepared for such eventualities."

"And rule number five. Show up. You say you're going to be somewhere, be there. You say you're going to do something, do it."

"It's so simple, you wouldn't think it needs to be said."

I couldn't tell whether he was joking with me or not. I don't think he was.

"Is that it? Five rules?"

"I'm still working on them."

After Willie left, I wrote *winsome* and *eventualities* in my notebook. I thought I knew what they meant and I was right.

After that night, I didn't see Willie as much. His business with the dolls was finished, and when his book, *Jungle Ways*, became a best-seller, he got into deep hot water because he said that he sat down to dinner with cannibals and could report that human meat tasted "much like veal." Turned out that a lot of the people who read that thought he was terrible for doing it. A lot more couldn't stand it that he ate a meal with colored people. The rest didn't believe him.

He still came back to dip his beak in the Five-Star from time to time. He got his final Continental Agency report from Mrs. Opperman in my office. She'd learned that Lily White did know a Sidney Abbey. She said she'd gone out with him once, but he frightened her, and she broke it off with him. She barely remembered the man and couldn't believe that he was so taken with her that he'd been involved with the doll. She got over her stomach problems, too. Whether it was Willie's voodooism or her thinking she was too fat the way some girls do, she was fine. She wound up having a career on the stage, too. You never saw her name up in lights, but she worked for a long time. I followed all the news and reviews about the Great White Way, even if I didn't go to many shows, and I saw her name in the papers. For a few more years, she played ingenues, then she was sisters and best friends, and finally mothers.

I can't say as much about Ruby Rose. I heard she took up with one of Carlo Gambino's guys, but I don't know that for sure, and I never saw her again.

Helen Stiles did the best of the three. She didn't get her own show like she wanted, but she was the lead singer for the WEAF radio orchestra, and she had a few more hit records. Nothing like "Meet Me in the Shadows," but people in New York knew who she was and they remembered her.

Later in the spring, Willie and Mink sailed back to France. By the time they left, he'd run up the biggest tab anybody ever had at my place, and he paid it with cash from his pocket.

Miss A'Lelia Walker died in August. Thousands of people came to her service in Harlem, and when they buried her in the Woodlawn Cemetery, the "Black Eagle" flew over and dropped flowers. He was a guy who was famous for parachuting out of airplanes. The story of him flying over the funeral was in most of the papers, but not the *Times*.

Me, I stayed busy with the speak and other things.

Chapter Thirty-one

Connie said that all the housekeeping routines she was beginning to understand at the Pennyweight house got tossed out the window after little Ethan arrived. Either Dr. Cloninger was there to see him or Oh Boy was driving the baby and Mrs. Pennyweight to the clinic. Two or three times a day, Miss Flora told anyone who'd listen that it was all more than she could bear. Then she'd call some of her friends and they'd sail off together.

The first shipments of special baby food arrived from Germany and Switzerland. Mrs. Conway ordered Mr. Mears, Oh Boy, and Dietz to wrestle a big set of shelves from a storeroom to the kitchen. Cloninger showed them what to do. He was a pale, blond knobby-jointed number who sported frog-eyed glasses and a white doctor's smock. He spent a day with Connie and Mrs. Conway translating the labels, and explaining how they were going to have to experiment with the different foods, all packed in small square boxes, to learn which ones the little fellow could keep down. He had checklists for them to fill out for every day of the week.

Mr. Spencer's work picked up at about the same time. Oh Boy drove him into the city for meetings with lawyers and bankers. At first, it was only a few times a month, but before long, the business telephone in the library was ringing all the time. Connie had strict orders never to answer it. Then the people from the city were coming out to Valley Green to talk to Spence and Mrs. Pennyweight, and Spence's city meetings sometimes lasted until dawn.

Every time Oh Boy sat down at the table and tried to snag a slice of uneaten pie or cake from one of Miss Flora's trays, he would tell Connie that something was up all right, something big.

In June, Connie was dusting in the big entrance hall on the first floor when she heard somebody drive up and stop by the front door. She figured it had to be one of Flora's pals. Tradesmen used the road that took them around back. Then she heard a heavy fist pounding on the big double doors, and it wasn't just one knock, the thuds went on and on.

Connie opened the door. He was a heavyset middle-aged man with a rosy swollen face, and a white apron flecked with blood. He shoved the door open, pushed her aside and stomped in.

"I'll see Catherine Pennyweight," he said, booze on his breath, paying no attention to Connie.

"Catherine Pennyweight," he repeated, his voice louder. "We must have a settlement."

He took two more steps forward and stopped when he heard Mrs. Pennyweight's voice slice down from the second-floor balcony that overlooked the hall.

"Remember your place. You will not address me in that tone. Wait there." The man froze.

Mrs. Pennyweight wore a long high-collared dress and came down the stairs slowly, her cane tapping each one.

Connie saw the anger drain out of the man as Mrs. Pennyweight got closer and tilted her head back to stare down at him. He wouldn't meet her eyes.

"Has there been some problem with payment?"

He unclenched his fists and wrung his hands as he nodded. "Yes, ma'am, in town, you know, there's talk, and people, you know, talk."

"Very well. Come with me." She led him toward the library, and turned to Connie. "That will be all, Nix. You can finish this later."

Connie hurried down the servant's stairs to the kitchen. Oh Boy and Mrs. Conway were at the table. Mrs. Conway grabbed Connie's arm, and explained that the angry man was Mr. Bartham, the butcher. Connie didn't bother to ask how they'd figured that even before she got downstairs. Word was about that Bartham and some of the other merchants in town had not been paid, and now they were losing their patience. What were he and Mrs. Pennyweight saying?

Connie told them that Mrs. Pennyweight had taken him into the library. Mrs. Conway told Connie to go and dust on the front stairs to the second floor. From there she could see them when he left.

Sometime later, Mrs. Pennyweight and Mr. Bartham came out and walked to the front door. Connie saw that he was folding a few bills into his pocket.

Little Ethan got better. Then the next day, he wasn't better. Mrs. Pennyweight worried that he wasn't gaining weight like he should, changed his food, and changed it again when he still wouldn't eat. New boxes arrived from Germany. Then the fights started between Mrs. Pennyweight and Flora, usually in the afternoon after Flora had knocked back a bottle of wine with lunch. The fights always began behind a locked bedroom or nursery door, but when Flora got frustrated at what her mother was saying, Flora yelled. Once Flora started yelling, she liked to stalk the halls and wave her arms. She also turned up the volume knob, and when that didn't get results, she threw things. If Spence wasn't there, she'd hit the button for Oh Boy to bring her car around, and she'd roar off in a spray of gravel. Flora's car was a sweet little green Ford coupe with a V-8. I always liked it.

If Spence was there, he could calm her down. Everybody knew that. But if he was at one of his meetings, staff stayed out of Flora's way.

Through the summer and fall, that was the pattern they followed. As Connie saw it, everything started with little Ethan. If they fixed up the right mealy German stuff for him, and he ate it and kept it down, then the rest of the household could relax. It he refused it or whooped it back up or got any of half a dozen other digestive ailments, then it was off to Dr. Cloninger's with him, and Flora was stomping around the second floor and yelling about why couldn't she just be a normal girl and have fun with her friends? What's wrong with that? Bring me my car.

Toward the end of the year, Spence was less likely to be there. His trips into the city got longer. There were more meetings at the house. They never knew when they'd need to take his meals to the library.

The next shoe fell one night around Christmas when Mrs. Conway called the staff together before dinner. Connie said the woman looked more worried than she'd ever seen her. Then the cook said, "I've got some very good news for us."

Oh Boy muttered, "Oh, boy."

Dietz drank his foul white liquor, and Mr. Mears drained his dago red. Mrs. Conway said that Mr. Spencer had secured the loans that Pennyweight Petroleum needed for new exploratory wells. Connie didn't know what exploratory wells were and figured Mrs. Conway didn't either. Those wells were so promising that Dr. Cloninger was also investing. Mrs. Conway stopped, and Connie could tell that she was about to get to the bad part. "Mrs. Pennyweight has explained these complex financial dealings and, because of them, all household funds have been frozen until Mr. Spencer brings in the new wells."

"What do you mean? We won't be paid?" Connie couldn't believe she was hearing this, and she couldn't understand why the others didn't look like it bothered them. Mr. Mears and Dietz just shrugged and finished their drinks.

Oh Boy said, "It's happened before."

"And we'll all receive generous bonuses when Mr. Spencer returns from his trip."

Mrs. Conway saw that Connie didn't understand or wasn't buying it. "He'll be flying in the company Tri-Motor to Louisiana and Texas and possibly to Mexico to see to the wells. After that, our wages will be brought up to date and everything will be fine."

Connie asked when that was going to happen. Mrs. Conway said soon.

Soon turned out to be the first week in March, 1932. Until then, Spence kept going to the city, and guys from the city came out to New Jersey to see him. Dr. Cloninger spent more time at the house in the library with Spence, not with little Ethan. Things got dicier with Flora.

With Spencer and Mrs. Pennyweight paying less attention to her, Flora invited more of her pals over and they spent more nights out on the town. Connie could hear some of the angry early mornings that Spence and Flora had in their room. She couldn't make out the words. She didn't have to.

By the end of February, everything was ready. Mrs. Pennyweight was sending out orders for this and that every fifteen minutes. Even Dietz had to pitch in with some of the housework. Late in the afternoon, Connie was moving some of little Ethan's rations from the pantry to the kitchen when she ran into Spence. It was the first time she'd seen him downstairs. He had an automatic in his mitt, a .45 with a couple of extra clips.

He was coming out of the gun room at the far end of the basement. Mrs. Conway had showed it to Connie in her first week, but the room wasn't on the cleaning schedule, and she'd forgot it was there. Spencer didn't look at her as he hurried upstairs.

Connie went back to the kitchen and spent the rest of the night cleaning dishes, and fixing more food for the second floor. She and Mrs. Conway were the first ones up the next day. The cook had a list of things that had to be done before Spence could leave that morning. As Connie got the big coffee pot started, Mrs. Conway switched on her radio and they learned that the Lindbergh baby had been kidnapped.

It hit Connie just like it hit me when I found out about it later that day. First, she thought she heard it wrong. That couldn't be right. Charles Lindbergh was the most famous man in the world. His son was the most famous baby in the world. They lived a few miles down the road in Hopewell. This was impossible. It could not be happening.

Thus began the craziest day of Connie's life.

She and Mrs. Conway just stopped what they were doing and stared at the radio until habit took over, and they went back to getting coffee and breakfast under way. As the rest of the staff showed up, they had to stop and fill them in on what was happening. Mrs. Pennyweight's light came on around eight.

When Connie brought the tray up, she found that Spence was with his mother-in-law and little Ethan. They stopped talking when she came into the room and told her to bring Mr. Spencer's tray. Connie went back downstairs, fixed Spence's breakfast and went upstairs again. She was just about to roll the cart into Mrs. Pennyweight's room when the door to Flora's room banged open, and Flora, in filmy pajamas, ran past her, screaming, "Have you heard? How could it happen to Charles and Anne? The radio says they strongly suspect it's the work of the underworld."

That last bit seemed to be directed at Spence personally. He tried to settle Flora down. "You can't let this upset you. This is the kind of thing that the police take very seriously. Every cop in New Jersey and New York is working on it."

"That doesn't matter. What about *us*? What about little Ethan?" She stopped and her eyes got wide and wild. "Little Ethan. My god, he could be next. If they can take little Charles, they can take anyone."

That was enough to wake up little Ethan and set him screaming. Connie left the tray in the hall and got back downstairs.

Less than ten minutes later, Dr. Cloninger's ambulance skidded to a stop at the front door and he went straight up to Mrs. Pennyweight's room. For the rest of the day, the staff got orders for one thing and another, and then more orders saying not to do that thing or the other. First, Spence would be leaving in the Tri-Motor that afternoon. An hour later, that was cancelled. Spence and Mrs. Pennyweight locked themselves in the library while Dr. Cloninger tended to Flora. Around three o'clock, Spence called Oh Boy to the library. He stayed there for an hour. When he went back to the kitchen, he told them that he had to go into the city by himself, and Connie needed to get one of the guest bedrooms ready. He said that Mrs. Pennyweight wanted them to move the baby's crib into the library.

Connie and Mr. Mears went up to Mrs. Pennyweight's room. She was holding the baby. He wasn't keeping anything down, she said. This excitement wasn't good for him. Connie and Mr. Mears took the bedding out of the crib, and wrestled it down the wide steps to the first floor and into the library. They had to wait for Spence to finish a telephone call.

He was saying, "There's no need for that. Sherman knows what to do on his end. I'm taking care of this part of it. Nothing has changed. Tell him to stay away. I don't want to see any of his guys around here, got it? Tell him that. I've made arrangements… That's right… Someone I trust will be here."

He told them to put the crib beside the desk near the fireplace. They went back upstairs for the mattress and blankets. Mrs. Pennyweight brought the baby when they'd put the crib back together, and tucked him in. He was quiet. Mrs. Pennyweight said Dr. Cloninger had made sure that the kid and Flora could handle excitement. Connie thought little Ethan looked dopey.

Mrs. Pennyweight said, "We've decided to move the baby into the library for the time being. The kidnappers took Charles Junior from a second-floor nursery. It's simply not practical at the moment for us to guard the grounds, but the library windows are barred and someone will be armed and near little Ethan at all times."

Spence held out a double-barreled shotgun to Mr. Mears. The old guy blinked and pulled away. Spence said, "This is only for a few hours. Oliver is bringing an old friend of mine from the city. I trust him completely."

Mrs. Pennyweight snorted.

Connie left Mr. Mears holding the shotgun outside the library door and went back to the kitchen. Mrs. Conway was banging pots and dishes in the sink. Connie could tell she was upset, and took over the washing. Mrs. Conway poured tea for herself and sat at the table.

"Cursed," she muttered. "We're cursed. We have been since… Turn that up."

The man on the radio said, "Cars entering and leaving New York on all of the tunnels and bridges are being searched. Authorities have nothing new to report."

Mrs. Conway shook her head. "What are we coming to?"

Connie turned the radio back down, poured tea for herself and sat across from Mrs. Conway. "Mr. Mears and I moved the baby to the library. Mrs. Pennyweight thinks it's the safest place for him."

"And Mr. Spencer has sent Oliver into the city to bring back a gun thug," Mrs. Conway said. "I know what they say about Mr. Spencer but I never believed it could be true."

The brindle cat bumped Connie's leg, yowled and went to Mrs. Conway for food. Connie's feeling that something was going wrong rushed back.

She spent the rest of the afternoon and evening helping with the mutton roast, and going up and down the servant's stairs to Mrs. Pennyweight and Spence, bringing more wood for the fireplace, drinks, food, any newspapers Mrs. Pennyweight hadn't seen. Every time Connie went into the room, Mrs. Pennyweight asked if Oh Boy was back.

Around nine o'clock, Mrs. Conway sent Connie to the first floor to see if Mr. Mears or Mr. Spencer needed anything. Mr. Mears was still in front of the library, holding the shotgun like he was afraid of it. He wanted his dinner. Spence was outside in the driveway. Connie saw headlights and thought it was Oh Boy, but it was Cloninger's ambulance. The doctor and Spence and Dietz were talking. Actually, Spence was doing all the talking. By the look of it, he was intent and serious, saying or explaining something important, and they were taking in every word.

Connie went back to the kitchen and asked Mrs. Conway if she knew anything about it. She didn't. Not long after that, Oh Boy showed up. He went straight to the mutton and wolfed down a piece before Mrs. Conway could run him off. Mr. Mears came in, without the shotgun, and Mrs. Conway poured a glass of dago red and fixed him a plate. Oh Boy said he'd brought an old friend, meaning me, to look after things while Spence was on his trip.

Mrs. Conway cut her eyes at Connie and said, "The gun thug, no doubt."

Oh Boy was about to say something when Miss Flora's light flashed. She probably wanted wine. Connie went up to her bedroom and took the order. Champagne on ice, two glasses. Right away.

Connie took care of that and went back to the kitchen to find that Mrs.

Conway had a tray on a cart ready for Mrs. Pennyweight. Up the stairs again. She was back in the kitchen when they heard the sound of a car outside. Oh Boy said, "It's Mr. Evans' Marquette." He could recognize most of the regular visitors by their engines. Mrs. Conway and Connie knew that their neighbor Fordham Evans wouldn't want to eat, but he would drink anything you put in front of him. No need for another plate.

But Mr. Spencer would certainly want something. They were getting it ready when they heard the commotion from the first floor, something big hitting the floor, and then from outside, a police siren getting louder and closer. Oh Boy jumped up from the table and went to the top of the servant's stairs to see what was up.

Connie heard people leaving and doors closing a few minutes later. Oh Boy came back and told them that Mr. Evans had been acting off his nut, and so Oh Boy's friend, who was not a "gun thug" had calmed Mr. Evans down. Nothing to worry about. The sheriff had been following Mr. Evans anyway, and was taking him home. Connie went back to the dishes and listened to the radio.

After eleven, Mrs. Pennyweight's light came on. Connie climbed the stairs again to collect the empty dishes. She pushed the cart away from Mrs. Pennyweight's room and went across to Spence and Flora's bedroom to see if their dishes were ready to go back. The door was cracked open, and the cart and ice bucket were just inside. When she was closer, Connie saw something move and she stopped. It was a reflection of two bodies in one of the big mirrors, or maybe a reflection of a reflection. She couldn't tell where they were but she knew what they were doing. Flora's filmy pajamas were on the floor, She was facing the mirrored wall. Spence, stripped to the waist and pants around his ankles, was tight behind her, his arms around her waist pulling her close.

Connie held her breath and backed away, quiet as she could be. She tiptoed the cart into the dumb waiter and went down to the kitchen. That's where she saw a good-looking guy, well turned out in a black pinstripe single-breasted and gray turtleneck, leaning on his stick and talking to Mrs. Conway.

Oh Boy said, "Constance, this is my friend Jimmy Quinn."

A week later, once Spence's business was settled, she came to work for me.

Two years after that, when she met Willie, Connie knew more about running the speak than I did.

Chapter Thirty-two

1933
NEW YORK CITY

The day after Connie and I saw Willie at Doctors Hospital, I got an invitation just like his in the mail. I sliced it open, then dug around in the desk drawer where stuff collects on its own. I sorted through the papers until I found Willie's invitation from two years before for his evening of "fantastical experiments and occult esoterica." Same engraving, same gold foil.

I looked up the number in the book and dialed the Continental Detective Agency. Mrs. Opperman still worked there but she wasn't in. She called my office that evening. I told her about the invitations. She swore.

"Did you keep an eye on Mrs. Garner after Willie's business was finished?"

"The agency billed Mr. Seabrook for another month of light surveillance. After that, I made it my business to bump into her from time to time, ask her out to tea, that kind of thing. We lost touch after she went to Florida for the winter."

"Did you ever convince her that Manny the Instructor was phonus bolonus?"

She didn't answer. Instead, she said, "What was the wording on the new invitation?"

"Bring an 'earthly treasure.'"

Mrs. Opperman thought on that for a time, then said, "I'll call you back."

Connie came in a little later and saw the invitation on my desk. "Is that...?"

I nodded.

196

Her smile was tight with excitement. "Now we don't have to weasel a way in with Willie. What am I going to wear?"

"If we both go, that'll leave us shorthanded on a Saturday night."

"Don't even think about trying to stop me," she said. I knew not to argue.

Willie came to the speak a little after ten that night. He stopped at the bar to talk to Frenchy, and to flirt with Marie Therese and Connie before he walked back to my table. He was wearing one of his bespoke corduroy suits and a red neckerchief instead of a tie. Looked better than he had the night before and his hand didn't tremble when we shook.

Marie Therese put a tall glass of Scotch and soda in front of him. Willie saw my expression and said, "My second of the day."

"Sure it is."

"All right, possibly my third, but it's mostly seltzer. Really, I'm fine. Everyone agrees I don't need to be there. They're discharging me next week. I've been able to sublet a furnished penthouse, not too far from here on East Twenty-Second."

He saw that I still wasn't buying it.

"Now that time and distance have given me some perspective, I see that my problem in France was the place and the heat. It's not right for a man, not for me, anyway, to be sweating all the time. But that's not why I'm here. It's the invitation. I've been asking around and it's quite mysterious."

"Yeah, I got one this afternoon."

"Really? You could sell it for a hundred dollars. Rumors and stories about this are flying all over the place. Everybody's talking about it but nobody actually has an invitation. I've learned the names of three women who are said to have been invited, but that's all I've been able to find. Those three are old and very close friends of Victoria Garner, and, for what it's worth, they're also widows and extremely wealthy. I suspect that the rest of the invitations have gone to her closest friends and that is a very exclusive club."

"So they can afford pricey earthly treasures that could add up to a respectable haul. I guess they invited you and me so they could screw us over. It's a good bet that Pool is still working with them. If he is, everything changes."

"How?"

"We know Manny and Sidney Abbey are confidence men. They're not going to hurt anybody unless they have to. Pool's a thug with a short fuse.

He sees something he wants, he'll take it and he'll kill anybody who tries to stop him."

"You may be right about him and Manny. But I still cannot believe that Abbey is a fraud. I know him better than you do. The man's search for deeper truths was genuine when I knew him. We only have Manny's word that he was involved with what went on at Tudor City."

"Damn, Willie, has the booze turned your brain to mush? He and Pool were ransacking your place after they robbed mine. We know that Abbey and Manny were working together in Florida before they came here. And Florida is where Mrs. Garner spends her winters. It figures that she still believes Manny can pierce the veil, or some such. Now, she's invited her carriage trade pals to take part in his little demonstration and each of them has to pony up an 'earthly treasure.' You know what's going to happen."

That got his back up. "No, I don't know. Look, I played a little game to show those women how easy it is to be fooled. But that doesn't mean that genuine psychic powers don't exist."

It was good to see that he could still get pissed off. "I am convinced that men like the Abbé and Crowley are on to something. They may be more theatrical than they need to be, but their search for other forms of knowledge is real."

"Like chaining up Deborah Luris and taking her clothes off and blindfolding her so she can detach herself from the sensory envelope?"

He laughed. "You don't understand, but that's not why I came here. You've got to explain what happened with Connie last night when you mentioned Pool. Refresh my memory. I hardly remember the man. He was with them that night in my apartment, wasn't he?"

Connie heard Pool's name and pulled a chair up next to Willie's.

"Pool and I were involved in some business that had nothing to do with you. Because of that, Pool was keeping an eye on my place while you were occupied with Lily White and the doll."

I turned to Connie. "I told you about this last night."

She said, "Don't mind me," and smiled at Willie. He smiled back.

"Now, here's the funny part that I didn't understand."

I explained that Pool had surprised me in the lobby of my hotel one night about this other business. He wanted to establish his bona fides, and so he told me there was a big guy wearing a watch cap who was following the other guy who was spending so much time at my place.

"When I told him your name, he said 'Wow, *The* Willie Seabrook, so he knew who you were."

Connie said, "Xeno and my brother got into trouble together in California. It's a long story. The important part is that Xeno gave me *Adventures in Arabia*."

Willie leaned close to her. "Tell me all about it."

She did. She didn't tell him the parts about growing up in the orchards and her mother and father, but she told him the rest of it about her older brother and Xeno Pool and going to work for the Pennyweights where she met me. Whenever she tried to skip over something, Willie stopped her and asked for details. It took her an hour.

When she'd finished, he fired up a smoke and waved for another drink. "Do you remember what I told you about our fan-shaped destinies?"

I nodded.

He turned to Connie. "Basically, it's the idea that every day we face endless possibilities and seemingly inconsequential choices can set us on a new and unexpected course. For example, your going to work at Stag's Leap Manor led directly to the employment agency that sent you to Jimmy and me. Or had reading the Arabia book already nudged you in that direction? When did Pool give it to you?"

"It was new, so that was five years ago?"

"Five years ago, a book makes an impression on a young man. He gives it to a girl and it inspires her to explore the world, leading her from California to New York. It also takes him from California to New York where he meets us, and—"

"Actually, he tried to shoot us."

Willie ignored me. "After all this, how can you doubt that there is something greater than blind chance involved here? Something with a purpose we lack the facilities to perceive. It can't just be coincidence."

Connie said, "If it's not coincidence, what is it?"

"He's working up to an infinite number of sidewalks and an infinite number of Jimmy Quinns," I said.

They paid no attention to me and kept on talking about Willie's ideas. I did not join them because I knew two things for sure and I couldn't stop worrying about them. First, I knew that Xeno and Manny and Abbey meant to steal those 'earthly treasures' and, second, they wanted to hurt Willie and me.

After they'd talked as much as they could for one night, Connie asked Willie what she should wear to a demonstration of advanced psychical powers?

"For you, it doesn't matter," Willie said, leaning close and giving her one of those smiles I'd seen him use a hundred times. It had the same effect it always did.

"Whatever you wear, those old doyennes will give you the shoulder. They may be wealthier, but, I promise, you'll be prettier than any of them. And younger."

I pulled out my notebook and wrote *dwa-yen*.

Chapter Thirty-three

1933
NEW YORK CITY

Saturday, I decided on a light gray single-breasted three-piece with a faint herringbone. It was a year or so old but roomy through the shoulders and the pockets were slightly larger than normal. Cream colored shirt, also not too tight, green and silver foulard tie, and my most comfortable rubber-soled brogans. It was not my best, but I knew that the weight of a pistol didn't affect the drape of the coat. When I knocked at Connie's room, she told me through the door she wasn't ready and she'd see me at the speak.

I stopped by the Cruzon kitchen and asked the guys to fix up something for lunch. They said the special was sausage, potatoes and spinach. I told them to send a tray down. In my office, I opened the safe and got out Connie's count of Friday's business. At first, I thought it was o.k., not great but o.k. Then I saw Connie's note. It said our take was off fourteen percent from the same December Friday the year before.

I thought, damn, how does she know that? And again, I had to admit that in some ways, she was smarter than I was. Then I checked her totals against the count I'd made before I turned it over to her. She'd skimmed her usual.

Lunch was up to the Grill's standard. I'd have appreciated it more if I hadn't been so edgy. After I finished, I went back to the safe and found my pistol and cleaning kit. I'd happened upon another Detective Special, a .38 with a two-inch barrel. I unloaded it, gave it a quick cleaning and put five rounds back in the cylinder. I slipped a sixth bullet into my vest pocket. Jimmy Quinn's earthly treasure.

I was about to lock the safe when I saw a shape wrapped in a rag on the back shelf where I kept that sort of thing. It was a little German automatic, the piece I'd taken from Pool the night he knocked over my place. I hadn't touched it since.

I popped out the magazine and ejected the round in the chamber. Couldn't really see down the barrel but it smelled dirty. Not being familiar with the gun, I had to mess with it before I figured that you pulled the trigger guard down to take the slide off. After that, it was simple. Using solvent and scraps of rags, I cleaned the slide and the barrel, oiled them and put it back together.

There were eight .22 rounds in a magazine that held nine, less the one I shot at the Abbé. I reloaded the piece, and set the safety.

Sitting there, I tried to work through what I needed to do and what I should do. Smart move—don't go. Nothing good was going to come of this, I knew that. If they want to screw with me, let them come here. But it was too late for that. I was in Willie's game. I'd been in it since I delivered the booze to the party for the late A'Lelia Walker. Connie had been in it since she met Xeno Pool. Maybe there was something to Willie's infinite number of sidewalks business, after all. It was sure feeling like it.

But there was still Saturday night to take care of.

I went downstairs and asked Arch Malloy to come to my office. He took a long questioning look at the pistols on the desk but didn't say anything. I poured him a tot of Spanish rum infused with absinthe, one of the most expensive bottles in the house, and a smaller tot for myself.

"And what is the occasion of this?" he asked.

I explained that Connie and I were going to some sort of affair with Willie out on Long Island.

Arch nodded. "She told Marie Therese all about it. She's quite excited."

"Yeah, well, it's not that simple. I don't know what's going to happen out there, but the last time I got myself involved in something like this with Willie, it didn't go so good. Maybe Frenchy and Marie Therese told you about it."

"You were robbed, I believe."

"They got past Fat Joe, cleaned out the register and the smokes."

"But as I heard it, you took care of the situation."

"You could say that, but, you know, these things never end as clean as you want. And I think the son of a bitch who did it is back."

"That is Connie's Xeno Pool?"

For someone who liked to talk, Arch liked to listen, too.

"Maybe I'll run into him on Long Island, or maybe, like the last time, he's using the business with Willie to distract us, and he's planning to hit us again. What I'm saying is, he doesn't like me any more than I like him. Be ready."

"Then you won't mind if I slip back over to my apartment to arm myself."

Connie got back around two. She looked swell in a new shimmery black blouse and a tweed skirt and coat. She was trying to act like this was the kind of thing we did every day, but I could tell she was excited. She kept moving around until I sat down with her on the divan and showed her the German automatic. That got her steamed.

"What the hell is this?" She never cursed until she met me. "We're going to a mansion on Long Island, not a cock fight."

"Humor me. Every time I've been around your pal Xeno Pool, things go south."

"You don't even know that Xeno is going to be there, and he's not my pal, but," she stopped, confused, then went on, "he'd never hurt me."

She was probably right about that. Dammit. She saw it on my face and smiled. "You're jealous. I haven't laid eyes on him in years and you're jealous."

"What if I am? Doesn't change anything. We don't know what's going to happen tonight. You've got room in your handbag and you know how to use this. Take it."

She stood up, said she wanted to make sure that Marie Therese had everything ready, and went downstairs. She didn't say another word to me until Willie showed up. Then she was all smiles again. Willie bought a quart of Black and White for the road, and we were off.

You couldn't see the little automatic in my inside vest pocket unless you were looking for it.

Willie had hired a black Cadillac limousine, a huge thing with white sidewall tires, spares mounted on the fenders, and a bar in the back. If Connie hadn't ridden in the Pennyweights' Duesenberg J, she might have been impressed.

It was raining and the driver held an umbrella for us from the door of the speak to the car. There was plenty of room for four on the back seat, but I took the jump.

We went over the Queensborough Bridge and onto Long Island. Willie worked on his quart of Black and White. I mixed a mild one for Connie and had seltzer myself. They talked about Willie's books. Connie wasn't too interested in the screwy stuff about magic and fate. She wanted to know about the people who lived in the desert and the woman who taught Willie in Haiti. I watched the road. If anybody followed us, I didn't see him.

I can't really say how long it took us to reach Collier's Neck, but it was getting dark when we drove through the three blocks of a prosperous, old-money burg. The main road ended at the Sound and a dock where motor boats and sailboats were tied up. I moved onto the seat with Connie and Willie so I could see where we were going. The big car and the smooth pavement reminded me of Valley Green, and I touched the Detective Special just to make sure it was still there. Connie noticed. Willie rattled on.

We turned onto a road that followed the beach for a few blocks. The sidewalks were red brick, and I saw a guy lighting a gas streetlamp in front of the bank. Other stores had electric lights so they must have kept the gas because they liked it. We drove out of the town, past a few little houses. Then the road climbed a steep hill and twisted between tall hedges until it ended at Couffinghal House.

It was a tall blue-gray wooden building on a bluff overlooking the Sound. In the fading light, I could see tall windows, a deep covered porch, and an etched glass front door. An arched glass skylight capped half the roof. There was something funny about the shape of the house, too. It wasn't square or rectangular. Looking at it from the drive, you couldn't say exactly what it was.

Another big car was unloading passengers at the front steps. When it was our turn, the driver rolled down his window. A guy directing traffic told him to go back down and park in the lot at the foot of the hill if he was going to wait. They'd let him know when it was time to pick us up.

We got out of the car into a wind that made you hold onto your hat. It was colder than the city. Inside, an older guy in a black coat and white gloves checked our names off a list and said in a low voice that the demonstration would begin presently. Mrs. Garner was next to him.

The only time I'd seen her was at Willie's black magic soirée, and then not face to face. She was sixty or so with gray hair, dark eyes, an unlined face and a dreamy sort of smile. She was wearing a dark hooded robe made out of coarse fabric with a rope belt. Despite the cold, she was barefooted. Willie stepped right up and grabbed her hand in both of his.

"Mrs. Garner, so good to see you again."

They talked about this and that for a few minutes and then she said that she'd never forgot that night at his apartment and the "parlor trick" he played on everyone. "Since then, I've often wanted to ask you if you deny the possibility of the supernatural."

"Not at all, I've seen too many things I cannot explain."

Her dreamy smile widened. "And you shall do so again tonight."

I got more worried.

A hallway led to a long room with French windows at the back of the house. The hall and the room were lined with flowers and potted plants. Added to the flowers, candles and burning sticks of incense gave the whole place a thick smell as ripe as an opium parlor. The French windows overlooked the Sound, gray water and gray clouds. There was a guy serving wine and punch and sherry at a table in the corner. The bottles looked real. Connie tried the sherry and said it was o.k. Steam trays were ready for food at another table. Willie's doyennes—who are older women who've made it to the top of the heap—were already there. Two more came in later. They were about Mrs. Garner's age, but dressed like regular women in dresses and skirts. I noticed that I was not the only one who needed a stick. Three of them used canes, and one woman used two. They smiled at us when we came in. Willie waltzed right over and introduced himself. A couple of minutes later, they were hanging on every word.

The woman with two sticks introduced herself to Connie as Mrs. Hendrixson. I wandered off to get a better idea of the layout of the place. After testing three locked doors, I figured that one end of the house was a single big room. Curious. Waiters and waitresses appeared carrying containers of food for the steam trays. Going against the direction they were coming from, I walked through a formal dining room to a smaller food preparation room. It had a dumbwaiter and steps that probably went down to a kitchen in the basement. An irritated-looking guy with a pencil mustache was in charge. He blocked my way and suggested that I join the other guests. He was checking his watch like he had someplace to be.

Still looking for another way out, I went back to the front door. Outside, I followed the porch around the house. There were rocking chairs in back.

A raised wooden walkway about twenty yards long crossed the brown grass and connected the porch to a set of wooden steps. The steps switched back and forth down the bluff to a private beach. Some of the boards on the porch felt spongy and rotten. The walkway and steps I could see looked to be in worse shape with lots of missing pieces. I was not tempted to find out how bad they were.

I went back inside and climbed a set of stairs off the main hall.

The second floor was laid out like the first, but the three doors that were locked downstairs were open. I went into a large six-sided room. At first, I thought it was empty. The ceiling was the glass skylight I'd seen as we were driving in, and the three sides that faced the water were mostly windows. More plants and flowers lined the walls. If the room below it was the same, it would have been where the Garners had dances and such. The room on the second floor would have been for the family.

In the center of the big room, twelve small tables were arranged in a circle like the points of a compass for the earthly treasures. Each table had a name card, engraved with the same careful writing as the invitation. I took a gander at the goods.

A Mrs. Paget had brought an old book. Mrs. Banbrock's treasure was a diamond and sapphire necklace. Mrs. Connell, a silver music box. Mrs. Reddy, a leather case with six gold Sovereigns. Mrs. Hendrixson—the woman with two sticks—a bird's nest. Mrs. Collinson, a cameo pin. Mrs. Banbrock, a diamond and sapphire tennis bracelet. Miss Fen, star sapphire earrings. Mrs. Grantham, a yellow diamond ring. Mrs. Garner, one of those gold Russian eggs that was open to show a little car inside.

Mr. Seabrook and Mr. Quinn's tables were empty.

I was taking a closer look at the golden egg when a voice close behind me said,

"Don't get light fingers, Quinn."

"Wouldn't think of it, detective."

Theodora Opperman had a pistol in her plump mitt. "Over here," she said.

We went back to a corner away from the windows. She had a chair and another table set up where she could watch the three doors and the goods on display.

She said that after she talked to me on the telephone, she went to Mrs. Garner's apartment house and found the doorman who'd helped her two years before. He told her that Mrs. Garner had been gone for most of that time. To Florida. She returned four months ago and the same things were happening. She was giving him checks made out to cash every few days. Might have added up to nine hundred dollars that he'd got for her. He didn't know what she was doing with the dough but there was a lot of mail and messenger activity, and she told him she was opening the family house on Long Island.

Mrs. Opperman arranged to be outside the building when Mrs. Garner came out for her morning constitutional. Over tea, she found out what was going on.

Willie had not convinced Mrs. Garner that the Instructor, aka Manny the Dip, was a fraud. Truth was, she'd been "heartbroken" when he disappeared like that. She knew the guy in Tudor City as Brother Emmanuel. When Mrs. Opperman tried to tell her that the man had been involved in an armed robbery, Mrs. Garner just stopped listening. That could not be true. The detective knew that if she argued, she wouldn't be able to do anything else, so she dropped it.

Mrs. Garner said that she'd known from the moment she met him that Brother Emmanuel was the genuine article. He could not have told her the things he did without being in contact with her dead husband and son.

It was so fortunate that, completely by accident, he ran into her in Florida a year after he decamped New York. Since then, their relationship had deepened. She claimed there was no mumbo jumbo. She and Manny simply sat in a slightly darkened room and talked about her family and what she'd been through. Sometimes he would see images of her past or he would hear her husband and son speaking to her through him. Sometimes he would fall into a full trance and then he would tell her the most amazing stories. He was certain that they had almost reached the point where a reunification of her family would be possible. His chances of "effectuating a passage between realms" were greatest at Couffinghal House where her son and husband had left this world.

"Manny is an ice-cold son of a bitch," I said.

"It gets worse."

Manny told the widow it would take a congregation of diverse psychical personalities to raise the level of energies to a spiritual boiling point. Perhaps Mrs. Garner could arrange for some of her acquaintances to attend. He'd never attempted this and could not guarantee it would be successful, but he knew men who could lay the proper groundwork at the house, if she was willing to try. Of course she was.

"What's his game?"

The detective said, "I don't know but I've managed to convince Victoria that it was only wise to provide some protection for these valuables, and I walked out of that tea shop with a signed contract."

"You just happened to have a blank one in your bag."

She sniffed. "No Continental operative leaves the office without a blank contract, flashlight, pistol and handcuffs. You never know what you're going to run into."

"What's Manny's excuse for the pelf?"

"He told her the earthly treasures are talismen, 'points of physical intersection.'"

"I'd guess this adds up to about, what, fifty, maybe seventy-five thousand dollars worth of physical intersection. What a racket."

"Stuff it. The woman has lost four children and her husband. Do not judge her. Or her friends. These women have known each other for decades. Several of them have outlived husbands and children just like Mrs. Garner, and most of them helped her after her son and her husband..."

The detective's voice got thicker. "The boy was electrocuted right there, out on that porch. He was trying to adjust the antenna for a radio he'd made himself. Her husband Bartholomew sliced open an artery in his thigh in the bathroom over there. And those came after the deaths of her three older children. How does anyone ever get over experiences like that? Can you blame her for searching for some sort of answer?"

Connie and Willie strolled into the room. He was about two drinks looser than the last time I'd seen him. I introduced Connie to the detective, and Mrs. Opperman went over what she'd told me about the earthly treasures.

"Actually, Manny could be right about the points of intersection," Willie said. "It is possible for certain physical objects to absorb emotional energies. You saw what I did with the puppets. Jimmy thinks this is nonsense, but the theory might have some validity. Just because Manny was forced into helping with the robbery of your place by Pool, that doesn't mean he's not the genuine spiritual article. I'm not saying he is or he isn't, but it's still possible. Remember what I told you about Rhine's experiments. In a setting like this where more emotions are in play and there's the threat of physical violence, who can say what will happen?"

"'You mean I'm the threat of physical violence?"

"Why do you think they invited you?"

He knew the answer to that so I said I was going to find something to eat.

Mrs. Opperman said, "Make yourself useful. Bring me a sandwich. Haven't had anything since this morning. I'm peckish."

They'd set up the steam tables downstairs. Willie went for the booze. There wasn't much to the eats, but I can't say that I cared. I knew trouble was coming. I didn't want to be overstuffed or run out of gas when it got there. Connie talked to the woman sitting next to her. I didn't know what they were talking about, but I could tell they were picking up a conversation they'd had earlier. So much for what Willie said about the doyennes. The old girl and Connie chatted like pals, and a few minutes later, she led Connie off. I went back to the food and loaded up another plate with little triangular sandwiches with the crust cut off. The detective was glad to get them.

I strolled back over to the goods. Willie had put a little cloth bag tied with a string on his table. I couldn't tell what it was. Mine was still empty. I took the bullet out of my vest pocket and stood it up on the table. I had some damn fool idea that when Xeno Pool came to steal the goods, he'd know that I was on to him. I was taking another look at the golden egg and thinking it would fit in a pocket when we heard a muffled gong from downstairs.

Mrs. Opperman said, "That means they show's about to start, and you can forget about the Fabergé."

"You misjudge me."

"You got away from the Agency once. It won't happen again."

Chapter Thirty-four

1933
COUFFIGNAL HOUSE, LONG ISLAND

Downstairs, I saw that Mrs. Garner was walking slowly from room to room. She had a gong in one hand and gave it a tap with each step. The nine doyennes were following her. The doors to the six-sided room were open, and that's where they were headed. I held back.

By then it was dark. There was a light on the big porch and I could see movement out there. A bus was idling by the front steps, and the waiters and waitresses were climbing aboard. The guy with the pencil mustache was hurrying them along. He still looked irritated.

I turned around and found Mrs. Garner right next to me.

"You're the last," she said with a dreamy smile. "This way."

The big room was dim. Connie was standing by the door. She whispered to me, "There's only room for twelve. I'll watch from here."

Hindoo music was playing, some kind of flute and twangy strings. There was a riser in the middle with twelve plain wooden chairs in a circle around it just like the tables with the earthly treasures over our heads. More flowers and plants were in big pots behind the chairs. Between the pots, more candles and long sticks of incense were burning. The room reeked. Some of the women were holding handkerchiefs to their noses. Mrs. Garner went to the riser, and I took the last chair. Willie was straight across the circle from me. He was so excited he was squirming in his chair as he gulped his drink.

Mrs. Garner said, "Good evening, everyone. I'm so happy you could join me this evening. Some of you are familiar with my friend. For others, this will be an introduction to a remarkable man. Brother Emmanuel…"

From where I was sitting on the circle, he was at two o'clock, to the right of Willie. The man seemed to appear in front of a pot of flowers. It wasn't like he was behind them and walked through them. One second he wasn't there, the next he was. The women next to me saw it, too, and they gasped. Murmurs spread around the room as others noticed him. Even though he looked taller, it was the same mug we braced in Tudor City and sent packing two years before. He was wearing a robe like Mrs. Garner's with the hood down. He walked behind the chairs, put a hand on one woman's shoulder and spoke to her.

As he stepped between two chairs, a light brightened over the riser. That's when the next thing happened, and I still don't know how to explain it so you'll understand.

He separated from himself. The guy in the robe stepped up onto the riser. As he moved, the same guy, in a white robe, hovered in that spot behind himself, and turned to stare at me. The woman sitting next to me gasped again and clutched her throat. Behind me, I heard Connie catch her breath. Across the room, Willie said, "My god," and jumped in his chair. Then the second guy was gone. The weight of the Detective Special in my coat pocket was not reassuring. Whatever I'd just seen scared the hell out of me.

Nobody did or said anything. I sat straighter, and tried to shake the dizziness I was feeling from the incense and the flowers.

Manny clasped his hands together and said, "My friends, this is an auspicious night. With your help, I am going to attempt to create a link, a bridge if you will, between our world and another, a completely different and separate plane of existence."

He opened his hands and a coil of smoke rose from one of them.

A young woman stepped up onto the riser beside him. I didn't see where she came from and I couldn't make out her face. Like the other two, she wore a robe.

"In the room directly above us are the earthly treasures you brought." He stopped and smiled. "I can assure you they are completely safe," he lied. The women's laughter was uncomfortable.

"Victoria has spoken to some of you and explained that these objects can facilitate the link that I propose to create. Even though they are inanimate, you have imbued them with emotional weight. I have studied them this evening." He stopped and pointed at one of the women.

"Mrs. Banbrock, you brought a necklace that your mother loved but never wore, and she forbad you from ever wearing it."

The woman gasped. It was the loudest gasp so far. "How could you know, I've never breathed a word."

He moved on, pointing to another woman. "Mrs. Grantham, I will not say anything about how you came to possess your ring." Even in the dim light, you couldn't miss her blush.

He went on with those teasing little bits until the first explosion went off.

It was loud enough but not close, outside somewhere. You couldn't feel it through the floor. Several of the women yelped, and Manny collapsed flat on his face. The young woman in the robe turned into smoke and disappeared, Mrs. Garner knelt beside Manny. Somebody yelled that he'd been shot. Connie grabbed my shoulder.

Willie charged up on the riser. Mrs. Garner yelled for someone to call a doctor. By then, all of the women were out of their chairs and milling around. Connie and I backed out of the room and went to the front door. From there, I could see down to the town, but I couldn't make out anything except scattered lights.

Connie said, "What's going on?"

"Brother Emmanuel is the same character I told you about, the one who was running the confidence game in Tudor City. Whatever's happening outside now is a diversion. Him and his pals want the loot upstairs."

"But what about what we just saw in there—the way he split apart? That was real."

"I can't explain it, but I know he's faking now. Come on, let's see what's going on upstairs."

Theodora Opperman had stubbed out a Fatima in one of her sandwiches. She had her pistol in her hand again. "What's the commotion outside?"

"Part of the plan they've got to steal all this. Manny had just started his act and he was waiting for the explosion. Dropped like a sack of cement."

Mrs. Garner came hurrying up the stairs. Willie was behind her. She ignored Connie and me and said, "Theodora, we need your help. Emmanuel is experiencing a seizure. He's prone to them when he's making contact with the other side, but this one is worse. The explosion or something has severed the telephone line."

The second explosion sounded farther away than the first.

It took the detective a few seconds to decide what she should do. She said, "Mr. Seabrook, I'm going to ask you and Quinn to stay here and make sure that these goods are safe. Can you do that?"

Willie squared his shoulders. "Of course."

She said, "Keep your eyes on Quinn," and headed downstairs with Mrs. Garner. Connie went with them.

The lights upstairs were as dim as they were on the floor below. There were curtains on the windows and walls. Willie and I searched behind them for light switches near the doors. I could hear women talking downstairs, and, closer, there was a hum or a whir like gears meshing. For a time, all I could do was listen to the hum. Then a light brightened behind me. I figured Willie had found a switch, but I turned around and saw that he was staring at a golden naked woman. She was on the other side of the small tables. Willie was close to her. He stared and dropped his Scotch. She wore a polished gold mask with silver eyes and had chains wrapped around her waist and thighs. Willie started babbling in French and stumbled toward her, knocking over a couple of the tables.

The hum got louder and a second figure appeared close to me. It was a misshapen man, green and orange, standing on one big elephant foot that split apart and became three feet. Its nose swelled and melted into its shoulder, and twisted into a thick arm and hand that reached for my face. I swung at it with the knucks. It was like I was sinking my fist into wet mud. I felt the contact but it wasn't solid and it sucked at my arm. I tried to pull back. The figure loomed closer, and it was all I could do to keep from screaming. But I couldn't breathe either and the weight of it pushed me to my knees. I went face down on the floor. The weight rolled over my back, and I could breathe a little better.

Leaning heavily on my stick, I got back to my feet and staggered away from the misshapen man. At least, I think I did. I can't say how long any of this lasted. I know I saw Willie trying to hold his golden woman, and I saw him another time with his hands over his head. I thought I saw Connie, far away on the other side of the big room, tearing at the flowers and reaching for something high on the wall.

I was just trying to keep away from the thing that was after me, and it seemed like we went at it for hours. The misshapen man didn't stay in one place. I think I knocked over one of the tables of earthly treasures and fell against a wall. Not sure where the thing was, I stabbed blindly with the stick. It hit something solid and broke through with a loud crack. I jabbed a second time. Something caught the stick. I pulled and twisted. It came loose but not completely. I pulled again and heard a loud tearing sound and a splash of cold air hit me in the face like a fist.

The orange and green figure sparkled, and Connie was beside me, pulling me away.

Holding a handkerchief over her mouth, she yanked at a curtain and it came away from the window I'd broken. More cold air poured in. Connie grabbed my tie, shoved my face into the draft and held it there. My head cleared enough to help her get Willie to his feet and move him to the window. The cold air didn't do much for him. The golden woman was gone.

Sweaty and wild-eyed, Willie grabbed both of us by the shoulder and said in a rush, "My god, did you see that? She is my vision, she knows every terrible desire, she is inside me."

The booze on his breath was thicker than the stink from the flowers.

Connie said, "Keep him here." She hurried to the nearest wall, reached up and turned the knob on a gaslight fixture. The fixtures weren't used for light and I hadn't even noticed them. She turned off three more of them before she came back and explained.

When they left us, Connie and the detective went downstairs with Mrs. Garner. They found that two of the women had turned Manny over and held him sitting up on the riser. He was rolling his eyes and shaking like he had the heebie jeebies. The rest of the women weren't doing much better.

Mrs. Garner said to Theodora Opperman. "I want you to find out what those explosions meant."

"That's a bad idea. I trust Quinn and Seabrook for a few minutes, but left alone, they'll get into trouble."

"Let me worry about them. I'm more concerned about the town. The nearest police station is in Whitefields, an hour away."

"You hired me to protect your friends' possessions. That's what I should do, but I am curious about what's going on down the hill. If you want me to go, I'll do it."

"Please."

Connie told me later that she thought the two women acted more like friends than boss and employee, and I knew what she meant. Mrs.

Opperman had her own way of doing things. She grabbed a coat and rainhat. Before she left, she told Connie to lock the door behind her.

Connie and Mrs. Garner went back into the big six-sided room. Manny was still babbling and some of the women looked worse. One sat sobbing into her hands. One jumped up from her chair, put her hands over her mouth and ran for a bathroom. Mrs. Garner followed, saying she'd help. Without saying a word, two women turned to face each other and started slapping each other.

Whatever was going on, Connie was feeling it too. The way the women were acting made her angry. Then her older sister was standing in front of her, eyes flashing, calling her "monkeyface" and reaching out to twist the skin on her arm. And Connie's mother was there, screaming "You stole from us and abandoned your family." Connie said she knew they weren't there, and she tried to blink back tears, but she couldn't. It was too real and the smell of the flowers was too strong.

Half blind, she backed out of the room. While all that was going on, she kept telling herself it wasn't happening. She handled it a hell of a lot better than I did. Once she got out of the six-sided room, she coughed and teared up and fought for air until she could think and figure what to do. After she got her breath, she crept back into the other room and tried not to look at the women. What else was in there?

Nothing caught her attention until she saw leaves and petals quivering on the flowers near the wall. The others were still, but there, at that one spot, they were moving. Connie took a deep breath, covered her mouth with a handkerchief and went inside. She pushed two heavy pots over and found the gas jet high on the wall. It was hissing. A lot of houses that were built before electric power had gas lights. They converted when electricity became available. Some of them ran wires through the gas pipes and made them electric lights. Some didn't, but most people left the fixtures on the walls.

Connie closed the valve and went on around the room to find the other fixtures. Then the ceiling shook when something in the room above banged hard on the floor. That was me.

While Connie and I were seeing things that weren't there, Theodora Opperman was running down the road to town and thinking she was on a fool's errand. At least, that's what she told Connie.

Through breaks in the hedges, she could see lights and movement, but she couldn't tell what was going on. She'd got about half way when she saw the fallen tree. As she got closer, she smelled it. First, there was the stink of the powder they'd used to blow it up, and there was the smoldering wood. She pulled a flashlight out of her bag and took a look. The tree was close to the road and somebody had dug a hole right next to it for the charge. The explosion had blown out a lot of dirt and the tree had toppled with a fat root ball. Funny thing was, it fell away from the road. If somebody meant to block the way to Couffignal House, he made a poor job of it.

The detective headed down the road against a strong gusting wind, and got into Collier's Neck ten minutes later, sweating and breathing hard. The volunteer fire department had their truck at the curb in front of the bank. She counted five men shining flashlights into the building and six kids standing around watching them. She could smell more of the explosive stink. Closer, she saw the same results. There was a crater in the brick sidewalk, and the stone façade and metal doors had been blackened by the blast.

She introduced herself to the firemen and said she was a Continental detective hired by Mrs. Garner. Mrs. Garner was concerned about the explosions and wanted to know why the telephone wasn't working. The firemen didn't know anything about the telephones. They were working fine in town. One of them said he'd call the switchboard operator and have her check the line to Couffignal House.

That's when the third explosion went off. This one was close. It was followed by a loud "whoop," and bright orange flames lit up the harbor a block away.

The firemen climbed onto their truck and drove toward it. The kids followed. Mrs. Opperman, still getting her breath back, chased them on foot. She slowed down when she noticed the guy by the four-door Oldsmobile on a side street.

He was just standing there next to the Olds, away from the light and not moving, the way a guy will do when he doesn't want anybody to notice he's there.

I finally found the light switches in the six-sided room upstairs. When I turned them on, Connie and I saw that we'd played hell with the earthly treasures. Willie and I had knocked over all the display tables and the treasures were scattered over the floor. Connie straightened them up. I helped Willie into the armchair where the detective had been keeping watch. The effects of the gas, or whatever it was they'd used to juice us, had worn off Connie and me. Willie was still spiffed from the Scotch, and he hadn't got over the golden naked woman. He kept muttering in French.

Connie told me to come downstairs to help her with the women. I figured we wouldn't be gone long enough for Willie to get into trouble.

Since Connie hadn't broken any windows or opened them after she turned off the gas, the room on the first floor still smelled thick and sweet. Some of the women looked to be asleep in their chairs. The two women who'd been slapping each other were hugging and crying, and Mrs. Garner and the woman who'd been about to throw up were still in the bathroom. Connie said it couldn't be good for them to keep breathing that air. We started with the ones who were awake and helped them back to the room where the food had been. They were dopey and didn't argue about it.

The riser was empty. Manny had scrammed.

Once we had the older women settled, I took Connie to a corner, slipped the little German automatic out of my vest, chambered a round, and gave it to her.

"The lever over your thumb is a safety. Push it up and it's ready to fire."

She frowned at me but put it in her jacket pocket.

I said, "Nothing's changed. No matter what Willie said, we know this is a set-up. Those guys want the goods upstairs. The detective guessed they're worth fifty, seventy-five thousand. All this other eyewash is supposed to keep us from thinking about that."

"Damned effective," Connie said.

"The doormen at Mrs. Garner's building said she has been cashing checks for months, and she has had men preparing this house. Figure those guys were Pool and Abbey, and maybe some others. For a payday this big, they could bring in more guys."

"You don't know that Xeno is here."

"He's here. Both of them are, or they're close. We should find them before they find us."

She agreed. I said, "Get Mrs. Garner."

Theodora Opperman got a better look at the guy standing by the Oldsmobile when the fire at the harbor flared in the gusting wind. Maybe thirty years old, dark hair, pencil mustache, black coat. He went around to the back of the Olds and put something in the boot. Then he got behind the wheel and drove up the road to Couffinghal House. The detective started to run after him, but, no, that wouldn't do any good. Thinking maybe Mrs. Garner's name would cut some ice with the firemen, she turned toward the harbor. She stopped when she saw the girl on the bicycle.

She told the kid she was a detective and she needed the bike. The kid said no. She even stupidly refused a five-spot, so Mrs. Opperman shoved her off and pedaled away after the Olds. The women in Couffinghal House need her help more than the girl needed the bike.

She caught up with the Olds at the downed tree. The guy had stopped there with the headlights aimed at the tree. He was on his knees and working at the base. She got off the bicycle and laid it down. The wind was making enough noise that she didn't even try to be quiet. He didn't know she was there until she spoke.

"Stand up and put your hands on your head."

The guy's hand darted under his coat. She put a bullet in the ground right in front of him. "The next one goes into your belly. Now, reach in slowly with your left hand, take out that gun and toss it on the ground."

He cursed when he saw her. "You're a woman." He sounded amazed.

"I'm a detective with the Continental Agency. Now, do what I said." She pointed her gun at his head. "Slowly."

He did what she said.

"That's a good boy. Now stand up and move into the light. You look familiar. I've seen paper on you."

He shifted his weight from one foot to the other while she stared at him.

"Flippo, Gustav Flippo. Age twenty-eight, height five foot seven, complexion dark. Arrested for arson. Now on parole from Dannemora."

"So what? I did my time. Now, I got a legitimate job. I'm a caterer."

"Sure you are," she said, and got the first idea about what they were up to.

Mrs. Garner looked like she was ready to spit nails at me. She sat next to Connie. "This is just terrible. Emmanuel was so close. You saw what was happening. He had established contact. My son was in that room with us." The hope in her voice was painful to hear.

"You don't get it," I said. "They were juicing the room with gas, something that made you see things that weren't there."

"Nonsense. Emmanuel told me everything. We have no secrets. The gas is an aerosol accelerant, a psychical lubricant developed by a close associate. The extra images came from his projection equipment."

I was about to level with the woman when Connie gave me a look. It said, Remember what she's been through.

Mrs. Garner gave me her own look and said, "He told me what happened two years ago. I know you ran him out of the city."

"He tell you why?"

"It was a misunderstanding about your establishment."

"Him and two other guys broke into my place. They beat the men and women who work for me. They stole money and cigarettes. I caught him red-handed."

"Why didn't you report it to the police?"

"I run a speak. I don't go to cops."

"There you have it," she said and crossed her hands across her chest like that explained everything.

Connie shrugged. I lied and said that whatever happened two years ago wasn't important now. "Is your boy Manny's disappearing act part of the routine he dreamed up like the 'aerosol accelerant'?"

"No." Then she looked confused. "The ritual had six more steps. The visible manifestations began sooner than he thought they would."

"He's been living here in this house, hasn't he? Where's his room?"

She shook her head. "No. His privacy is sacred."

"I just want to see if he's there, if he's o.k." I lied. "That's all. Or do you know where he is?"

She shook her head and I could tell that underneath her anger at me, she was scared. She said he was in the master suite upstairs, down the hall.

I had a good idea I wouldn't find him there but I went upstairs anyway.

The master suite was locked but the knob had one of those simple little afterthought locks you can open with a flathead screwdriver or a penknife. It turned out Manny still had the same steamer trunk he'd taken to Penn Station. There were more robes, the magician's jacket, crystal ball and other props. The trunk was standing open in the middle of the floor. The other stuff was all over the room. There was a packed suitcase on the bed. In the bathroom, I found fake beards, mustaches, and eyebrows, and face paints. No razor or toothbrush. He was ready for a quick exit.

There were two other bedrooms at that end of the hall. Both of them looked like they'd been used but I didn't find anything in them. A fourth door opened onto a narrow staircase that led up to a third floor. It was for servants' quarters. Small rooms, all unlocked and empty.

I went back down to the six-sided room. Willie was gone. So were the earthly treasures.

Theodora Opperman told Gustav Flippo to give her the keys to the Olds and get in the driver's seat. She stayed outside and cuffed his left hand to the steering wheel before he realized what she was doing. Then she got in beside him and told him to drive to Couffinghal House.

He blustered, demanding to know what she was doing. Sure, he was on parole but she couldn't just kidnap him. "I told you I ain't done nothing. Finished my work. I had to get my crew to the bus back to the city. I was just leaving myself when they tried to rob the bank and I hung around to watch."

"Horse feathers. Nobody's robbing a bank. You made it look like that to keep them busy. Now you and your partners are after the loot that Mrs. Garner's friends brought tonight. The only thing I haven't worked out yet is how you're planning to get away."

He was sweating hard. She could smell it. "You got me all wrong, sister. I arranged the food and drink for Mrs. Garner. You can ask her."

"Don't worry, I'm going to. Another thing I can't work out is why you're still trying to bring a tree down over the road. It could mean you've got another escape route. You tell me about it now, I can make it easier on you later. Believe me, whatever you clowns have planned, it's already gone bad."

"You got me all wrong. I was just coming back here because I forgot my wallet."

"This is your last chance, Flippo. Once we get back to the others, I won't be able to do anything. What's it going to be?"

She watched him argue with himself until he muttered a curse and said, "Somebody had to make one more trip into town."

Then he explained everything to her.

A few minutes later, as they rounded a curve and the house came into view, the detective saw the lights on the second floor wink out. After that, the lights in the big room on the first floor went dark. A second later, the front hall and porch light went. She told him to stop and took the key out of the ignition. As she was getting out of the car, Mrs. Garner and the other women came out the front door. The ones who could climbed down the steps. The others waited on the porch out of the rain.

I went through the six-sided room more slowly and found the bird's nest, the lock of hair and Willie's pouch on the floor, but none of the other earthly treasures. I'd seen Connie put some of them back on the tables, but I really hadn't been paying attention. And, hell, the truth is that I didn't care that much. Sure, I might have pocketed the Russian egg if the opportunity presented itself, but such things get noticed, and it's been my experience that stealing them is more trouble than it's worth. I had more important things to figure anyway.

Once Connie pointed out the business with the gas, the rest seemed obvious. Manny arranged to meet Mrs. Garner when she went to Florida, and he picked up where he'd left off in Tudor City telling her he could contact her family. But by then, Xeno Pool was pushing Manny and Abbey to go for a big score. If they could convince the widow to invite a bunch of her wealthy pals to bring their earthly treasures to this remote house, they could pick them clean. Pass a little gas, knock them out, grab the goods and away we go.

But why invite Willie and me? Because Pool wants to kill me. That I could understand.

Willie was in the dining room behind a glass a Scotch. His eyes were bleary, wide and bright, and his hands were shaking so bad he couldn't light a cigarette. I took his matches and held one for him.

"I can't describe what happened in there," he said.

"You know we got gassed. They were pumping something through the gas lights. The flowers covered up the smell of it."

He shook his head. "It doesn't matter. For me, it was real. You don't understand how these pieces are fitting together in a pattern I've seen before. It's not magic, it's truth. Not a simple truth but a deeper, more complex truth that appears to be magic."

I knew that once Willie got rolling with something like this, he could gab for hours. I had to stop him.

"Here's something you don't know," I said. "The jewels and the gold upstairs? They're gone. You may not remember it, but while you were going goofy over the golden naked woman, we busted up the place a little. Maybe more than a little. Somebody came in after that and made off with the goods. Did you see anything else after Connie and I left?"

He thought for a long time before he shook his head.

"How long have you been in this room?"

"I'm not sure. Is that really important?"

"No. Besides, Pool's here. It's time to get him out in the open."

"Have you seen him?"

"No, but I've been through the house. I know where he is. The basement."

"What?"

"You think you had a real vision, and maybe you did, but everything else has been a trick, a magician's trick. We're seeing what he wants us to see. The important things are happening behind his back, on the other side of the curtain. In this place, that's the basement where the gas line—"

I stopped when I heard a solid click. Then there was a second click and the lights in the front hall went out. Third click and the lights in the dining room went dark. A shape appeared in the doorway. I knew it was Connie.

"There you are. Didn't you hear me yelling for you? I just saw headlights. There's a car coming up the hill." She fumbled her way closer.

I remembered seeing a candlestick on the sideboard and struck one of Willie's matches. There it was.

I lit it and said to Connie, "Stay by the front door. Keep it locked and don't let any of those women out until you know who's there. I'm going to check the basement. Willie can explain it."

The servants' stairs and the dumbwaiter to the basement were in the food preparation area at the other end of the dining room. The door between the two rooms was locked. I gave Connie the candlestick, switched my stick to my right hand to support my leg, and kicked the door in trying not to make much noise. It took two smacks with the sole of my shoe and it wasn't quiet.

Connie carried the candle to the stairs. There was no light at the bottom.

I said, "Take care of Mrs. Garner and those women. Let me worry about the rest of it."

"I heard you say Xeno's down there. If he is…"

I kissed her as hard as I could before she said, "don't kill him."

I was slow going down narrow steep stairs that ended in a dark kitchen. When my eyes adjusted, I saw moonlight coming in through windows. There was another door at the end of the kitchen. I took out the pistol and eased the door open.

The rest of the basement had been used as a storage area with a concrete floor and a dozen or so twelve-by-twelve wooden support posts. The lights were still on in there. It was cluttered with boxes, old toys, lawn mowers, and the like. I figured it to be right under the two six-sided rooms.

Hanging from one of the ceiling joists was a department store mannequin that had been painted with gold gilding. The hair was coiled copper wire and the eyes were silver.

Xeno Pool and Manny were by the fuse box. They were not happy. I stayed behind a twelve-by-twelve where I could see them, and listened.

Manny moved over and unhooked a rubber hose from a tall gas cylinder. The other end of the hose was taped to the pipe that fed the gas lights. Using a big brass wrench that wouldn't spark, he tried to reconnect that pipe to the main gas line. The pieces were not cooperating and he was getting mad.

Manny said, "You gave them too much. I stayed down below the worst of it and it still got to me. Old ladies like that, it could have killed them."

Pool said, "Who cares as long as we've got the goods."

"They're in my suitcase. Most of them." Manny muttered that last part under his breath.

Pool turned from the fuse box. "What do you mean, most of them?"

Manny backed away. "I couldn't find the egg. Seabrook got a double dose. He knocked over the tables. We've got everything else. The sovereigns are worth more than the egg, anyway. So are the bracelet and the necklace."

"You useless bastard. I ought to kill you right now." Pool backhanded Manny, knocking him against the wall. Manny hit the tall gas cylinder. It fell over and clanged on the concrete.

Manny covered his face with his arm. "Christ, Xeno. It's up there. Lemme go and find it."

Pool hadn't changed. When he got mad, he lost control. He took another swing at Manny, then whipped his foot around and kicked the smaller man in the gut. At least he'd got rid of those ugly two-tones.

Manny spun away from him and whipped out a straight razor. He rushed Pool with a pigeon-toed lunge and slashed him across the stomach.

It surprised Pool so much he just stood there and Manny cut him again. Pool backed away. With blood on his shirt and his hands, he pulled an automatic and shot Manny in the face twice. Manny collapsed in a boneless heap under the golden mannequin. You could tell he was dead before he hit the concrete.

Before I could do anything, Pool swung around and hurried a quick shot at me. Splinters burst from the twelve-by-twelve. I stayed behind the post. Pool shot it again. I leaned around the other side, raised the Detective Special and took aim at the center of his body. The report of the .38 echoed off the floor and made me deaf for a few seconds. I hit him, I know I hit him, but like the time in Lansky's garage, I didn't shoot him good enough.

Pool turned and disappeared behind a stack of wooden crates.

Chapter Thirty-five

1933
COUFFIGNAL HOUSE, LONG ISLAND

I heard the same hum or whir that I heard right before the crazy pants stuff started with Willie and me on the second floor. I cocked the pistol and moved in the direction Pool had gone. Willie banged through the door from the kitchen. He opened his mouth to say something but stopped when he saw the golden mannequin. I left him to it and followed Pool. A few feet past the wooden crates I came to an open door. Cold rain was blowing in. I closed and locked it, and went back to Willie.

He was staring at the bloody mess of the dead man on the floor, and at the mannequin dangling above the body, his eyes moving from one to the other and back. His breathing was fast and shallow. "What, uh…"

I knew he shouldn't be seeing that. "Pool shot him." Willie acted like he didn't hear me. "Come on, we can get Pool. Willie, move. There's nothing to do for him."

Willie's focus still shifted back and forth between Manny and the golden woman. He didn't move until I got in front of him. "Help me. Upstairs. Now. They need you."

He wasn't moving so well. I pushed him back into the kitchen and up the stairs. I figured the combination of the laughing gas, his "vision," the booze, the mannequin and the body was more than he could handle. And I wanted to keep him safe from Pool.

It was still dark on the first floor. We heard voices by the front door and went to them. Connie and the older women were outside, some on the porch, some by an Olds. In the light of the car's headlights, I saw they were talking to the detective. Willie was walking wounded but I thought I could keep him busy.

"I need you to do something," I said. "Go out there and tell Mrs. Opperman that Pool shot Manny. I gotta go back to the basement and turn the lights back on."

"But what about Pool?" Willie still wasn't firing on all cylinders.

"We need the lights first."

Willie stumbled outside. I went back to the basement. Blood fanned on the concrete around Manny's head. The smell was terrible. I screwed the fuses back in and tried not to look at the body as I went into the kitchen and upstairs, but I could see him clear enough in my mind. Still can.

Connie stopped me by the front door. "What's going on? I heard shots, and Willie says Manny's dead. He says you shot him."

"No, Pool shot him. Where's Mrs. Opperman?"

"She's got a guy in the car. She says he's an ex-con working with Xeno and Manny. He set off the explosions in town. She's got him cuffed to the steering wheel. There's something else but she didn't get to it. Now, what happened to Manny? I don't understand."

It was too complicated to explain then so I said, "They argued over the split. Manny had a knife. Pool had a gun. Tell Mrs. Opperman that Pool is heading to the big room upstairs. I'm going to stop him."

She grabbed my arm. "What? Why?"

"To tell you the truth, if I thought he'd just run away, I'd let him. What do I care? But he hasn't got everything he wants and he likes to hurt people."

There was no more time for talk. I gimped up the stairs, moving carefully and trying to avoid surprises. When I saw the mannequin in the basement, I figured that they'd used some kind of lift to move it from there to the big room on the second floor. If Pool and Manny had several weeks to "prepare" the house, it wouldn't have been hard to rig something. Hell, a big place like that, it might have had an elevator. If that was right, maybe Pool used it to get out of the basement, not the open door.

At the top of the stairs on the second floor, I edged around the first door to the six-sided room. It didn't look like anything had changed since I'd been there before but I couldn't see the whole room. The second door, the one closest to the chair the detective had been using, was closed. I pushed it open all the way with my stick. Nothing. Couldn't hear anything, either. I stood outside long enough to wonder if I'd been wrong and Pool was somewhere else. There were the little tables, the plants and flowers along the walls, the broken window, the chair and even the plate of sandwiches where Mrs. Opperman had stubbed out a smoke. Still being as careful as I could, I was slow edging into the room.

Pool brained me with a clay pot.

It shattered on my shoulders, neck and head. It didn't knock me out but it stunned me and my vision shrank down to nothing. I fell to hands and knees. The stick went flying. I held onto the .38 but my finger tightened on the trigger and I fired a shot at nothing. I'd love to say that I leapt right back to my feet, but that would be a lie. I crawled away and wasn't able to stand until I bumped into a chair and used it to pull myself up.

Pool wasn't much better off than I was. He was on his knees, too, and he was shaking. He'd been standing somewhere behind the door with his stomach bleeding and that heavy pot over his head for a long time. His shirt was more red than white, and he was holding himself where Manny cut him and I shot him. He still had his gun and it was pointed at me.

"Xeno, no," Connie yelled and put four rounds through a window so he'd know she was serious. Damn, I love that woman, even if she should have shot him.

I saw the way his expression changed when he heard her. He turned to look at her and I know he would have shot her on the spot if he hadn't recognized her voice.

"Constance Nix? What are you, this is, no..."

I understood his confusion. I'd felt the same way when she told me she knew him. I didn't know what to say, either.

While nobody was paying attention to me, I brought my pistol up, cocked it and aimed it at him. Sweat slicked my hand.

Connie noticed. "Jimmy, don't."

"Put it down, Pool. I won't kill you if you do."

His eyes cut back and forth between me and Connie, and he winced at the pain in his gut. After what seemed like a long long time, he put the gun back in a belt holster, and stood up. He staggered back toward a window, the one Connie had shot. He wrapped the curtain around his hand, and broke out the rest of the glass. More of the biting cold rainy air flowed into the room.

He looked at Connie and shook his head. "This is just nuts. Hell, it's..." He looked at me and snarled, "You son of bitch" before he crawled out onto the eave over the porch. By the time I got to the window, he'd dropped to the porch.

I didn't know what he was up to but I wasn't going to let him back in the house. I found my stick and gimped down the stairs and out the front door. Mrs. Garner and the other women were standing by the car. Somebody yelled at me. I ignored her and kept moving around to the back of the house. In the moonlight, I saw Pool halfway down the wooden walkway. Hunched over and holding his gut, he was making his way to the steps down to the beach. I went after him down the long straight part of the porch lined with rocking chairs. Remembering the rotten boards I'd seen earlier, I was even slower than usual. I used my stick to test the ones that looked soft, but I really couldn't see anything, so I tapped the stick like a blind man with a bad knee.

I kept tapping once I got on the walkway and leaned on the handrail against a gusting wind that cut through my coat. Since I could see that Pool was going away from the house, I didn't try to close the distance between us.

Out on the water, a boat horn sounded, two short blasts. Pool stopped. So did I.

A speed boat was coming toward the shore at half speed. It looked to be close to the point of land that separated the little beach from the Collier's Neck harbor. I could see running lights that were bouncing in the water. A moment later, a bobbing spotlight appeared but it was too far away to show anything.

Pool hunched along faster and yelled out. The boat horn answered. I heard another voice behind me. Theodora Opperman was running off the porch as fast as her stumpy legs would carry her. The walkway was shaking until she hit a soft board and went straight through it.

She landed with a loud thump, and I could tell she was hurt. As I went to help her, Pool shot at me. The sound of the boat's engine changed.

"Forget about me," the detective yelled, "Get him."

Pool was near the top of the stairs. I could barely see him, but it was enough to bring everything back—the way he tore up my place the first time, putting me out of commission for weeks, trying to rob me, fooling around with Connie when she was too young.

I stalked toward him. He shot at me again, and a third time. That must have been his last bullet. He threw the gun away and ran. I didn't hurry and I didn't hesitate. I hooked my stick on the rail and with a solid two-handed grip, I aimed and pulled the trigger. I heard the bastard grunt, but he didn't fall. He kept going until he reached the steps and flung himself down them.

I followed, still walking slow and stopped at the top of the stairs. He was moving fast, half running, half falling. I shot at him again, hit nothing, and watched the end of it play out.

Pool made it all the way to the bottom of the steps. He collapsed and got up. On the water close to the beach, the boat's running lights still bounced up and down. The searchlight snapped on and I was close enough to see that a bald man was aiming it at the beach. Pool yelled, waved his arms and ran into the water. Shin deep, knee deep. His arms sawed. He fell forward and swam toward the boat.

The searchlight swung around toward him. I saw Pool thrashing through the water. The engine burbled and the boat eased forward toward him. He swam harder.

I raised the pistol again and used my last shot to shatter the searchlight. A moment later, the engine revved. The dark shape of the boat wheeled around and it headed out into the Sound.

I went back and helped Mrs. Opperman get up onto the walkway. She couldn't put any weight on her knee and had to lean on my shoulder back to the house.

She said Willie had gone crazy.

Chapter Thirty-six

1933
COUFFIGNAL HOUSE, LONG ISLAND

Connie met us on the porch and we got Mrs. Opperman into the house. By then, Mrs. Garner and her friends were inside, too. It seemed like all of them were talking at the same time. I finally came to figure out the parts that I hadn't seen.

After the detective braced Flippo in the Oldsmobile, he told her what their plan had been.

He said that Manny was an old pal from the time they worked as dips together in Herald Square. Manny looked him up and told him that they needed a fourth guy for a sweet job out on Long Island. It was a table-rapping number. The mark was a rich old lady. They already had her on the hook. She lived in the city but she was letting them use her house on the North Shore. Manny and his partners Pool and Abbey had it all set up. Flippo wouldn't get a full share, but he didn't have much to do. The mark had already arranged a caterer for the food and wine. Flippo had to make sure the waiters and waitresses stayed out of the other side of the basement and were on the bus and away from the house by nine. Then Flippo would drive Abbey from the house down to the harbor. Abbey had picked out a speedboat he was going to steal.

There weren't any cops in town, but Pool, who was in charge, wanted a distraction anyway. They'd set off a few loud black powder charges. Those would keep the men in town busy and after it was all over, they'd add to the confusion.

The way Manny explained it to Flippo, they'd talked the mark into inviting a bunch of her rich old lady friends to this little gathering. Each of them was bringing something valuable.

Once they had everything in place, Manny would go into his act, and they'd pump a little laughing gas into the room where he was contacting the spirit world. As soon as he heard the first explosion, Manny would pretend to have a seizure and the guys in the basement would crank up the juice. Manny told him it was harmless. It was just like the stuff you got at the dentist, only it made you see things that weren't there and if you got a big whiff of it, you passed out. Manny figured he'd stay low, and control his breathing so he wouldn't get the full effect. When the old rich gals conked out, they'd gather up the goods and make tracks down to the beach where Abbey would be waiting with the speedboat.

Flippo would drive back to the city and get his cut later.

At least, that was the plan until they learned that the mark had hired a Continental detective to guard the goods. That's when they decided to run the laughing gas up to the second-floor room, too.

Abbey knew what he was doing with the gas. He showed them how to connect his cylinders to the lines to the gaslights, and how to unhook the main natural gas line from the furnace. When they had the goods, they'd let the natural gas leak into the basement where Flippo, also an arsonist, had placed a timed fuse that would set it off. They'd move the old ladies outside while they were still doped up. Oh, and there was one other thing. Two guys are coming—Willie and me—and Pool and Abbey wanted to screw them over good. Flippo didn't need to worry about that part.

But, Flippo swore, he didn't set the fuse. Yes, he said, he made one with a kitchen timer and a Ronson lighter, but he was sure it wouldn't work.

By then, the detective and Flippo were approaching the house in the Olds and she saw the lights going out. The women inside ran out as the car stopped. What was happening with the lights, they asked? Was the power out in town? Mrs. Opperman knew it wasn't a power failure. She'd seen the lights go off one floor at a time. Like me, she figured somebody was monkeying with the fuses. Then they heard the gunshots, Pool killing Manny and me plugging Pool. Mrs. Opperman took out her pistol and said everybody should stay with the car. She could tell something was going on inside. That was me hustling Willie out of the basement and then going back downstairs to turn the lights back on.

Then she saw me talking to Connie by the front door, and going up to the second floor. She also saw the gun in my mitt, and figured I was going after somebody who was up to no good. That wasn't important. She still needed to know what had gone on in the basement.

She grabbed Mrs. Garner's shoulder and said, "Listen to me. You've got to stay outside. All of you. It may not be safe in the house. I'm asking this as your friend. Please promise me that you'll stay here."

She knew that if the basement was filling up with gas, all of us were too close. She'd seen what gas explosions could do in the city. But she couldn't smell gas, and she didn't want the gimpy women wandering around in the dark on their sticks.

The detective ran to the basement door, the one I'd locked. She broke a pane of glass with her pistol. Inside, she could smell gas, but only faintly. Willie was sitting on the floor. She ignored him and Manny's body, and went straight for the main gas line. The smell was stronger there. She saw that Manny or Pool had left the ninety-degree valve cracked open. The brass wrench was on the floor where Manny had dropped it. Once she had the main gas line shut completely off, she went to Willie who had collapsed in a corner. He must have gone back to the basement as soon as I left him. He stared at Manny's body and the golden woman hanging from the ceiling joist above it.

He said, "She ate him. She killed him and she ate him. She's a cannibal, you see. Once you taste human flesh, you're changed. All women are cannibals. They devour us."

She was trying to jolly him to his feet when she heard gimpy footsteps on the porch over her head. That was me chasing Pool. She figured I needed more help than Willie, and she was right on that one.

When we got back into the house, Connie took Mrs. Opperman to the big room and called Mrs. Garner and the other women inside. Finally having a moment to consider the situation, I realized I was starving. I went to the kitchen downstairs and found stale bread, mustard and cheese in the icebox. The sandwich I made was so good I made two more, and put them in my pocket. After delaying it as long as I could, I went on into the basement and saw that Willie had passed out on the floor. I found a canvas tarp and covered Manny's body. Willie came around enough for me to pull him to his feet and shove him upstairs again. He got as far as the dining room where he stretched out on the table and went to sleep. I gimped into the big room and found the women rehashing everything that had happened.

They were still at it when the fireman who'd been in charge down in Collier's Neck drove up to the house to tell Mrs. Garner that they couldn't figure out what was wrong with her telephone. The problem had to be at her end. It was. Right outside where Pool cut the line.

By then, Mrs. Opperman had explained things to Mrs. Garner. The woman didn't believe me when I tried to tell her, but hearing it from the detective made a difference. Still, you could tell that it cut deep when the widow finally understood how Manny had played her for a sap. Nobody likes to know they've been taken.

Mrs. Opperman also took the fireman aside, and explained there was a body in the basement that needed to be taken care of. If they wanted to investigate such things, they'd find the pistol outside. The fireman asked Mrs. Garner what she wanted him to do. She said she supposed they should contact the chief of police in Whitefields. He was a personal friend. What she really wanted was for the entire matter to be settled as quickly as possible. And quietly.

That's what they did. When the cops showed up, Flippo swore he had nothing to do with any explosions. He was but an innocent caterer. Mrs. Opperman didn't dispute him because Mrs. Garner told her not to, and Flippo drove away in the Oldsmobile.

I don't know this for a fact, but I've heard that the county coroner eventually ruled that Manny committed suicide. Truth is, since he had a record that stretched from Manhattan to Miami, nobody really cared who killed him.

Whatever they thought about the body on that early Sunday morning, nobody tried to stop us when we were ready to leave. I told the fire chief about the arrangement for parking the cars somewhere in town. He said he knew about it and sent a guy to get them. Fifteen minutes later, a line of long cars paraded up the hill, and picked up the women.

As for the earthly treasures, most of them were in Manny's suitcase on his bed. I found them wrapped in a couple of shirts—the gold sovereigns, the book, the diamond necklace, the earrings, the tennis bracelet. But not the Russian egg. I gave the stuff to Mrs. Garner and she gave them back to her friends. And you know what's funny? They didn't care that much. Manny and Pool and Abbey concocted this crazy scheme to steal the stuff, and these women were yawning about it. Even Mrs. Garner wasn't upset about the missing egg. Yeah, it was hers, but she'd always "found it much too ostentatious." Go figure. Ostentatious means gaudy and vulgar.

And speaking of the crazy scheme, if you think that this was the dumbest idea for a heist you ever heard, I won't argue with you. But I've got to say you don't know how dumb some of these guys can be. And to me, Flippo's version that he told the detective doesn't hold water. If Pool really was the brains, I think he planned all along to gas the old ladies until they were out cold, turn on the natural gas, and set the fuse. Then he'd be in the speed boat with Abbey on the Sound when the house went up in a ball of fire. If they'd killed Manny and Flippo at the same time, the split would have been even easier to figure.

But nobody can say about that. They never found a body in the Sound. I know that Pool had a bullet wound and a bleeding stomach when he ran down to the beach. The way I saw it, he wasn't close enough to get in the speedboat after I shot the light out. And the boat turned around and left right after that. So, I can't tell you what happened to him. And you may also be wondering why Pool didn't shoot me when he had the chance on the second floor instead of bashing me with the clay pot. That one's easy. He didn't want to kill me, he wanted to hurt me. And he did. Just like Abbey, or the Abbé, wanted to hurt Willie, and he did a lot more damage than Pool did.

You see, because Willie and I humiliated them, they wanted us to suffer, and then they were going to kill us. If it hadn't been for Constance Nix and Theodora Opperman, they'd have got away with it. Like I said, sometimes a woman's just got to stick her arm out in front of you.

At the end of that long night, we got Willie into the back seat of the car he'd hired. Mrs. Opperman came with us, as gimpy as me with a swollen knee, and the driver took us back to the city. Connie and the detective wolfed down the cheese sandwiches I gave them.

The first stop was the Continental Agency's office on Broadway. The detective said she had a report to file, knee be damned. Then we drove back to the speak, and made a bed for Willie on the divan where I'd spent all those weeks two years before. Connie and I stayed with him, taking turns dozing.

The next afternoon, I called Doctors Hospital and left a message for Dr. Lambert. When he called back, I told him that Willie had gone off the rails.

He said he'd send an ambulance. If Willie wanted a drink when he woke up, I should give him a weak one, but I shouldn't let him go back to his apartment.

That's what happened. Willie woke up bleary and teary. He said he knew he had work to do with the doll in the basement, but he was afraid of the golden woman down there. I gave him a weak Black & White. When the guys from the hospital showed up, he pretended like he didn't want to go with them, but he didn't fool anybody.

They took him back to Doctors Hospital, and two days later, the fifth of December, the day Prohibition ended, they drove him upstate to the Bloomingdale Asylum to dry out.

Yes, it's funny that he would go there on that day, but what's even stranger is that after Willie got out, he wrote a book about it. It's called *Asylum*, and it was maybe the biggest success he ever had.

You see, nobody had written about being an alcoholic, and Willie was able to do what he did best. He told people what he'd done and where he'd been and how he felt. They felt it too and they wanted to know more about it. To do that, he told the truth and he told lies. Sometimes he was such a great liar that he fooled himself. I loved the man. He was my friend. I was with him at his best and worst. I understood him and he was a stranger to me. I didn't see much of him after that. Too many strong memories or nightmares, I guess.

But I'm getting ahead of myself again. On that Sunday after the ambulance drove away, Connie and I walked back to the Chelsea and went up to her room. She said she wanted to take a shower. I said I was too tired and stretched out on the bed. But even with the sound of the shower lulling me, I couldn't sleep. I turned on the radio and found a station that was playing a slow dance band, music that was exactly the opposite of my mood. It didn't help.

Everything we'd been through at Couffignal House kept coming back to me, out of order and confused. I stripped off my clothes, got under the blanket, and eyed Connie's things where she'd left them on the chair by the bathroom door. Then I was remembering the night with Willie in the diner when he talked about the infinite sidewalks, and that Sunday morning when the guy plowed through the intersection. Yeah, you think you've figured how it all works, and you forget it's a crazy world where things happen for no reason at all. And then there was Connie.

When she came out wrapped in a towel, the late afternoon sun hit her just right, tinting her brown skin pink and highlighting her black hair. She caught me staring and smiling, and she smiled back. She draped the towel over the chair, sauntered to the bed and slipped under the covers beside me.

"Can't sleep? Still thinking about last night?" she asked.

"I guess so. From the time I saw the invitation, I figured it was going to be unusual, but nothing like that."

She mumbled an agreement, and stuck her hands under my back to warm them.

"One thing, though," I said.

"Yeah?" She scooted up, kissing my chest.

"The egg. Is it in your bag?"

She looked at me, trying to read my expression. She moved so she was stretched out on top of me, and didn't say anything. Then she put her fists together and propped her chin on them so she could study me.

"No," she said. "I put it in the safe while you were asleep, on the bottom shelf where you never look."

"Probably for the best." I rubbed my hands on her naked back.

She sat up, straddling me. "Do you know a fence who could handle it?"

"Maybe. Why?"

She smiled. "I want to go to Paris."

Acknowledgements

Many people helped in the creation of *Jimmy's Rules*:

Simeon Doukrou, Thomas Ilecto and Wendy Scheir at The New School gave me a look at Willie's apartment.

Lisa Borok at the California State Railroad Museum Library shared invaluable information about train travel in the 1930s.

Dennis Hoffmann reacquainted me with the Detective Special.

Curt Gathje helped with the history of Tudor City.

Rachel Warren Ratliff and Robert Kintz read early versions of the manuscript and made it better.

Thanks to my agent, Agnes Birnbaum and the Bleecker Street Agency.

Some of Willie Seabrook's works are available in print and as eBooks. Most of the out-of-print books can be found in used book stores. Hunting for them is fun. For me, the best book about Willie is Joe Ollman's excellent graphic biography, *The Abominable Mr. Seabrook* (Drawn & Quarterly. 2017)

Read on for an excerpt from Michael Mayo's next book

Jimmy's Place

Chapter One

NEW YORK
JUNE 5, 1934

The first guys they sent to kill me weren't so good. That's what happens when you hire cheap, but you could see why they thought it. Two big lugs, armed, against one short good-looking gimp with a stick—ought to get the job done, right?

It happened about half past one in the morning. Business had been on the slow side so we closed Jimmy's Place early. I was walking back to the Chelsea. The sidewalk on that part of West Twenty-second Street is narrow. On one side you've got steps going up to the stoops of the brownstones and iron fencing in front of the doors to the lower floors. Trees close to the curb on the other side.

The two men were trying to read a little map that they were holding up under a lamppost near the corner. The map might have been one of those that they give you on the double decker tourist buses, but these two didn't look like tourists. Heavy-set guys, maybe thirty or forty, hard to say at night. Regular clothes, suits and hats. They'd been drinking, not drunk, not sober. I knew the look, but something wasn't right, something about the way they were standing. Then one of them nudged the other when he saw me and they both stared at me.

The first one pulled the map away from the other, switched on a big friendly grin and stepped quick toward me. His right hand was under the map. If I'd been farther away, I might have turned and run. But it was too late and maybe the bad mood I was in had something to do with it. Hell, in a situation like that you want to be the guy that lands the first shot, anyway.

I grabbed the stick with both hands, brought the tip up and went straight at him as fast and hard as I could. He wasn't expecting it and hesitated. I aimed at the middle of his tie and tried to jab the tip of the stick straight through his body. If he really was from out of town, well, welcome to New York.

He staggered back, dropped the knife he'd been hiding, and fell into the guy behind him. I kept pushing forward, lowered my shoulder and stabbed him again. He reached for the stick. I reversed it and rammed the crook end into his neck. He went backward and landed on his side choking and grabbing at his throat. No threat there. I went for the second guy.

He was reaching inside his coat as he backpedaled. I switched my grip, got in close and cracked his arm and his head twice. Jab to the soft spots, strike to the hard. The second one caught him near his eyes and drew blood on his forehead.

By then I could hear the first guy stumbling to his feet and running away. Realizing he was alone, the second guy sprinted the other direction.

I stood there under the lamppost looking one way, then the other until I was sure they were gone and my own excitement calmed down. Without thinking, I picked up their hats. I noticed then that the second guy had bled on the front of my shirt and my coat sleeve. The bastard.

Over the next day or so when I told people in the bar what happened, they'd shake their heads and say that with the end of Prohibition and Repeal everything was changing. You wouldn't be surprised by something like that a few blocks away, west of Ninth Avenue, but here? What're you going to do?

If I'd thought more about it, I might have figured that those two had been waiting for me where I walked just about every night. But I didn't think about it. I had other things on my mind. And like I said, those were the first guys.

They got better.

About the Author

Michael Mayo has reviewed films for numerous publications, including The Washington Post. He has worked extensively in radio and was co-host of the nationally syndicated Movie Show on Radio and Max and Mike On the Movies. Among his books are *American Murder*, *Videohound's Horror Show*, *War Movies*, and the *Jimmy Quinn* suspense novels.

www.ingramcontent.com/pod-product-compliance
Lightning Source LLC
Chambersburg PA
CBHW011116100726
47898CB00011B/3116